ISHMAEL'S SON

BY

NELSON ADRIAN BLISH

PALO ALTO
2003

Published by Palo Alto Books, a division of The Glencannon
Press
P.O. Box 341, Palo Alto, CA 94302
Tel. 800-711-8985
www.glencannon.com

First Edition, first printing.

Library of Congress Cataloging-in-Publication Data

Blish, Nelson Adrian, 1945-
    Ishmael's son / by Nelson Adrian Blish.– 1st ed.
      p. cm.
    ISBN 1-889901-29-6 (pbk.)
      1. Terrorism--Fiction. 2. Governors--Fiction. 3. Houston
(Tex.)--Fiction. 4. United States. Navy--Fiction. I. Title

    PS3602.L57184 2003
    813'.6--dc21

                                                    2002193144

ACKNOWLEDGEMENTS

The author gratefully acknowledges the help he has received from a number of individuals in the writing of this book. Some read a chapter or helped with strategizing, but all provided enthusiastic support. In no particular order, those giving of their time and energy include Laura Hunt, Shelby Edwards, Lieutenant Commander Jeff Edwards, Roxanne Stern, Edwin Stern, Major Jay Blish, Wendy Buskop, Corrine Chorney, Phillip Tomasso, and Major General Marshall Ward. Sharon Stiller did much of the heavy lifting, read the entire manuscript, and provided detailed comments for revision. In particular, I would like to thank my publisher, Ms. R. B. Rose, and my editor, Mr. Bill Harris, for giving me this opportunity.

And he will be a wild man;
his hand will be against
every man, and every man's
hand against him ...
                    Genesis 16:12

Contents

PART FIVE — RETALIATION

PART ONE

THE PLAYERS

2 ISHMAEL'S SON

CHAPTER ONE

LIBERTY IN ITALY

He slouched in a scarred, wooden chair, one leg crossed over the other, and one hand in his lap with the other lying lightly on top. His body was loosely, but neatly arranged. The only rigid part of him was a cigarette pinched between his index and middle finger. He cupped it close to his palm, and languidly brought his hand to his mouth, covering half his face. Affectation and anonymity. His right eye squinted against the acrid smoke from the glowing tip.

Through the smoke he watched the back-lighted dancers trying to dislocate their hips as they gyrated to the ear-wrecking music. Haze and flashing lights made them seem surrealistic. The small concrete apron in front of the band approached a world record for couples per square centimeter. Back to belly, and hip to hip, the close quarters left no room to wiggle their bodies, but they did.

His name was Khaled Hassan, not a well-known name, but in his profession anonymity was an asset. Some in the intelligence community, the alphabet people, KGB, CIA, FBI, may have known his name, he could never be sure, but not the man in the street, or the woman, or more important, the news media. When your picture was published, the game was up. Then it was only a matter of time until someone turned you in to save his or her own hide, or, as likely, for money or revenge.

The world knew the name, however, of Hassan's organization, Abu Nidal. Abu Nidal, the name of his leader as well as the name of his group, meant, "father of the struggle," in Arabic. That was not Nidal's real name, of course, but it was how the world knew him. It had become his calling card. "Abu Nidal" struck fear into the hearts of infidels and he had used it so long that even he would have had to look around to identify the person being addressed if someone called him by his real name, Sabri al-Banna.

Hassan's swarthy skin and black hair made him look Italian, which suited him well. In Naples, it pleased him to look Italian. His clean-shaven face had the dark, shadowed look that heavy facial hair gives many men. He was handsome, but not extraordinarily so. That would have made him standout, a detriment in his trade.

He took another drag from his cigarette and looked around. There were many more of the fair-skinned Americans than Italians in the club, but that was what brought him to the bar — American servicemen and women. He held the smoke in his lungs for a moment, relaxed and let it trickle out through his nose.

The Americans were also what attracted the Italians, most of whom were women. The women in turn were what attracted the men, a nice symbiotic relationship. The U.S. servicemen, mostly sailors, were out to persuade a few of the women to have sex with them if they could, pay for it if they had to, and get drunk while doing it. The women, on the other hand, were out to separate the men from their money, preferably in a manner that would result in the money ending up in their pocketbooks, giving sex if they must.

An American sailor put his hand on the extra, empty chair at Hassan's table. "You mind if I take this?" He turned his back and dragged it to the next table before Hassan could waive a casual assent with his hand. Hassan felt a stir of anger, but forced himself to relax. He knew who would live and who would die tonight.

The crowd filled the Kit Kat Club. It was usually crowded on the nights when the fleet was in. But it was not as packed as it would be on the weekend. If there were too many people he would not be able to leave quickly when the time came.

Khaled Hassan came prepared. He touched the shoulder bag under the wooden table with the toe of his Gucci loafer to reassure himself of its presence, caressing it with the soft leather of the shoe. He got a sensual feeling from touching the bag, like fire running up his leg to his groin.

Attention to detail mattered and the shoes were what the with-it Italian men were wearing. Likewise, Hassan's gray broadcloth shirt, unbuttoned to the belly, matched a thousand others on the street. Another anonymous Italian in Italy.

The shoulder bag, crafted from hand tooled, old Moroccan leather, resembled a purse. Similar to the bag carried by many Italian men. He had picked it up in the market, second hand, several days ago. Such a bag was often used in Europe to transport a wallet, comb, change purse, and assorted other objects that many American men stuffed into their pockets. Most young Italian men, both gay and those not so inclined, wore tight fitting jeans to show off their posterior, and, rather than having their pockets bulge with lumps caused by keys, wallets, and whatnots, they carried a bag. It was a year for men with good asses, and the Italians were showing theirs off, good or not.

The bag Hassan carried contained more important cargo than keys and a comb. The twenty pounds of plastic was a powerful explosive, equivalent to more dynamite than he would care to haul around the city streets in a shoulder bag. The chemical name was cyclotrimethylene trinitramine, but it was usually called RDX or more often, simply plastic. It was more than enough to level the Kit Kat Club. Of course, to level the building, the plastic would have to be divided properly and placed at key structural supports. Hassan was not interested in destroying the building, however, only as many of the people in it as possible.

Many men would feel uneasy about sitting with twenty pounds of plastic explosives at their feet, but Hassan was as relaxed as he looked. He took another drag on his cigarette. Cool but alert, he had that extra awareness athletes have when they are about to begin a contest, excited, but not nervous, ready, but relaxed. When you have been to the best schools in the bomb business, and worked with the stuff, you know exactly what it can and can't do.

His memory of his instructor at the terrorist school, discussing the properties of plastic, was still vivid. The school was run by the Palestine Liberation Organization, before Abu Nidal had his own training facilities, before the PLO had gone soft on terrorism and got into bed with the Americans.

The instructor had assembled a group of five students around a fire for an evening lecture. In another part of the world, such a group might have been young men gathered at an Eagle Scout outing. The instructor stood by the fire and told war stories about how bombs made with the same amount of plastic he held in his hand, had been used to blow up a certain airplane or a particular building or an armored car full of diplomats. Hassan remembered the feel of the gray putty-like substance as the students, sitting cross-legged in the sand, passed the fist sized sample around. Excitement ran through him at the power he held in his hand.

When the instructor had the sample back, he said, "Plastic is a dangerous explosive and must be handled with extreme care at all times." The fire light reflected from his eyes. With a wicked smile, he tossed the plastic into the fire. One of the students with faster reactions than the rest, rolled backward and away from the fire. Hassan and the rest of the students simply froze in place, their breath caught in their throats.

The plastic caught fire and burned brightly. But, of course, there was no explosion. An explosion occurs when a material burns rapidly and the by-products are contained, if only briefly. Even an atomic bomb must be contained in a metal sheath for a short time to allow the reaction to occur in order to achieve an explosion.

"The point," the instructor said, "is that there is more to a bomb than a quantity of plastic, or gunpowder, or refined uranium."

The plastic in Hassan's leather bag was encased in metal tubes blocked at both ends. Each tube had a detonator wired to a timer and batteries. The wires were all the same length to ensure that each tube detonated at the same time. Attention to details. Even though the electronic signals traveled very fast, nearly the speed of light, it was better not to leave anything to chance. If one stick went off too soon, it could destroy the other sticks rather than detonating them.

Attending to the details made Hassan a successful man in his business. He used only the very best equipment. The timer attached to the tubes was the most accurate on the market. This one was manufactured in Switzerland. It was a special order shipped to Libya, to a corporation more than glad to front for the Abu Nidal organization, but more afraid not to.

The timer was also the most expensive available, but that fact mattered not at all. The oil rich Islamic nations on the Persian Gulf funneled all the money needed to the Abu Nidal group and others like it. It assuaged their conscience that they were not doing more in the Arab struggle against the infidel and the Jew. It also bought them peace at home. For a time.

Before he entered the bar, Hassan had set the timer for twenty minutes. He had also activated the anti-tamper mechanism so that the bomb would detonate if the wires were cut between the timer and the trigger. Another circuit would detonate the bomb if it were dropped or thrown after it was armed. If Hassan were detained, he would throw the bag against a wall and escape during the confusion after the explosion.

"Another drink?" the waitress asked with a smile, bending over to make herself heard above the band and conversation. And to give him a view of her cleavage, which strained against her low cut white blouse. The blouse hung down enough to let him see she was bra-less, which he was certain was her intention. He could just see her nipples brushing the front of the fabric.

"No thank you." The smile he gave her was genuine. He watched her haunches strain against the black, imitation leather mini-skirt as she walked away. She was certain to sell many drinks. Just watching her was enough to make a man thirsty. She would have to hurry though. He looked at his watch and sipped the last of the seltzer water. Muslims weren't allowed to drink alcohol, but that was not why he had ordered the non-alcoholic beverage. He would do what he wanted, rules were for others and mattered little to him, but alcohol and bombs don't mix well.

Hassan consulted the stopwatch feature on his wrist-watch again. He had activated it when he started the timer on the bomb. Five minutes to go. He double-checked the backup watch on his other wrist. Leave nothing to chance. If your first watch stops you might be sitting there looking at it when the bomb explodes.

He would get up from the table three minutes before the bomb was set to detonate. There were six tables between him and the door, approximately thirty-six feet. With the number of people milling about in the darkened nightclub it should take no more than forty or fifty seconds to walk out the door. He could safely watch the explosion from across the street.

The problem with amateurs was they were often more concerned with their own safety than getting the job done right. They planted the bomb and left thirty minutes before it was scheduled to go off. Then someone noticed the suspicious package and called the bomb squad to deactivate it. Or they were in such a rush to get out of the building that they made themselves conspicuous, or worse, got themselves detained. Once caught, the fools would wind up revealing the bomb's location to save their own skins. Even the Nazi generals that planted a bomb to kill Hitler had not done the job right. They put a briefcase with explosives under a conference table for a briefing that Hitler was scheduled to attend. The officer, Claus Stauffenberg, left without even waiting to see if Hitler would get to the meeting on time. Hitler lived and the conspirators died.

Hassan had given himself sufficient time to ensure there were plenty of American servicemen in the nightclub before leaving the bomb. He wanted to see them and count their bodies while they were still alive, before they were nothing but charred meat. He watched their smug faces as they bought liquor and left the bartender tips that were as much as the bartender earned in an hour. He watched as they pressed themselves against women on the dance floor and leaned against the women at the bar, rubbing the women's arms and legs and asses. Soon those smug looks would be gone from their faces.

With three minutes to go, Hassan leisurely slid back his chair and stood. The bag was pushed far under the table. In the dim light, with the tables close together, someone would have to get down on their knees to see it. Unless someone sat down at the table in the next few minutes and kicked the bag with their foot, it wouldn't be discovered. Hassan left his drink on the table, almost full, and a cigarette smoldering in the ashtray, so that anyone looking for a table would know his was occupied.

As Hassan started to walk between the two adjacent tables, one of the Americans lurched to his feet. As he stood, the chair slid back into Hassan, which caused the drunk to stumble forward into the table. The edge of the table caught him at his crotch. His elbows kept his face off the table but his ample belly hit his glass, spilling it.

"Watch where the fuck you're going," the drunk slurred, whirling to face Hassan. He balled up his fists close to his big belly. One of his friends stood and put a restraining hand on the drunk's arm.

The rush of adrenaline tightened Hassan's stomach. Two minutes forty seconds. "I'm sorry," Hassan said holding his hands up, palms out in a placating manner. Hassan's English was good. No one would know the slight accent was not Italian.

"Damn right you're sorry," the drunk said, trying to shake off the restraining hand. "You are one sorry fucking dago son of a bitch."

"Hey, cool down," his friend said in a placating tone. "Shore patrol," he added, motioning with his head to two sailors in bell-bottom Service Dress Blue uniforms. The white web belts the men wore showed they were on duty. They were just inside the door of the club casually looking around, their nightsticks in holsters at their waist.

"I'm sorry, I was very clumsy," Hassan said, backing away.

The drunken sailor looked over at the shore patrol. "Just don't let it happen again," he said sitting down, forgetting why he had stood in the first place. "Fucking fag," he added loudly and laughed.

Hassan walked the long way around the table and continued to the door, taking care not to hurry. He carefully avoided eye contact with the shore patrol as he passed them on the way out. If he did not make eye contact, it was likely the shore patrol would not remember him later. That assumed that the shore patrol would remain alive long enough to remember anything.

The evening air felt cool on his skin as he walked across the street. After the stale cloud of cigarette smoke in the club, the cool night air was enough to make his lungs hurt. He hooked his sports coat over his shoulder with his fingers. Outside the nightclub the noise from the band was reduced to a bearable level, but the beat of the drum was still loud enough to echo in his bones. The subsonic beat provided rhythm without melody, but there was no need to yell in someone's ear to be understood.

The streetlights provided little illumination, barely enough to see the shore patrol standing just inside the door. Hassan checked his watch and lit another cigarette. He closed his eyes and inhaled deeply. He left his eyes closed holding his breath until he heard the deep-throated rumble of the explosion. Like a mortar round going off. Like the end of the Earth. Like death.

The tinkle of glass from the blown out front windows followed, like rain falling from heaven. Then silence. It was like the world was waiting, heart paused in midbeat. Waiting to see if it was really over.

A loud thud followed as something fell on the hood of a car near him, breaking the spell. Hassan opened his eyes to see the carnage he had caused. He sighed, letting go of the smoke. The object that had fallen on the hood of the car appeared to be part of a leg. What remained of one of the sailors in uniform, the shore patrol, was lying in the middle of the street in a twisted heap, limbs tangled and body bent in a shape that even the manic dancers from the Kit Kat Club couldn't manage. The head was missing. Hassan looked around for it but did not see it.

The moaning and wailing was starting as Hassan walked away. It would only be a little while before the sirens started, off in the distance howling like dogs on the way to a kill. Hassan planned to be miles away when the police and ambulances arrived. He walked away at a leisurely pace, humming some tune he could not have named, careful not to draw attention to himself. Hassan was happy, and it was the only emotion he had shown all evening.

Hassan caught himself and became silent. He put his head down and moved close to the wall. He walked slowly away, careful not to stand out in the gathering crowd.

CHAPTER TWO

SWIFT SWORD

Lieutenant Commander Joshua A. Clark, United States Navy, parked his car on the south side of the Pentagon. He carefully locked the doors of the 1989 Ford Taurus, mostly through force of habit. It was well worn and probably not worth stealing, but no sense taking a chance that it would be vandalized. It had served him well. It was only the second new car he had ever bought, and he kept it in good condition. It was like an old friend and the thought of some crack head ripping out the radio for a few bucks was painful.

His footsteps echoed as he crossed the parking lot toward the five-sided building. With Reagan International airport shut down for the night and no traffic on I-395 yet, the silence was eerie. The still, moist air, on the edge of turning to fog, was typical of the area. It carried the scent of the river, moist and earthy.

Five a.m. was an ungodly hour to be coming to work. Belay that, 0500. Sarah had him thinking like a civilian; he had been ashore so long. At this time of night, or morning, the parking lot was virtually empty. Even the stressed out, over-achievers that the military sent to the puzzle palace would not arrive for another hour. Just the cars of the people on the night watch, and others called in, like he was, to handle a problem.

The full moon glinted on the Potomac and he paused for a moment to look for the Jefferson Monument. It was on the other side of the river, but he forgot that it was not visible from here. His eyes were night adjusted and the moonlight was enough to make everything as bright as day. In the fading night, with the lighted spike of the Washington Monument standing out in the distance, and the haze of automobile exhaust not yet clouding the air, Washington, D.C. was as nice as the picture postcards in the souvenir shops portrayed it.

Lieutenant Commander Joshua Clark, USN, watched his reflection march up to the glass double doors at the side entrance to the building. The reflection was dressed in the dark, almost black, Service Dress Blue, Navy uniform. Two gold stripes, with a smaller stripe between them circled the wrist on each sleeve of the reflected officer. A handful of ribbons hung heavy on the left chest, and a white hat with gold eagles and anchor, contrasted with the somber suit. His mahogany colored face was almost invisible in the dark glass.

The reflection reached out to touch hands with Clark as he pushed the heavy glass door open. He couldn't help being a little critical of the medium height, five-foot eleven inches, medium build figure that looked back at him in the glass. He let the door swing shut behind him. A daily workout kept his weight down to one hundred seventy-five pounds; not great, but pretty solid. The problem was that even with exercise the muscle was starting to shift around, mostly to the little pouches at the top of his hip bones. Love handles, that's what Sarah called them. He shook his head as he thought about finding more time to exercise. Each day was a battle to prioritize what had to be done, what he wanted to get done, and what would be left undone.

The amount of free time available to personnel stationed at the Pentagon wasn't great, but if you set your priorities, there was time for a workout. You made time for the things that were important, like your health. Twenty minutes of jogging in the neighborhood before coming in was all that it took to keep the heart in shape, but he was going to have to find time for some sit-ups and weights to firm the upper body. He would have to work in a visit to the Pentagon Officer's Athletic Club.

Many of the people in the pressure cooker atmosphere of the Pentagon didn't even take twenty minutes a day. They were willing to buy health insurance, and pay for life insurance, but they weren't willing to contribute a little time for the price of good health, which was the best, and cheapest, insurance of all. They lived on a steady diet of cigarettes, coffee, stress, and more coffee. They were keeping Maxwell House healthy, but killing themselves. They looked trim, but the weight they were putting on was in the fatty deposits on the inside of their arteries.

The guard at the entrance to the military section of the building, past the entrance to the Metro, looked carefully at Clark's badge as he passed the checkpoint. The light brown face on the Navy Lieutenant Commander matched the picture on the laminated Pentagon badge. Clark had forgotten the badge once and once was enough. All he had then was his green military ID card. With the military ID you went through the metal detector. That meant removing all change, keys and belt buckle before being allowed to pass. With the Pentagon badge, a wave of the hand from the guard and he was through.

Clark took the up ramp to the E ring, first level. His footsteps echoed hollowly in the empty hall. He followed the E ring to his corridor and marched inward toward the quadrangle in the center. Famous Naval heroes looked sternly down from the pictures on the walls.

He was still new enough to the Pentagon staff that he had to consult the three dimensional map in his head to find his way to his office. It was even harder finding his way around the Pentagon than finding his way around his first submarine. On a submarine, there was only forward and aft, and up and down two or three levels. In the Pentagon, there were five levels up and down, five concentric rings on each level, and numerous corridors connecting the rings, most of which looked alike. It was very much like a beehive, both for the geometrical complexity and the frenzy of constant activity. He breathed a sigh of relief as he located his office in the Navy section and put his briefcase down on his desk.

First things first, he thought as he headed for the coffee pot. In the Navy the ships might run on petroleum products, but the sailors ran on coffee. He took the two-gallon metal coffee pot from its shrine near the sink and poured out the cold remnants of yesterday's brew. Filling the pot to the mark with water, he assembled the basket and added a filter and ground coffee from the one gallon can in the cabinet above the sink. He plugged the pot in anticipating a steaming cup of elixir. The pot gave a groan as the coil started heating the water.

The groan echoed in Clark's head as he realized relief would not come soon. The pot didn't seem to be brewing any faster with him watching it as much as he wished it otherwise. There was time to check the message traffic before the meeting started although he was reluctant to leave the coffee maker. The message board, however, might give him some clue as to why he had been summoned. Besides, there was probably fresh coffee in Radio. That was the deciding factor.

Walking down the broad, yellow-lit corridor to the radio room, he rang the buzzer. An enlisted man looked at him through the glass panel in the metal door and opened it to let him in. The din in the radio room from the Teletype machines was loud enough to make him wish for earplugs, a sharp contrast to the silence in the halls.

Enlisted men in Navy blue jumpers tore paper off printers, changed perforated paper tapes on other machines, and filed flimsy, paper copies of messages on clipboards, with rings that could easily hold stacks of paper three or four inches thick. U.S. civilian industry may have discovered the paperless office, but this was the U.S. Navy, thank you very much, and if a few forests had to give their lives in the defense of the free world, so be it. That was the price of peace.

He walked over to the Radioman First Class in charge of the watch section. "What have you got for Counter Intelligence? I got a call at home that something had come in for immediate action."

"If you'll sign the log Lieutenant Commander, I'll get the traffic for you."

"Certainly," Clark said, bending down to write his name and rank in the log. "You mind if I have a cup?" he said pointing to the pot at the end of the counter with his chin. He was careful not to salivate.

"Help yourself, sir, but it's only the dregs left. We should be perking a new pot for the oncoming watch soon if you want to wait."

"I've got one perking myself down in my section. I just need something to keep me awake until it's done," Clark said, pouring some of the dark, black brew into a white Styrofoam cup.

He blew the steam off the hot coffee and took a sip. The bitter taste made him grimace. Clark could see the First Class trying not to smile as he watched him from the corner of his eye. Clark had been an enlisted man himself and he knew the sailor was thinking something like, "You can't tell these officers anything, they already know it all."

"Here's the Secret board, sir." The clipboard for secret radio message traffic was slim, thank God.

"Thanks." Clark continued to alternate blowing on and sipping the liquid as he flipped open the cover of the message folder. SECRET NOFORN was printed in half-inch high black letters across the top. Loosely translated, No Foreign Nationals.

Clark always half expected to see "Burn Before Reading" on some of these messages. They did everything except give you a Captain Marvel Secret Encoder Ring before you were allowed to read radio messages classified Secret or above. Half the time the same story was on the front page of the Washington Post the next day, usually with more details. Sometimes the message traffic made the news the day before it was on the message board.

He paused with the cup half way to his lips, his mouth open. No wonder people were being called in. The message was enough to insure that most of the military types would be at the Pentagon all weekend.

152330Z JUN
FLASH
FM CINCLANT
TO LIST 1

//BT//

1. BOMB EXPLODED APPROXIMATELY 2100 LOCAL TIME AT KIT KAT CLUB, NAPLES, ITALY. NINETEEN U.S. SERVICEMEN KILLED IN THE BLAST.

2. PRELIMINARY ANALYSIS OF BOMB DEBRIS BY LOCAL NATIONALS INDICATES INVOLVEMENT OF TERRORIST GROUP ABU NIDAL.

//BT//

Short, sweet, and to the point. Here is one big mother of a problem. He blew his breath out through pursed lips. The new President had clearly announced his intention not to take anything from terrorists. Now there had to be US retaliation. The President had locked himself into his rhetoric.

Clark decided that his first action would be a call to his boss to tell him he needed to come in. You certainly can't read a secret message over the telephone, so he would have to diplomatically tell the Captain in charge of his section to come in, without telling him why. He looked at his watch. Just time to make the telephone call, lock the message in the safe, and then get to the meeting. At least now he knew why he had been called in. He should have watched CNN before he came in, he could have got more details.

CHAPTER THREE

FIRST STEP

Ahmed Mohammed felt the thick, metal plate beneath the blankets cooling as he woke. The lump of coal that he carefully banked under the plate the night before had died a natural death sometime in the stillness of the early morning. The heavy slab of metal would soon begin to conduct heat away from the bodies toasting on its surface, reversing direction, and sucking back the nocturnal warmth it had supplied. A crude method of keeping warm at night, but effective. Also very inexpensive.

He shivered and pulled the thin wool blanket close, drawing his knees toward his chin, his arms across his chest. The early morning dampness made the blanket smell like the sheep that gave their coats to provide the material for the cover. He sneezed, covering his mouth with his hand. The blanket always made his nose itch, but it was warm, therefore worth it.

Giving up the struggle to stay warm, cold overcoming the desire for more sleep, Ahmed crawled out of bed. He was careful not to wake the children who were still bundled in the blankets. He put his blanket over them and tucked it underneath them. The chill morning air bit into his skin as he slipped into his robe and sandals. He pulled the robe around him and rubbed his arms.

The pale, gray light of dawn came through the opening in the concrete wall that passed for a window, unhindered by pane of glass or screen. Later in the day a cloth covering would be pulled across the opening to keep out the sun and sand. It didn't do either very well.

Safia, his wife, was already busy at the small gas stove heating water for tea. Their eyes met as he dressed. The color of her eyes never ceased to amaze him, an amber-bronze hue that defied exact description. Two children and still her eyes could stir a fire in his soul and body.

He walked up behind her and kissed her neck, the clean smell of her long, black hair filling his senses. Putting his arms around her, he hugged her gently, surprised again, as he always was at the sense of serenity that holding her gave him. His chin rested lightly on the top of her head. Her short and supple body fit comfortably against his taller frame. Allah had made them as two parts of a puzzle, and then fit them together. She paused at her work and leaned her cheek against his arm where it came around her shoulder.

"Good morning," he said.

She put a finger to her lips. He released her and began preparing for work. Usually neither spoke, a predawn ritual in their small, one room apartment. The children would probably sleep anyway, but the habit was well established. The quiet fortified him for the long day at the plant, where the noise level was so high that conversation had to be conducted in shouts that left him hoarse by the end of the shift.

It was at these times he was almost glad that they could not afford the radio or television that played all day in the homes of some of their neighbors. Almost glad. Radios and televisions were treasures despite the fact that they had to be bundled in plastic baggies when not in use to keep out the powder fine sand that quickly ruined all things mechanical or electrical. But those who had electronic devices played them incessantly whether or not they were listening. A constant background din. They wanted to be sure their neighbors heard and knew they could afford them.

He pulled the comb through his jet-black hair. Pouring water from a pail into the basin, he dipped a bristle brush in the water, then stirred it in the soap mug. The face that looked back at him from the small circular mirror nailed to the wall looked like it had not been touched by a razor in several days, although he shaved every morning. Ah, the price of virility. The face in the mirror smiled at him.

He carefully scraped the hair off his chin, cheeks, and neck, leaving only his lip untouched. Safia had started asking him to shave his moustache, but he resisted. He remembered how he had looked like an adolescent before he grew the moustache. Of course, he had been an adolescent then, but he had a feeling deep in his stomach that he was much more manly with it. Besides, much as he loved her, it was not a woman's place to tell him what to do.

When the tea was ready, they sat across from each other on rough cut wooden stools. Ahmed had a piece of hard bread with his tea. Safia had tea only. She would eat later with the children when they woke. Cereal grain with hot water, dates if there was money for them, and a vitamin.

Ahmed had insisted on vitamins for the children. Safia relented only after a long and bitter struggle. It was the only thing they had seriously disagreed on in their marriage. Safia was deeply religious and believed that giving vitamins was interfering with the will of Allah. If it is the will of Allah that the children grow tall and straight, they will, if it is not, then they won't. *Inshallah*, if Allah wills it.

Administering medicine was interfering with the will of Allah. The Koran was silent on antibiotics and vitamins, but the Koran contained all knowledge. To admit that something as important as antibiotic, or vitamins, was not in the Koran was blasphemy. It was only when Abdel, their son and first-born child, was sick with fever, that her love of the child overcame her belief that the practice of medicine was heresy.

He looked at Safia over the cracked porcelain cup he held to his mouth. He was never sure how she had reconciled her religious beliefs. She never offered that information. Ahmed never questioned her about her change of heart, unwilling to give the appearance of triumph in this, their first small disagreement. It was only later he heard the story from others. When Abdel could no longer breathe because his throat was swollen with infection, Safia had taken him to the doctor. The doctor said he would die without medicine. Safia obtained the medicine. Soon after, she started giving the children vitamins.

Ahmed shook his head at the thought. There were so many inconsistencies in their religion he could not accept. It was good to believe in something, but when it went against common sense, it was wrong. And the fanatics who used religion as an excuse for killing others who did not believe were the most illogical of all.

Safia cleared the table and poured water into a metal basin. She washed herself in preparation for prayers. Face, hands, arms, and feet. Ahmed went through the ritual motions, willing to please her in this matter despite his own lack of belief. Besides, one had to bathe whether or not one believed.

They had barely finished when the call to prayer came from the minaret, the tall, slender tower of the mosque near their home. The muezzin's voice was harsh and shrill, but quite clear in the quiet confines of their room. "God is great. I testify that there is no god but God. I testify that Mohammed is the Prophet of God."

The call to prayer, amplified electronically, always caused Ahmed a feeling of embarrassment. It made the religion like a stage show. It seemed no different than the amplified sound of the rock groups that the decadent Westerners flocked to in place of religion. Even though he did not believe, it annoyed him to see Islam run like a carnival.

Of course, he could not express his views about Islam in public. To do so would bring him scorn and derision and, perhaps, jail or death. To disparage Islam in Libya would be as bad as making derogatory remarks about the great leader Kadafi. There were easier ways to commit suicide.

Safia unrolled the small prayer rug, knelt and touched her forehead to the floor. Ahmed knelt beside her, both facing the east wall of the kitchen. Somewhere in that direction lay Mecca. Safia had used an instrument to mark the exact direction. Ahmed prostrated himself at the proper times, saying the proper words, but letting his mind wander where it would. Tradition would have him speak the words loudly, but he could not. Safia was happy he said them at all.

Ahmed looked east and saw a concrete wall, peeling paint visible in the morning light. He looked at Safia. She saw something else he couldn't see. Seeing her, however, filled his needs. Her dark, coffee colored skin matched her black hair and amber eyes perfectly. He could not imagine changing a single thing about her.

Even her black dress was appropriate. Not because it enhanced her beauty, but because it hid it. It was one of the precepts of Islam with which Ahmed totally agreed. When Safia left the house, she would be covered from head to foot in a black dress. Even her hair would be covered, and her face would be veiled. Only her eyes would show and that was bad enough. Ahmed did not want other men to see those eyes and fall into them, heart and soul, as he had done, but there was nothing to do about that. At least other men would not see the rest of Safia.

Prayers finished. They stood. Ahmed rubbed his knees where the cold floor had sucked the feeling out of them. Safia rolled up the rug and put it away. The house was always well kept. The amenities were not many, but everything was clean and tidy. A little oasis in a disordered desert world.

He kissed the children good-bye and they stirred in their sleep. Safia waited for him by the door. She turned her face to him and let him kiss her. He knew this was a great concession. Her strict view of religion limited her contact with men, even her husband. Ahmed appreciated her desire to please him as much as the affection. He had a strong desire to stay there with her and stretch the moment out forever.

She handed him his lunch, a sack with bread and cheese. Plain fare, but nourishing, and the sack to be brought back at the end of the day. He took one last look at her, fortifying himself for the world outside and pulled the door shut behind him.

CHAPTER FOUR

COUNCIL OF WAR

Joshua Clark was not surprised that the meeting started late, it was Saturday morning. Several of the section heads were late arriving, most of them O-6s, captains and colonels, with a few 0-7s, admirals and generals, sprinkled in the group. At that elevated rank, and at zero dark thirty in the morning, the senior members of the military did not move as fast as they once did.

Clark's own section head had gone fishing. When Clark had called his boss, the captain's wife explained he had left for the lake late last night. Since there was no phone at the cottage, good Navy wife that she was, she had gone to retrieve him, but no telling when or even if she would reel him in.

Clark used the extra time to read the intelligence file on Abu Nidal. There wasn't much. He then signed on to the

Internet, typing his password "elocin," his wife's name, Nicole, spelled backward. Security might not like something so easy, but at least he could remember it. He selected LEXIS from his list of "Favorites" and entered Headline (Abu Nidal), and ran his search on the current news library. There were sixty-two stories with Abu Nidal in the headline within the last two years. More than he expected, but there was no need to narrow his search. He called up the first one and read quickly. It gave him what he wanted. An important terrorist organization based in Libya. More than ninety documented terrorist acts. Number three on the State Department's list of terrorist organizations. It had slipped over the past several years due to increased activity of other groups. One article speculated that the organization might have moved to Iraq. That was enough for now, he would do more research later. Clark signed off and went to the meeting.

An Army brigadier general stepped to the front of the small amphitheater, his back to a large wall map of Libya. Clark looked at his watch. Time, tide and terrorists wait for no man, not even captains and admirals. It was time to start the meeting. The general looked at the faces in the tiers of chairs gathered in a quarter circle facing him in the small amphitheater. He waited for silence.

It didn't take long. The officers in the room were anxious to be brought up to speed on the situation. Knowledge was power, and while information was not the same as knowledge, in the Pentagon it was status. Even more than the audience's desire for information, the demeanor of General George C. Armstrong demanded quiet. He had a commanding presence. When he looked around at a group of men, even senior officers, they usually fell silent waiting for his words. With his prematurely bald head and short stature, he did not stand out in a crowd, until you saw his eyes. When he looked at you, you could not look away.

"Gentlemen." General Armstrong added as an after thought, "and ladies." There were two female officers in the audience, but Clark thought that the tone of Armstrong's remark was condescending rather than inclusive. "Yesterday a bomb was detonated in a club frequented by U.S. servicemen. Nineteen U.S. sailors were killed." He looked around the room to judge the effect of his words. No one showed surprise. Many, like Clark, had read the message traffic before they came to the meeting. Those who had not weren't about to let on that they didn't have access to the latest scoop.

"You all have read the newspapers and know that the President has stated that any acts of terrorism directed against American citizens, anywhere in the world, will not be tolerated." The general's voice was not particularly loud or deep, but it carried throughout the medium sized room. Penetrating was the word that came to mind, or perhaps cutting. "Gentlemen, justice will be swift and it will be sure.

"What many of you don't know, and up to this point, didn't have a need to know, is that several contingency plans have been prepared for this eventuality. Several targets were selected in various Arab nations and strike plans developed. The operations were structured so that attacks could be carried out quickly once the nation that launched the terrorist attack was determined."

Clark's attention was riveted on the general, just like the other officers around him. The atmosphere was electric. Like watching a storm gather on the horizon, filling the sky with black from edge to edge, you knew what was coming.

Clark remembered the day that he heard President John F. Kennedy was assassinated. He was in Geometry class in high school. One of the students, Lee Conte, had just returned from the administrative office. Lee was one of the students who carried a slide rule on his hip and pencils in a plastic carrying case in his shirt pocket. He was always running some errand for the teachers. Lee came into the classroom, went straight to Mrs. Potter's desk and whispered in her ear. Mrs. Potter slumped in her chair for a moment, straightened up, and announced that President Kennedy had been shot. Clark could remember it as if it were yesterday. The cloudy day, the sudden silence, the unbidden thought that this could mean nuclear war. This would be a day like that. History would be made.

"An analysis of the bomb components," the general continued, "combined with analysis of message traffic to and from the Libyan embassy, leaves little doubt that Abu Nidal was behind the attack. Although they frequently shift from country to country, the Abu Nidal organization presently has a base of operations in Libya.

"Libya is the target for the retaliatory raid."

The military men and women stirred like wheat rippled by the wind. They looked around at each other to judge the effect of the general's words. To assure themselves they weren't alone, to confirm their feeling of awe, elation, trepidation, anticipation.

The general again waited for silence. To reach this rank he had become many things. He was warrior, leader, but now mostly politician. Clark watched with admiration as he played the crowd with pauses and the pacing of his words.

When General Armstrong had them again he continued. "The President has chosen the name Swift Sword for this operation. The name itself, as well as all aspects of the operation, is Top Secret."

The general moved to the large, full-length wall map, "This operation has been preplanned. The target selected is a chemical factory in Libya." He used a wooden pointer to show a location in Northeast Libya.

"The factory is believed to be making chemical weapons for Kadafi. Kadafi claims the plant produces fertilizer. Kadafi is full of shit gentlemen, but his factory is not, nor of any other kind of fertilizer. But it is a good cover. The technology used to make fertilizer and the technology to make chemical weapons is pretty much the same.

"Our human intelligence section, spies if you will, has no first hand information on this factory and Kadafi is not about to let us or any neutral outside observer inside to check it out. Knowing Libya's declared intention of exporting terrorism, the probability that this target is a chemical weapons factory is pretty good. We are not going to give Kadafi the benefit of the doubt." The general smiled. Clark, sitting in the second row, was sure that, rather than the benefit of doubt, what made the general smile was the thought of giving Kadafi a planeload of bombs. Shark-like was a good description of his grin.

The general faced the auditorium squarely, feet spread, the pointer held in both his hands behind him. "War is, of course, an extension of politics." Clark noted and admired the general's shift into pedantic mode. Now he was quoting Clausewitz and acting the college professor. "This operation is no exception. We have picked this factory because we believe it is a military target.

"At the same time, we want to minimize the number of civilian casualties, although there are bound to be some." Armstrong aimed a pocket control device at the wall to bring down a grid map.

"The factory is located in the suburbs of the town. It is likely that it was placed there to make us reluctant to use an air strike. Every effort will be made to avoid hitting civilian targets. Anti-American sentiment in this area of the world is already bad enough, we don't want to make it worse. The public relations people will put the right spin on the news and blame any civilian casualties on Kadafi for locating the plant in a populated area.

"The attack will be a coordinated strike," the general said, returning to the geographic map. "The first wave will be submarine launched cruise missiles. Using a submarine, the Navy's stealth platform, Tomahawk missiles can be launched without moving surface ships into the area and arousing suspicion. The Tomahawks will follow the terrain, several hundred feet off the ground, and are virtually undetectable until they fly through the front window of the factory. They are accurate enough that we can even pick which window. We have several nuclear powered attack submarines in the Mediterranean, and they are making high speed runs to move into launch range."

Clark looked around him at the collage of different colored uniforms in the audience. The dark blue trousers and light blue shirts of the Air Force, the forest green uniform and tan shirts of the Marines, the drab olive suits and mint colored shirts of the Army, and the black uniform and white shirts of the Navy. With a mixed group like this it must be difficult for the general to find the right balance of too much information and too little information. At least there were no blank stares.

"The next wave will be the F-117 Stealth bombers," Armstrong continued. "They will be in radar range of Libya at the time of the cruise missile attack, but of course, they are virtually undetectable on radar. The primary targets for both the Tomahawks and the Stealth bombers will be antiaircraft defenses. These include antiaircraft guns, antiaircraft missile sites, and airfields." The general indicated air defense sites on the map with the pointer as he spoke. "The Tomahawks will target missile and gun sites, and the Stealth aircraft will concentrate on the airfields, cratering the runways to prevent interceptor aircraft from taking off. We will be destroying as many aircraft on the ground as we can.

"Following the Stealth will be B-52 bombers staged out of England. The B-52s will be used to hit the factory. The B-

52s will be protected by F-14 Tomcats and F-18 Hornets on the run in. The USS *Forrestal* is moving into launch range. Any questions?"

Clark held a hand in the air and stood. "General, the Tomahawks are so accurate they could probably knock out the factory without exposing U.S. aircraft to Libyan air defenses at all. If we send aircraft over Libya, there is a very good chance that at least some will be shot down no matter how good a job we do with suppression. Then there will be United States servicemen held prisoner in Libya. Why not use only Tomahawks for the whole operation?"

The general looked at the lieutenant commander who had asked the question. Clark knew Armstrong was trying to intimidate him, but refused to look away. He also suspected that the general would recognize him from the newspaper and magazine articles about the abortive attempt to seize the submarine USS *Martin Luther King*. Clark had received the Navy Cross for his actions in that episode. If it had occurred during a war, it would have been a Medal of Honor. He had been promoted to lieutenant commander from chief, ostensibly through the Navy's Limited Duty Officer program. He had been stationed at the Pentagon for public relations purposes, but what the hell, he was here. Clark would do his job as he thought it should be done and not sit quietly merely because he was supposed to be window dressing. It dawned on him as he stood there, and the general drew the silence out, that he was the only lieutenant commander and the lowest ranking officer in the room. And the only one who had asked any questions.

"Good point Lieutenant Commander, however, there are some internal politics involved here as well as external politics. This may not be a great war, but it's the only one we've got." The general's laugh invited others to join in. Some did. "So all the different branches of the military are eager to contribute to the war effort. It will make their next appropriation bill go down easier in Congress if each service can point to some success in Libya. The Tomahawk, at least the submarine launched version, is a Navy weapon. If we win the war with a Navy weapon, what good does the Air Force get out of it? Therefore, the Air Force gets to send in the Stealth and the B-52."

He smiled. "If I could think of any way to do it, I would send some Army Apache helicopters in to take part in the raid, but there are none based within strike distance of the operation." That got a few more polite chuckles. "I like the idea of hitting Kadafi with Tomahawks and then sending in the Apaches. It has a certain symmetry." The tension exploded into laughter.

"There is another factor to consider." The general's tone turned serious. "By suppressing Kadafi's air defense before knocking out the chemical weapons factory, we destroy a lot more of his military assets. He has a pretty big pocketbook, but it's not unlimited. If he has to spend money to rebuild his air defenses, he will have that much less to spend on terrorism.

"In addition, the Tomahawk is preprogrammed and is only good against fixed targets. Planes, on the other hand, are under human control and the pilot can reprogram targets on the fly, so to speak. Having said all that, the plan does include putting a few Tomahawks on the factory floor for insurance. Rather than merely blowing up the building, we are going to be sure that no stone is left on stone.

"Remember, the object here is not just to knock out a chemical factory, but to kick ass, and we are certainly going to do just that," the general finished emphatically.

CHAPTER FIVE

HOUSTON

Craig Jones gave his wife, Elizabeth, a perfunctory kiss as he left their suburban Houston home. She stood in the door still dressed in her robe, rollers rampant in her tired yellow hair. The bunny rabbit blue, cotton robe was one she had owned just short of forever. He couldn't remember seeing her out of it recently. He was no longer sure he wanted to.

She had to get the children ready for school so there was no reason to get dressed just yet, still, Jones found it annoying. After getting the children off it would be time for coffee and the newspaper, front to back. Then time for a nap. The nap would be followed by telephone conversations with other, similarly situated ladies, and who knew what else. With luck Elizabeth would be dressed by the time he returned from work. She would also have a list of complaints about how hard her day had been. He would have to listen, or at least nod his head at appropriate times.

Jones folded his five-foot ten frame into the old Ford. He left his trenchcoat on since he didn't have time to warm the car. Even Houston could get cold. Guaranteed to get down to freezing at least once every year or so. He even saw a snow flake, once several years ago, from the forty-third floor. Still, his body had adjusted to the warm climate and forty degrees seemed frigid.

Backing out of the driveway, he slowed to a crawl to avoid scraping the rear bumper where the driveway dipped steeply at the curb. It would have been so simple to slope the driveway at a smaller angle all the way from the house when it was being constructed. It should have been obvious that any medium-sized car would drag its rear end every time it went in or out, but common sense and expediency did not mix well in Houston during the oil boom days.

He put the car in drive and headed for the interstate. The construction philosophy used for the driveway was really no different than that used for the house, just enough to get by. Almost good enough. The homes in this neighborhood all sold for two hundred-fifty thousand dollars, yet they were all rather plain-jane. The fronts were brick, at least up to the first floor, and the sides and back were wood siding. Inside accents included cheap carpet, linoleum, and the lowest priced kitchen appliances the contractor could find. All on less than a quarter acre lot. Lots of show and not much substance, but in the days when oil was bumping $35 per barrel, the contractors could not build them fast enough.

In Houston there were two main variables controlling the price of a home, size and distance from the center of the

city. You could buy the same house five or ten miles farther out for half the price, or a bigger home for the same
price. Of course the fact that Houston was the biggest city
in the United States without zoning laws didn't help. If your
neighbor wanted to turn his home into a hair styling salon,
adult video store, or a junkyard, and the restrictive cov-
enant had run out, there wasn't much you could do about
it. This pushed everyone out to the newer suburbs where
deed restrictions were still in force. City Council frequently
debated implementation of a limited form of zoning, but
he would believe it when he saw it. Fortunately the homes
in his subdivision still had deed restrictions which offered
some protection.

Traffic started backing up before Jones reached the on
ramp. On I-10 itself, the traffic was a used car salesman's
wet dream. Cars as far as the eye could see. Actually, traffic
was a misnomer. Traffic implied movement and there was
none. It was an eight-lane parking lot. Bumper to bumper
on the four inbound lanes and not a car moving. The cars
would periodically limp forward at five or ten miles per
hour for a hundred feet or a hundred yards, and then pause
for another rest. It would be like this until just inside the
I-610 Loop where the interstate widened to ten lanes. Jones
turned off the heater, which recirculated the acrid exhaust
fumes from the rusted out Pontiac in front of him.

Of course it was the people coming in from the more
distant suburbs that clogged the highway. They had to leave
home more than an hour before work to have half a chance
of getting there on time. The knowledge that all the inbound
traffic arteries around the city were like this didn't ease the
frustration. Jones felt his knuckles strain as he gripped the
steering wheel tighter. He hit the brakes as a pickup truck
with several dents forced its way in front of him. The rules

of the road were that the biggest vehicle with the most dents had the right-of-way. His jaw started to ache as he clenched his teeth. White knuckle driving. You were exhausted by the time you reached the office.

The city couldn't seem to get its act together on mass transit either. The voters finally passed a referendum a few years ago approving a rail system, but the ex-Mayor, who supported mass transit, appointed the chief opponent of the plan to implement it. Predictably, he killed it. He then ran for Mayor with a pledge to kill rail transportation, and won. Most Texans preferred to drive and they were all out crowding the highway at once, one to a car or truck or sports utility vehicle. They didn't seem to realize that a rail system would not limit their driving, but would take some of the other drivers, who might want to read the newspaper on the way to work, off the road. Texans were an independent lot.

Jones eased off on the gas pedal and let the interval between his car and the next increase to a full car length as the speed picked up to a stunning twenty miles per hour. Much more than a single car length and two cars would swerve in to fill it, one from the right and one from the left, and he would be right in the middle of a pile-up. And he would probably be the cause of it for leaving the proper interval between cars.

He turned the radio on, tuned to K-LITE, and put his mind in neutral. No use worrying about gaining a few minutes by weaving in and out of traffic. It usually turned out that the lane you changed to was the one that was ready to come to a complete stop. The police didn't bother patrolling the interstates in Houston during rush hour. Even though the speed limit was fifty-five miles per hour, no one ever reached anything approaching that.

The music stopped for a traffic report. It was hard to keep your mind off the traffic with updates every ten minutes, but it sometimes helped to avoid major bottlenecks. Usually the radio just told you what you already knew, that you were in the middle of a traffic jam. Jones turned up the volume to catch the details. A two-car pileup on 290 inbound, a car stalled on the inbound lane of the Southwest Freeway at Gessner, a minor accident on the outbound lanes of the North Freeway that was holding up traffic in both directions due to rubber-necking.

Jones shook his head. It sounded like a battlefield out on the highways today. In other words, a typical day. At least the Katy Freeway, the name for I-10 on the West Side of town, had no accidents. Just the usual stop and go. Mostly stop.

The sun was starting to paint the bottom of the corn row clouds purple and pink, as he passed the I-610 Loop. He picked up speed as the traffic cleared. He smiled as his hands relaxed on the wheel. Sometimes you concentrated so hard on the traffic that you didn't notice how beautiful a sunrise could be.

He started humming along with the song on the radio. Another five or ten minutes to the office. Michelle should be getting there just about now. Anticipation pulled him along as he mounted an overpass and the city itself came into view.

The tall metal and glass buildings looked like the Emerald City rising out of the green area around Buffalo Bayou. Houston was so flat you couldn't see even the seventy-five story Chase Tower from ground level more than a mile or two away. But the effect was magnificent as you approached the city on the highway, drove up an overpass, and saw it rise up out of the morning light for the first time.

40 ISHMAEL'S SON

PART TWO

ACTION

42 ISHMAEL'S SON

CHAPTER SIX

LIBYA

The line at the security checkpoint was more than twenty people long when Ahmed joined its end. The swarthy men in front of him shuffled along at a slow but steady pace in the gathering heat. Dressed in plain, baggy trousers and faded, short sleeve shirts they were not much different from factory workers in any other part of the world.

Ahmed shaded his eyes with his hand against the strong, morning sun as he looked at the line in front of him. It was still early, but the sun was already pouring energy into the sand and the buildings. They would fill up with heat, like a sink, until later in the day, when they too would radiate energy, cooking everyone unlucky enough to be outside.

Sand had drifted over parts of the concrete walk that led to the factory. It seemed to have a life of its own, working its way into your shoes, socks, pockets, and every aspect of your existence. It clogged your nostrils, ears, left a fine grit on your skin, and penetrated to the roots of your hair.

The clumps of weed-like vegetation that grew in a few places along the edge of the walk were not enough to hold the shifting soil. By afternoon the sand and the concrete would be hot enough to burn your feet through the bottom of your boots.

Guards stood at the gate in the twelve-foot high, chain-link fence, checking identification cards. As he waited his turn, Ahmed let his eyes wander to the coil of barbed wire strung in a spiral along the top of the fence. The security was tight for a fertilizer factory. Who would want to steal fertilizer? There was more to the factory than the workers were told, of course, but it was best not to be too curious about anything in the People's Republic of Libya.

The officer in charge of the checkpoint pulled on the end of his full, black mustache as he read badges and lists. Many soldiers had grown mustaches after Saddam Hussein invaded Kuwait. Most kept them even after Saddam lost the war. It was astounding that Hussein could lose a war with the United States and its allies and still be a hero in the Arab world. The number of mustaches in many Arab countries these days was only exceeded by the number of male babies named Saddam.

The army officer looked closely at the identification badge that Ahmed wore clipped to his shirt pocket. He carefully checked the name against the list of employees and compared Ahmed's face with the picture on the badge, even though he had checked Ahmed through the gate on many other occasions.

The two enlisted guards stood casually watching the check in process, their *Kalashnikov* AK-47 assault rifles slung over their shoulder. They rocked on the balls of their feet and tried not to look bored as the first shift of factory workers passed by. The officer finally marked Ahmed's name off the list and waved him through.

Ahmed's spirits lifted with the change in temperature as he stepped into the cool interior of the solid, concrete building. The building was cool only by comparison with the outside temperature, but even Hell would be cool by comparison with the outside temperature in the Sahara Desert on most days. The temperature was kept constant for the chemical operations that went on in the plant, not for the benefit of the workers, but whatever the reason, Ahmed was thankful.

Ahmed climbed the stairs that led to the second level overlooking the factory floor. The male secretary didn't look up from his papers as he walked past him into the manager's office. The inner office had floor to ceiling plate glass windows that gave the plant manager a clear view of the factory floor, his little kingdom.

Koch, the plant manager, was a chemical engineer from what used to be East Germany. He was studying piping diagrams at his desk when Ahmed entered. It was eight o'clock and although the temperature in the factory was moderate, at least by Libyan standards, Koch was already sweating. The perspiration stood out on his fat face like raindrops and his perpetually pink skin made him look like he had just climbed a set of stairs. Probably carrying that mass of blubber around everywhere was much like climbing stairs, Ahmed thought. The Germans used swine as a derogatory word, and Koch was a perfect caricature of the animal. It somehow seemed like poetic justice. Ahmed waited patiently, standing in front of Koch's desk.

"The current batch of chemicals being processed will be finished at nine o'clock," Koch said, handing Ahmed a piping diagram. He finally looked up at Ahmed. "The plant will then be shut down to reconfigure the pipes to produce a new chemical."

"What is the new chemical we will be producing, Herr Koch?" Ahmed knew Koch liked to be addressed as "mister," in fact insisted on it. A little flattery never hurt, although with Koch it usually didn't help much either.

"Your concern is not what chemicals are produced, but how the piping is rearranged," Koch said, irritation apparent in his voice. He wiped the back of his hand across his forehead to remove the sweat. Even his hand was fat.

"You would be wise not to be too curious about what goes on at this plant. Just take care that you don't come in contact with any of the new product," he said pointing his pudgy finger at Ahmed. The perspiration on the blond hairs of his fingers made them glisten.

"Your group will be responsible for changing several of the elbows around to realign the pipes. The changes are highlighted with yellow marker on the drawings." Koch stood and leaned across the desk. He pointed out the piping changes on his copy of the diagram on his desk. Ahmed forced himself not to draw back from the strong, pungent smell the German exuded. Water was not so precious that you could not bathe regularly. Perhaps the German could not smell himself. Perhaps a bath would not make much of a difference.

"You must be careful that all the flanges are tightened to the torque specified on the drawings." Koch thumped the list of figures in the corner of the blueprint. "After the flanges are tight, you must personally recheck all of them yourself. There must be no leakage. Do you understand?"

Ahmed nodded his head. "Yes, sir."

"Do not over torque," Koch continued. "Too much torque or too little torque and the flange will leak."

Ahmed remained silent. Why was Koch lecturing him on his job? He was the foreman; he knew what to do.

"Do you think you can get it done without screwing it up?"

Rage boiled up in Ahmed's throat and he felt his teeth clench together. Koch usually ended his instructions with an insult. Ahmed had come to expect it, but it didn't make it easier to take. Koch examined him closely, waiting for a response. Ahmed slowly nodded his head, not speaking.

"Good. I will check the flow path and the torque settings myself when you are done."

Ahmed knew that he would. If nothing else the German was thorough. Satisfied that Ahmed understood, Koch dismissed him with a wave of his hand, sat down, and went back to reviewing the drawings.

Ahmed forced his jaw muscles to relax as he climbed back down the stairs. He had trouble concealing his dislike for Koch, but the job paid very well, enough to endure the several times a day he had to deal with the man. Even with the higher wages that a worker could earn in Libya these days, the job as a work crew leader in the factory was good. While Brother Leader, the term Kadafi applied to himself, had promised to do many things, raising wages was one promise he kept.

Ahmed crossed the factory floor. The noise at the factory was no worse than usual. That is, it was very loud. The steam preheaters were leaking again, and gave off a steady, high pitched sound, exactly like a teapot. The boilers provided a constant, deep-throated roar. The hundred humans in the building, yelling back and forth to each other above the din, added little to the overall noise level.

Ahmed's four-man crew waited for him in the assembly room drinking strong, sweet coffee. Ahmed didn't like

the sweet liquid, which was almost like syrup, but he sometimes drank it just because it was there, and because it was
free. Another benefit of the worker's state.

"Today we will be realigning pipes to produce a different chemical," Ahmed said. He spoke slowly, firmly making sure they understood. "We will pick up the blank flanges
and pipes from the supply shop and move them to the
proper place in the factory to be ready for the shutdown."

The men nodded and finished their coffee. No questions. Ahmed sighed at their lack of curiosity. To them it
was just a job, something to fill the hours and pay the bills.
He waved his hand for them to follow him.

They picked up the large, stainless steel sections of pipe
in the storage area. The pipe sections were loaded on a
heavy, metal frame, hand dolly for transport to the proper
locations in the plant.

At the first stop a long, three-inch diameter elbow was
unloaded by two of the workers. Ahmed took one of the
men aside while the rest waited with the dolly. Pulling the
drawing from his pocket, Ahmed pointed out the connec-
tions for the new pipe.

"When the plant is completely shut down," Ahmed said,
yelling to be heard above the preheaters, "We will remove
the blank flange that covers the end of the pipe here." He
indicated the pipe on the drawings and then tapped the
actual pipe with his hand. "I will come back and we will
remove the old elbow where it connects these two pipes."
He again touched the appropriate pipes with his hands.

Rachmiel, the man Ahmed was instructing, nodded his
head and looked at each pipe as Ahmed placed his hand
on it. Ahmed watched his eyes as he gave instructions.

"Do you understand?" Rachmiel's eyes had their usual
dull, glazed look and it was difficult to tell whether he understood, but he nodded again.

"Very well," Ahmed sighed. "Put on your mask before removing the blank flange, and wait until I return before starting to remove the old pipe section. It will take three of us to unbolt the old elbow and lower it to the floor without damaging it."

Ahmed moved off with the dolly and the rest of the crew to the next location, where he left another section of pipe and another worker. At the final stop Ahmed helped the last two men unload the remaining pipe sections and tools, and waited for the processing plant to shut down.

The preheaters were the first to be taken off line, followed quickly by the boilers. The quiet in the plant, or at least the absence of the constant background roar, was unnatural, but not unwelcome.

The announcing system, which was often hard to hear, and even harder to understand when the plant was operating, was clearly audible. "Commence change over. Realign the pipes." Koch's accent was unmistakable, even over the amplifier. Ahmed could just see Koch across the plant standing at his office window.

Ahmed pushed his mask against his face with one hand, and pulled the rubber straps snug behind his head with the other. He held his hands over the air intake openings and inhaled to test that the mask was airtight. The rubber mask collapsed against his face. Good, no air leaks.

Satisfied that his mask was sealed properly, he checked that the masks on the two men with him were on correctly. He held his hands over the filters, which stuck out on each side of the mask, and made each man, one at a time, breath in to collapse the mask. The large, clear plastic lens over the eyes, the circular filters on each side of the head, and the green rubber of the mask made them all look like men with grasshopper heads. All the pipes had been flushed prior to changing out the sections, but it was good to be careful. There was always a possibility that chemicals would still be left in the loops and low points, and breathing the vapors could be harmful. Also, Koch insisted on observing all precautions.

The first blank flange came off easily. Ahmed made sure that each of the bolts that was removed was in good shape, and that the threads were not damaged and were free of corrosion. They would be used again.

The pipe section they were working on was difficult to separate and remove. One of the nuts refused to move on the bolt. Ahmed directed one of the men to slip a cheater bar, a hollow length of steel pipe, over the end of the wrench to increase its effective length and the amount of torque on the nut and bolt. Even after the nut started turning, it moved very slowly and had to be coaxed along at every rotation. Ahmed made a mental note to replace that nut and bolt.

By the time all the bolts were removed Ahmed was sweating, as much from anxiety as from the exertion. The job had gone much slower than it should have. Koch would be down soon yelling at everyone to hurry.

They were just lifting the new pipe into place when the sirens went off. The high pitched wail was loud enough to cause his head to hurt, and the two men with Ahmed placed their hands over their ears to shut out the sound.

They had all practiced gas leak drills many times and Ahmed started putting on his white, chemical resistant coveralls immediately. Without looking around he knew that everyone in the building would be donning gas masks and nonessential personnel would be leaving the plant. The casualty team would obtain equipment located at strategic places around the plant and converge on the scene of the leak.

Ahmed and his crew were part of the casualty team. They already had their masks on and their tools with them, so they were a step ahead of the rest. Ahmed looked at his men as he finished fastening his coveralls. One of the men had started putting on his coveralls, but the other still held his hands clamped tightly over his ears. Ahmed shook his arm and pointed at the coveralls stored in a box on the dolly, angry that he had to remind him to get moving.

Ahmed and his men were all fully dressed even before the sirens had stopped wailing. All that was necessary was to wait for information on the location of the leak.

"Sensors indicate a chemical leak on the main floor near the superheaters," the public announcing system boomed out. "Casualty team assemble at the site in gas masks and protective clothing."

Ahmed grabbed the front of the dolly and started pulling it behind him at a trot, as the others pushed from behind. The dolly retraced the path it had taken earlier in the day dropping off sections of pipe. The superheaters were near the first location where Rachmiel was working.

Ahmed felt a sense of foreboding. Rachmiel was not the most intelligent of his men. His fears were confirmed when he saw him stretched out on the concrete floor as they approached. He stopped the cart beside Rachmiel and bent to check his condition. He was still conscious, but his breathing was labored and ragged as he twisted in pain on the floor. It sounded like plastic being wrinkled each time he took air into his lungs and exhaled, and blisters covered the left side of his face. His mask was off. Looking around, Ahmed saw that it was still on the cart. He had never put it on. Ahmed felt a moment of anger at himself for not making him put it on before he left him.

Ahmed examined the pipes, looking for the source of the chemical leak. The medical team would arrive shortly and there was nothing that could be done for Rachmiel until they arrived. The leak was not hard to find. A brownish liquid bubbled out of a flange that connected two sections of pipe. Some of the fluid was collecting in a puddle on the floor, but much of it had vaporized into the atmosphere. A yellow brown cloud hung over the group.

"Wrenches," Ahmed shouted, as he pulled tools off the dolly. He placed one wrench on the bolt head and motioned for one of the men to hold the plate in place. Using a second wrench, he tightened the nut as much as he could. No time to worry about proper torque settings now. Fuck Herr Koch.

Ahmed moved his wrenches to another nut and bolt, one hundred eighty degrees around the circumference of the pipe from the first one. Tightening opposing pairs would ensure the flange was firmly seated all around its edge.

He was careful not to let the liquid get on his clothing. Chemical resistant coveralls, were not the same as chemical impervious coveralls. Rachmiel's moans provided a constant reminder of what this particular witches brew could do. Fertilizer! Right!

The hiss of the liquid fizzing out of the joint gradually diminished and eventually stopped as Ahmed tightened the bolts one at a time. As he went back and tightened all the bolts one last time he had time to think. This was one of the elbows that was scheduled to be changed. Why was it under pressure? Someone had screwed up badly.

The rest of the casualty team, Koch in the lead, arrived as they finished. Koch looked like a doughboy in the white coveralls. At least he comes to the scene for the emergency, Ahmed thought, rather than hiding in his office.

"Cover the spill," Koch ordered.

Ahmed felt like tapping his head to see if it was still there. He should have thought of that. The men in the casualty team started throwing chemical absorbing paper towels over the liquid on the concrete floor to prevent more of it from vaporizing.

Koch bent to look at Rachmiel as the medical team started working on him. "Why wasn't this man wearing a gas mask?" he demanded as he turned to face Ahmed.

"He was instructed to put on a mask," Ahmed said.

"He doesn't have one on," Koch said, shouting. "You did not supervise him properly!"

"I was with the other men removing a section of pipe." Ahmed refused to be intimidated. "Why was this section of pipe under pressure?" Ahmed said, raising his own voice. "Why wasn't the chemical flushed from the pipe before the order to change out the pipes was given? And what is this chemical that has fallen on my man!" Ahmed's voice grew louder as he asked each question. Without thinking about what he was doing, he moved up chest to chest with the taller Koch.

Koch took a startled step backward, glancing at the large Crescent wrench Ahmed still held in his hand. Ahmed was a few inches shorter than Koch and eighty pounds lighter, but formidable in his anger.

"You don't need to know about the chemical," Koch said, lowering his voice to a normal tone.

"What is the chemical?" Ahmed stepped closer so that he was still toe to toe with Koch. "One of my men may be dying and I want to know what is killing him."

Koch looked around and stepped away from the group. He motioned Ahmed to follow. He whispered, "The chemical is mustard gas. Its purpose is to kill people. That is why I have insisted on everyone wearing gas masks when the piping is opened.

"You are not supposed to know what the chemical is. Officially only fertilizer is produced here. We actually do produce fertilizer, but only when the inspection teams come. It will go bad for you if it is found that you know what is produced here and I will deny that I told you." Koch pointed his finger at Ahmed's chest.

Ahmed was stunned. "What of my man? Will he survive?"

"I am sorry about your man. His chances are not good. The mustard gas destroys the lungs. He should have had his mask on."

Koch held up his hands as Ahmed started to speak. "I know that the pipe should have been depressurized and flushed. I will find out who is responsible for that and they will regret their negligence."

CHAPTER SEVEN

CASE FILES

Craig Jones checked his watch as he pulled up to the automatic gate at the parking garage. Seven-fifty. Forty-five minutes door-to-door, not too bad for a fifteen-mile trip, especially in Houston. He slipped his magnetic card into the slot, waited for the arm to lift, and started up the circular, racetrack ramp to the seventh level. Another five minutes out of the day wasted driving up to the seventh level. Minutes a day out of your life mattered and there were only so many allotted to each individual. Even Einstein could not get around that imperative.

After spending almost ten times that on the trip in, however, it hardly seemed worthwhile paying an extra twelve dollars a month to park one or two levels down. Besides, Michelle parked on the seventh level. He seldom saw her in the parking garage, and she wouldn't let him walk her in if he did, but it was nice to think she might be on the same floor. Still, he looked for her car as he circled level seven, finally finding a slot on level eight.

He took the crosswalk to the tower. The first bank of elevators was for people going to floors forty-nine to sixty-nine. To go all the way to the top, the sixty-ninth floor, you had to change elevators at the fifty-fifth floor. An architect once told him there was a physical limitation on the equipment, in particular the cable which held the elevator, which prevented running the elevator from the first floor to the sixty-ninth floor. It sounded reasonable.

He was last on and next to the door, but as the door opened on the fifty-fifth level, he and the other men squeezed to the side to let the ladies out. After they were out, he trooped over with the others to wait for the next elevator to continue the trip to the top. He smiled as the men stood aside letting the ladies on first. Texas etiquette, the ladies all get on the elevator first and stand in the back, and then the men, who are last on, go through contortions to let them off first when the elevator stops.

Jones got out at sixty-one and fished in his wallet for his magnetic security card with one hand while holding his briefcase under his other arm. He had just finished his one-hand extraction of the magnetic card when the chime announced the arrival of another elevator. He looked over as Michelle Stern got out of the elevator.

"Why don't you keep your card in your pocket, Craig? It would be easier than fumbling around in your wallet each time you go in or go out," she said, reaching inside the coat pocket of her business suit for her card.

He noticed she wasn't even wearing an overcoat. She warmed up her car at home while drinking coffee, she previously told him, was in the unheated parking garage for only a minute, then to the heated overpass, to the heated office. Why bother with a coat? A cold day in Houston is only in the thirties or forties anyway.

Also, an overcoat wouldn't show off that fine figure as nicely, not that he minded. At five-foot eight she was almost as tall as he was but had a figure that looked more like a model that a professional. Not the overstuffed Playboy kind of figure, but the well-proportioned women you find in fashion magazines.

"I tried that. Every time I changed shirts or changed suits, the card was always at home in the other garment. Then I would have to hang around the door until a beautiful engineer came by to let me in." He smiled broadly.

"I bet you say that to all the engineers." She returned the smile as she inserted her card into the card reader. The magnetic lock clicked, releasing the door and Jones pulled it open to let Michelle walk past him.

"Since you're the only female engineer in this corporation, I would get in trouble telling it to any of the other engineers," he said, struggling to catch up and stuff his wallet and card back in his pants pocket at the same time. Those long legs cover some distance. He drew abreast of her two doors down the hall.

"Not true," she said. "This is Houston and some of those engineers, especially the ones that live in Montrose, would love to hear some of your flattery."

"I bet they would, but they would start sending me flowers at the office and I don't think I could handle that."

She looked at him as they continued down the hall. "We just passed your office."

"I know, but I thought I would walk you to your office. Visit for awhile."

She walked a few more steps, stopped, and turned to face him. She held her lightweight, leather briefcase in front of her with both hands as she carefully chose her words.

"Please go back to your office."
"Do you really want me to?"
"Yes."

Michelle stood for a moment watching him retrace his steps and then continued to her office. She set her briefcase down on the desk and looked at her phone, one arm across her chest and her other hand cupping her chin. She picked up the phone and dialed four digits.

"Jones speaking."

"I didn't mean to be so rough on you in the hall, Craig, but you can't hang around me at the office. I told you that when we started this."

"But I never get to see you," he said, sounding cross.

"You see me every day at work, five days a week." She smoothed her skirt under her as she sat down and crossed her legs.

"That's not what I mean. I never get to spend any time alone with you. I never get to touch you or kiss you or just be with you."

"Well you were the one that started this." She wondered sometime if he really paid attention to what she said.

"You knew how difficult this would be," she continued. "Having an affair with someone you work with is the stupidest thing I can imagine."

"Would you like to go to lunch today?"

She sighed. He was not listening. "What did you have in mind?" she asked running one finger around her lower lip to check the lip-gloss.

"We could go over to the Hyatt and check out their room service."

He sounded so hopeful she smiled in spite of herself. "You have already spent your lunch money for the week. We had 'lunch' at the Doubletree on Monday. Elizabeth is going to catch you putting the children's pop-tarts in your coat pocket and start wondering what you do with your lunch money."

"Screw Elizabeth!" he said with feeling.

"That's your job," she laughed.

"Besides, we were at the Hyatt two weeks ago," she said. "If we keep going back the desk clerk is going to start remembering us. Or someone from the office will see you checking in or checking out. Then it will be only a matter of time before one of the secretaries figures it out.

"That's all some of those girls live for," she said. "They get a whiff of an office romance and they will follow you around, stand outside your office to listen to your conversations, and open your personal mail. Even though we walk over to the hotel at separate times one of them will follow one of us. There are already enough clues, like why do you and I always seem to be on the phone at the same time?

"Coincidence?" he suggested.

"Some of the secretaries have both of our extensions on their phone and will notice sooner or later that they both seem to light up at the same time, rather frequently, and then go out at the same time." She flipped her head to the side to clear her shoulder length, blond, naturally curly hair from her face where it had fallen over one eye. "If we didn't have a conference call light on these new phones to show when someone else is listening in, I wouldn't talk to you at the office at all."

"I still want to see you," he said. "You won't take me over to your place, we can't be seen together at lunch, the hotel is out. Where can we go?"

"You'll think of something."

She twisted the cord around her finger and looked around her small office as she waited for him to answer. The Ansel Adams photo on the wall always made her feel good. The sharp contrast of black and white in the picture made the neutral beige of the walls come alive. Baxter Oil was too cheap to buy office decorations for the employees, but it would have been too depressing to have to look at the bare walls of the interior office with no decoration. Adams was expensive, but if you were going to buy something, you might as well do it right.

Jones was talking again. "I just want to see you. I think of you all the time."

"I think about you too." Her voice was matter of fact.

"I'll tell you what," she said. "I have to pull some files out of storage. If you just want to see me you can meet me in storage. I'll take the service elevator and you take the fire stairs. I'll let you in when you get up to storage."

Jones closed the file he pulled out of his credenza when he arrived. He thought about putting it away, but decided to leave it out. With the file on his desk, if the associate general counsel for his section walked by, he would know he was at work. Baxter had a clean desk policy that required that all work be cleared from the desk every night. It was a hassle, but it was a good security measure. It also helped keep you organized, he grudgingly admitted. Also, if you had a file out, you must be somewhere around the office working. *Ipso facto*, the fact speaks for itself. Lawyer logic, but it worked.

He reached behind the door of his office, took his suit coat off the hook and put it on, and straightened his tie. Through force of habit, he ran his hand through his straight, dark brown hair to make sure it wasn't sticking up. Good thing there wasn't a mirror. He didn't want to have to look at the flecks of gray contaminating the color. He put a wintergreen lifesaver in his mouth and smiled. He felt like he was going on a date.

After waiting a few minutes to give Michelle a head start, he walked around the corridor that separated the interior offices from the offices on the outer wall. Through a large window in an empty office, he could see the city stretching south and east to the Houston Ship Channel. On a clear day, like today, you could see, not forever, but at least to the Astrodome.

Reaching the fire door to the emergency stairwell behind the little coffee kitchen, he looked up and down the hall to make sure no one saw him. It was early, but several people were already at work. He pushed the door open and started up.

The storage room was only four flights up but he was winded by the time he finished the climb. It may have been the physical exertion, but more likely it was excitement at the thought of seeing Michelle. Probably a combination of both.

He tried the fire door. Locked. Women were always late. You could enter the stairwell from any level, but the doors were locked on the inside for security purposes. More than one company leased space in the building and it was not a good idea to give one corporation access to the offices of another though the back door, the fire door. You could only exit the stairwell at ground level. Or if someone opened the door from the office side for you.

Michelle opened the door with a file in her arms. Jones leaned through the door, kissed her.

"Honey, I'm home," he said.

She laughed and took his hand. "Not here. Let's go back in the stacks. We can hear if anyone comes into the Baxter section."

The file storage section of the building was functional. It had no exterior windows and had not been finished, or built-out as the construction workers phrased it. Different companies rented space on this level, for a nominal amount, to store files and used office furniture. It contained all the typical clutter that a business might buy, wasn't using, but wasn't ready to throw away. It was the attic of the office world.

Michelle led him to a wall that divided off one entire end of the floor. It was plasterboard from the floor up to eight feet, and then heavy, mesh wire to the ceiling. Michelle unlocked the door and relocked it behind them. Rows of storage bins stood ten feet high. The rows stretched from the plasterboard walls to the wall of the building, divided by corridors at each end and at the middle.

Michelle took his hand and led him the length of the stacks, all the way to the back, as far from the door as they could go.

"Now what was it you wanted to talk to me about, Craig Jones?" she said, turning to face him and putting both her hands behind his neck and leaning back against the stack.

He slipped his arms around her waist and pulled her close. "I just wanted to tell you what a fine engineer I think you are," he said smiling.

"And?" She rested her forehead against his and ran her fingers through his hair. This close he could not bring her face into focus. The familiar crystal blue color of her eyes stretched from horizon to horizon.

"And I love you."

"You don't know me well enough to love me," she said, ending the discussion with a kiss.

He drew out the kiss, running his tongue around her mouth and sucking on her lower lip. He felt himself stir where his hips pressed against her. He slid his hands down her back and pulled her hips closer. The tight fabric of her wool skirt felt good against his hands, almost like skin.

Almost. He slipped his hand under her jacket and pulled her blouse out of the waistband of her skirt. He ran his hands up her bare back.

Jones leaned back and looked at her. She had her eyes closed and her head tilted up, a slight smile on her face. An enigmatic smile. What thoughts were floating through her mind?

She ran her hands slowly up and down his back and under his coat. He kissed her again and slid one hand around to cup her breast. He held his other arm tight around her waist as if afraid he would lose her. He lifted her white lace brassiere and traced slow circles around her nipples. She sucked her breath in sharply as he touched the tip of her nipple.

He leaned back to look at her again. Her eyes were still closed, her mouth parted slightly. He expected her to tell him to stop, someone might come in, your hands are too cold. He kissed her neck, moving his mouth down to her shoulders, both hands now on her breasts. His hip pinned her to the shelves. His fingers brushed lightly over both nipples, which were erect and hard.

Moving both hands around to her back, he pulled her skirt up, a hand full at a time. When her skirt was at her waist he slipped his hands inside the waistband of her panty hose and underneath her panties. The feel of her skin under his hands made his mind go blank. It was like the high you get from the first shot of whiskey, warm and filling.

He shifted his mouth back to hers as he moved his hand down her bottom as far as he could reach. His arms just weren't long enough. He slid his hand around to the front and was still quietly amazed that she had not stopped him and afraid she would.

She was always moist. He let the tip of one finger slide part way inside her as he caressed her. She moved her hips in counterpoint to the stroking motion of his hand. Using his other hand he pushed her panty hose down below her thighs. He unzipped his trousers, loosened his belt, and drew himself out of his shorts. She leaned back against the file stacks, hands behind her head, gripping the shelf.

As he slipped inside her he thought it is physically impossible to make love while standing, with each partner having both feet on the floor, and the woman having her panties half way off. The angle was all wrong. Yet here they were, four on the floor, pedal to the medal. It was wonderful disproving the laws of physics.

CHAPTER EIGHT

SPRINGFIELD

The USS *Springfield* (SSN-716) sprinted through the water at more than thirty knots. Even with her hull fouled by eighteen months of marine growth and barnacles, she was a fast lady.

Thirty knots may not seem fast compared to a car, which most people drive at seventy mph now that the speed limit on the Interstate has been increased to sixty-five mph. But a knot, or nautical mile per hour, is more than fifteen percent faster than a standard mile per hour. Since the *Springfield* was more than six thousand tons displacement, compared to the two or three thousand pounds for an average car, thirty plus knots was impressive. An amazing amount of steel to be moving at any speed, and with her ample girth she had momentum which would make Sir Isaac Newton proud.

Pushing the big Los Angeles Class submarine through a hole in the ocean, with one hundred forty-three men on board, was like driving a bus through a tunnel and making the tunnel at the same time. The nuclear reactor that provided the power to do this was big enough to supply the electrical power for a small city.

Seaman Rosalles O'Grady didn't care how fast thirty knots was, what he cared about was that he couldn't go to the head. He shifted his five-foot seven-inch body around in the padded chair, trying to find a more comfortable position. It was hard enough to sit in one place for several hours on watch, but with a full bladder it was almost impossible. The cold air blowing on the back of his neck from the air conditioning duct behind his seat didn't help either.

With the ship making a high speed run to launch position, the executive officer, or XO, wasn't allowing any watch reliefs. Normally when O'Grady was the helmsman, which was the watch he had, he could shift control of the rudder and the fairwater planes, the large winglike structures attached to the submarine sail, to the planesman. The planesman sat just outboard of O'Grady at the station closest to the hull, and had the capability to operate everything from his station while O'Grady made a pit stop. Another option was getting the messenger of the watch to relieve him for a few minutes, if the messenger of the watch was qualified as helmsman. But that was at normal cruising speed, five or ten knots.

O'Grady took a quick look around the darkened Control Room. Everyone was more alert than usual because of the high speed run. There was little of the usual background chatter. At this speed, any small accident, like loss of hydraulic control to the stern planes, could send the ship on a depth excursion of hundreds of feet in a matter of seconds.

With the *Springfield* presently running at 500 feet below the surface, if the stern planes failed on full dive, the ship would quickly head for the bottom at thirty knots with a forty-degree down angle. That could easily place the ship below crush depth without immediate action by all members of the control team. Going below crush depth, the depth at which the ship imploded, was an evolution that even the *Springfield* would not rise from.

"Diving Officer, request permission to make a head call," O'Grady said, holding the control yoke with his left hand and his crotch with his right. He put as much emotion into his voice as he could. He hated to be the first one to ask. It wasn't macho to have to ask to go to the toilet, but he was not going to last much longer. On a ship with an all male crew, macho was even more important than if there were females aboard. Submarines were the last male bastions in the Navy. Surface ships all had women assigned to their crews, but on submarines no women, no way.

The diving officer, Lieutenant Smith, hunched forward in the control chair, elbows on his knees, and chewed on his gum for a few seconds without answering. He was seated between and slightly behind the helmsman and planesman. He swiveled his head around almost ninety degrees to look over his shoulder at the XO on the Conning Stand to see if the XO had heard the request or if he was going to have to repeat it.

The XO, second in command of the ship, was also officer of the deck (OOD) for this evolution. Like most executive officers in the nuclear Navy he tried to stay on top of everything by doing everything. The ship was short one qualified officer of the deck this patrol, and the XO was taking his turn in the watch rotation rather than have the two other qualified OODs stand port and starboard, six hours on and six hours off. One of the new junior officers was almost qualified to stand the watch, and O'Grady was glad he was not getting the pressure that guy was getting.

O'Grady suspected the XO also wanted to be sure all the preparations for launch were completed properly, and a good way of doing that was to stand the watch. When a ship had a good XO, and this one was, all the captain had to do was be the morale officer and make sure the crew was happy.

"Hang tight, Rosy," the XO said. "We'll be slowing for a sonar search in a few minutes and then we will get a round of relief for everyone."

O'Grady groaned. He didn't like being called Rosy, but it was much better than the nicknames some of the men had acquired, such as Greasy, Sugar Bear, and Warhead. Pilots picked their call signs, but sailors called each other names. Besides, with his Hispanic complexion, brown skin and black, curly hair, given to him by his mother; and his striking blue eyes, inherited from his Irish father; the name fit. He wore it as best he could.

He gritted his teeth, determined not to ask for a break again no matter what it took. It was a vicious cycle. Standing a one in three watch rotation, six hours on and twelve hours off, meant his sleep period rotated forward each day until he finally had to stay up twenty-four hours to equalize. The result was that he had to have a couple of cups of coffee to wake up before going on watch. You "stood" your watch sitting in a padded seat, so you had a couple more cups on watch to stay awake. Then you paid the price if you couldn't get relieved for a head call. Never again will I drink that much coffee before watch, he thought, which he had thought many times before.

"All ahead one-third," the XO ordered.

"All ahead one-third, aye," O'Grady replied, acknowledging the order and repeating it back to show he heard it correctly. Orders to change the depth and angle on the ship were given to the diving officer. Orders to change course and speed were given directly to the helmsman. O'Grady twisted the engine order telegraph from the Flank position to the One-Third position. The pointer on the EOT (Engine Order Telegraph) clicked over as maneuvering moved their speed indicator to match.

"Sonar, Conn," the XO called over the MC, "Slowing to one-third speed. Search around and report all contacts."

"Conn, Sonar, aye," the squawk box replied.

"Chief of the Watch, give everyone a relief who needs one," the XO ordered. "Start with O'Grady before he embarrasses all of us."

The messenger of the watch was in Control, listening to the conversation, and stepped over to O'Grady's station. "Ready to relieve," he said, hanging his clipboard on a hook on the sheet metal bulkhead.

"Speed twenty knots, slowing to one-third, depth five hundred feet, course one-seven-zero degrees. I stand relieved," O'Grady said, running the words together as he unclipped the seat belt holding him to his chair.

"Whoa, horse," said the diving officer, putting his hand on O'Grady's shoulder as he stood to leave. "You have permission to relieve the watch."

O'Grady's face flushed at the mild reprimand for forgetting to ask permission for the relief. "I have permission to relieve the watch, aye," he said. He was out of Control and sliding down the handrails to crews berthing, several inches above the metal steps, almost before the words were out of his mouth.

The pace in Control picked up as the crew prepared to launch missiles. "Left ten degrees rudder, come left to heading zero-six-five," the XO ordered.

The XO listened to the reply while picking up the microphone. "Sonar, Conn. Coming left to zero-one-five. When the towed array straightens out, search astern."

The big submarine banked into the turn as the rudder moved left, much as an airplane tilts in the direction it is turning. Although there was no visible horizon for reference almost everyone on board felt the turn. Those who didn't could watch the coffee in the cups sitting in the metal brackets attached to the bulkhead, climb the side of the cup.

Making a high speed run, you were essentially blind. Your eyes, the passive sonar receivers, were unable to detect any noise from other ships over the sound of water rushing past the bow. After slowing to a speed at which the sonar was operable, making sure you were not being trailed by another submarine was high on a submariner's priority list.

O'Grady stepped up to the diving officer. "Request permission to relieve the watch," he said.

"Rosy, that was the fastest head call I have ever seen you make. You didn't think we were going to start without you, did you?

"Permission granted to relieve the watch."

"Speed twelve knots," the messenger reported. "Slowing to one-third. Left ten degrees rudder, coming left to zero-six-five degrees. Depth 500 feet." The messenger picked up his clipboard as he slipped out of the chair. O'Grady repeated back the speed, course, heading and depth and took his seat.

"Of course I didn't think you would start without me, Diving Officer," O'Grady said smiling. The hydraulic oil hissed softly in the lines as O'Grady shifted the yoke back and forth to test his control of the fairwater planes. "After all, the reason for having your best helmsman on the fairwater planes at Battle Stations, is to make sure the job gets done right."

"What makes you think you have the inside scoop on when we are going to set Battle Stations, Rosy? Did the mess cooks give you the latest rumor when you went below?"

"Hey," O'Grady said. "The mess cooks may run the rumor mill, but they are usually right. I also saw the captain up and getting a cup of coffee when I made my head call. Getting the captain on station and arrival at the launch point are all we need to do it. My momma didn't raise no dummies."

"Captain in Control," the quartermaster of the watch announced from his position near the plotting table at the entrance to Control. Everyone in Control concentrated a little harder on his job as the captain stepped into Control from the passageway to his stateroom.

"XO, what is the status of preparations to launch missiles?" the captain asked in a quiet, throaty voice, as he stepped up on the platform that held the periscope, in the center of Control. The CO's (Commanding Officer) voice wasn't loud, but everyone in Control was focused on what the boss was saying, in addition to what they were doing.

"Good morning, Captain," the XO said, turning to face the balding, middle-aged man.

Dressed in blue cotton coveralls, the only thing that distinguished the *Springfield*'s short, stocky commanding officer from civilian middle level managers, besides the silver commander oak leaves on his collar, was the ramrod straight posture and self-confidence that only near absolute authority gives. Ashore there were civilians, and even military officers, that commanded more men. But ashore, there was always a more senior manager, or officer, or board of director, or Congress to second guess everything you said or did. At sea the captain was king. No messages went off the ship without his signature. If a man on board was cited for a violation of any of the rules, the captain was both the judge and the jury.

The captain of the *Springfield* had a name, but to the crew, he was simply "Captain." He was a commander, but the commanding officer of any ship was always called "captain," even if he was only an ensign. The authority of the captain was as close to absolute as you could get this side of a dictatorship. Many officers who advanced to squadron commander or higher, firmly believed the high point of their career was when they were captain of a ship.

"Sir," the XO continued. "We are in launch position, completing a search astern. No contacts reported. Four Tomahawk cruise missiles were loaded in the torpedo tubes during the midwatch according to your night orders. Thirty minutes to scheduled launch time."

"Very well, man Battle Stations."

"Man Battle Stations, aye," the XO repeated. "Chief of the Watch [COW], man Battle Stations."

"Man Battle Station, aye"

The COW twisted the red, plastic coated handle for the klaxon on the Ballast Control Panel. The ear numbing blast from the horns rose and fell throughout the ship, sounding like an amplified electronic egg timer. The sound was one of several used for all hands evolutions, each separate and distinct, but all incredibly loud. The Battle Stations alarm was followed by the COW's voice on the announcing system. "Man Battle Stations." The COW turned the klaxons, the electric horns located through the ship, back on and let them run through several more cycles. Even the devil himself would have had trouble sleeping through that noise, O'Grady thought.

Personnel in Control unwound coiled telephone cords from sound powered phones, and plugged them in as additional watch standers arrived. With the voice powered mike mounted on a chest plate and the earphones mounted in ear muffs, the sailors soon looked like a cross between an old fashioned telephone operator and Mickey Mouse. The electricity might fail throughout the ship, but the old, tried and true technology of the voice powered phone system would still enable the officer of the deck in the Control Room to receive reports about the status of the ship, and give orders.

"Sonar, this is the Captain," the CO said, picking up the microphone connected directly to the Sonar Room. "Have you completed your search astern?"

"Captain, Sonar." O'Grady recognized the voice of the chief sonarman on the speaker. "We've completed our search astern. We are just starting to pick up a surface contact in the first convergence zone. It appears to be the freighter we held between us and the beach that we detected prior to the last high speed run."

"Captain, aye."

"Diving Officer, make your depth 100 feet," the captain ordered. "Helmsman, right fifteen degrees rudder, make your course one eight zero degrees."

"Captain has the Conn," the XO announced to make sure that all the watch standers were aware that operational control had been transferred to the captain.

"Make my depth 100 feet, Diving Officer aye," the diving officer said.

"Right fifteen degrees rudder, make my course one-zero-eight degrees, Helmsman aye," O'Grady repeated.

"Planesman, ten degree up angle," the diving officer ordered. "Helmsman, make your depth 100 feet." O'Grady knew the Captain liked to change depth promptly and the diving officer was using a bigger angle on the ship because the speed had decreased.

"Ten degrees up," the planesman repeated, pulling the yoke back to bring the bow up. The angle on the stern planes, located at the very aft end of the ship, and far from the center of buoyancy, began to change the angle on the ship almost immediately.

"Make my depth 100 feet, aye," O'Grady replied, pulling the yoke back. The big fairwater planes, located closer to the ship's center of buoyancy, had less effect on the angle of the ship, but a greater effect on the depth. O'Grady kept the wheel on the yoke turned to the right as he watched the depth gauge and the course indicator.

"Maneuvering manned for Battle Stations, Control aye," the enlisted man serving as phone talker repeated into his sound powered mike, holding the button on the mouthpiece down. The reports were coming in from all over the ship as all the men on board the *Springfield* manned the extra positions required to prepare the ship for battle. The phone talker gave the reports to the XO as they came in and another sailor kept track of the compartments that were ready on a plexiglass status board.

"Captain, Battle Stations manned," the XO reported after the last compartment called in. The XO had been relieved as OOD and was now serving as approach officer, his assignment during Battle Stations. Other personnel in Control and throughout the ship had been relieved by personnel on the Battle Stations watch bill, and in turn had reported to their own Battle Stations. The best qualified man was now at every station on board the ship. O'Grady was proud to be the best at his assignment, battle station planesman.

"Very well. Has all the target information been downloaded to the missiles?" the Captain asked.

"Yes sir."

"Very well.

"Weapons Officer, has a course been programmed into each of the missiles to fly them around the surface contact between us and the beach? I don't want some Libyan freighter giving anyone an early warning that there are incoming missiles."

"Course corrections have been programmed, Captain," the weapons officer replied.

"Very well. XO, launch missiles in sequence at preassigned targets."

"Launch missiles in sequence at preassigned targets, aye." The XO relayed the order to the weapons officer who stood behind the Weapons Control Panel, not more than three feet from the captain and the XO.

O'Grady listened as the weapons officer began a well choreographed, much practiced drill, that would culminate in the ship launching the four Tomahawk cruise missiles at their targets. Holding a checklist, the weapons officer read each step to the Firing Panel operator and to the watchstanders in the torpedo room located amidships.

In the torpedo room the watchstanders followed duplicate checklists and lined up valves and performed operations that they could have all done from memory. The evolution resembled a pilot going through a preflight check prior to takeoff. Each item on the list was checked off one at a time so that no switch, valve, or toggle was left unturned.

O'Grady felt like he was in the twilight zone. The dim artificial lights and the room full of men standing around seemed unreal, as they listened to the weapons officer read from a prepared script that would mean the end of the world for the people on the receiving end of the missiles. The calm voices of the men belied the fact that they were about to launch warheads, which would rain down hundreds of kilograms of high explosives on the enemies of the United States. The only saving grace was that this time, the cruise missiles carried conventional warheads rather than nuclear weapons. O'Grady surreptitiously touched his forehead, heart, and chest, left to right. He kept the motions small so no one would notice. Killing people was different than killing floating targets with practice missiles.

Finally the preparations were complete and the exchange of orders and information between the weapons officer and the other members of the firing team came to a halt. The weapons officer checked his watch for the launch time. If the cruise missiles were launched too soon, or too late, they might run into other friendly missiles or planes over the target. Like a well choreographed play, all elements of the assault must arrive on time.

Checking his watch one last time the weapons officer ordered, "Standby."

"Standby, aye," the panel operator repeated, moving the firing handle to the Standby position.

"Shoot," the weapons officer ordered.

"Fire," the firing panel operator repeated and moved the firing handle to the right.

The ship shuddered as an air operated piston forced a slug of water into the number one torpedo tube, flushing the Tomahawk missile out into the ocean. O'Grady moved the fairwater planes down to compensate for the increased buoyancy caused by launching the missile. His part in the evolution was to keep the ship at its preassigned depth.

Just to his left the chief of the watch was electronically opening valves to add water to internal tanks to adjust the buoyancy of the ship and return it to neutral.

The Tomahawk missile, free of the ship, bobbed like a cork toward the surface of the ocean, shedding its stainless steel protective canister as it popped out of the water. Free of the metal casing, the booster motor started. The cruise missile balanced above the waves on a finger of flame, hesitated and leapt upward, rapidly accelerating. As the booster burned out and dropped away, the Tomahawk's turbofan cruise motor ignited.

The Tomahawk cruise missile is an almost perfect weapon, and just about unstoppable. It is sufficient unto itself. It knows where it is when it is launched, it knows where the target is located, and it knows how to get there. The position locating equipment on the *Springfield* was among the best in the world. Developed for the U.S. Strategic Missile Submarine Force, it was subsequently installed on all Navy submarines. The ship's position was known accurately to within feet, and this information was loaded into the Tomahawk's onboard computer.

The Tomahawk skimmed the wave tops a mere two hundred feet off the deck at a speed just below Mach One. The speed was not great compared to high performance jet fighters, but the cruise missile was almost undetectable. It popped out of the water just offshore, carried by one of the oldest stealth platforms in the world, a nuclear powered submarine. By keeping low, the missile was flying under the horizon of most land-based radar. Any detection by airborne radar would be by accident, and probably too late.

Crossing the shoreline, the missile began looking for landmarks as it scanned the ground with its onboard radar. The Terrain Contour Mapping equipment in its computer had certain features, such as hills, valleys, and isolated buildings, programmed into its memory. If it didn't cross these checkpoints in just the right place or at just the right time, it made adjustments in its flight path to correct.

As the missile made its final approach, it armed itself. The contact fuse would now detonate the warhead after striking the target, with a small time delay to allow it to penetrate a concrete wall.

The Tomahawk, which had hugged the ground during most of its flight, began a sharp, steep climb as it neared the target. Detection was now irrelevant, since it was unstoppable at this point. Gaining the necessary height, the missile started the terminal dive to the target.

Able to penetrate the steel reinforced concrete walls of a military bunker, the Tomahawk easily penetrated the ceiling of the chemical factory. Herman Koch, sitting in his office, was looking out his glass window at the factory floor and actually saw the missile when it stabbed through the ceiling; otherwise he wouldn't have had time to look up from his desk before the warhead detonated. As it was he didn't even have time to be afraid.

The warhead leveled the building, killing everyone in the factory and most of those in the immediate vicinity. The second cruise missile also detonated on target a few minutes later, merely stirring up the rubble. The decision makers had decided that a little overkill, or even a lot of overkill, was better than taking a chance that the highly accurate Tomahawk might malfunction. A publicized miss might mean less of the gold plated weapons in next year's budget.

CHAPTER NINE

ASHES TO DUST

Ahmed walked briskly along the dirt street in the early morning light. The sandstone buildings were dark silhouettes on both sides of the narrow, winding street. The sunrise was ahead of him and it colored the cloudless horizon orange and pink. The sky changed from blue to purple to black directly overhead, as the dawn chased the night from the sky.

His boots stirred up little dust this early in the morning. Even in the desert there was some moisture in the air that was condensed out by the cold, desert soil at night. During the day, the sand absorbed the energy from the sun and was often hotter than the air, but during the night, the sand radiated heat back to space, leaving the desert colder than the cold, night air. It was then that the moisture in the air, what little there was, condensed on the sand, holding down the fine dust.

Breathing deeply, Ahmed looked up at the deep blue sky of early morning. The fresh, sweet air burned into his lungs. It is good to be alive. A wife who loves me, two beautiful children, a job that was not too hard and paid well, what more could a man ask.

He smiled as he thought of his daughter, Sofie. He brought her colored pencils for her birthday, and she sat for more than three hours sketching pictures, women in bright colored clothes, flowers with long, skinny stems. Some of the flowers had impossible, iridescent blossoms that she drew with a special marker. She brought every picture to him, leaning on his leg while she waited for approval. It made his heart swell to think how much he loved that little girl.

On such a morning a man could almost believe that there was someone greater than himself that looked after all men. Even Koch would not be able to spoil a day like this.

The thought of Koch brought him back to earth. Yes, Koch *would* be able to dampen even such a fine day as this. The German was the one great negative aspect in his life, always hanging like a dark cloud at the edge of his mind. Koch did not like being in Libya, did not like the Libyans, and, in fact, showed his contempt for them in everything he did and said. Koch stayed only for the money.

Koch did, however, do his job thoroughly. He was the first at the factory in the morning and the last to leave at night. He did his job well, but hated it. How do you explain that, Ahmed thought. This German was a strange man.

The smell of sweetmeats and melons announced to him his arrival at the marketplace. Merchants came down from the living quarters above their shops and began setting up goods in the street as he entered the narrow, winding lane that was the market for the city. It was not enough to leave everything inside and wait for the customer to enter, the goods had to spill out into the street to attract the passerby. If that was not enough the merchants would soon be standing outside the doors to hawk their goods.

Costume jewelry, fine jewelry, cloth, clothes, and food, everything you wanted. The whole street would be crowded in another hour. He had heard that in European countries and in the United States, all these things were sold in one very large building, and the building was owned by one person and all the other people worked for him. Ahmed shook his head; it was such a strange concept.

An old woman was arranging jewelry on a wooden table near the far end of the market. She held out gold earrings to him as he passed.

"Gold earrings. Only the finest quality."

Her eyes peered out from a window formed by the black, faded cloth that covered her hair and face. The rest of her body was covered in the same cloth, from her head to her feet.

He waved her away and kept walking. It would soon be time to buy something for his wife, Safia, for her birthday, but there was no time today. If he stopped to look at the earrings, he would have to spend an hour bargaining about the price. To buy without haggling would be almost an insult.

He stopped and turned around to look back at the woman. There would not be any better day than this to buy the gift, and he could walk fast and only be a little late. Koch thought all Libyans were unreliable whether they were at work on time or late, so why not prove him right.

"The earrings are beautiful," he said as he returned to the stall. Custom required that he admire the earrings before any mention was made of price. He squatted to bring himself down to the same level as the woman, who sat on the stone steps leading into the shop.

"These earrings and the others in the shop are all made by hand and of the finest gold." The crone put the earrings in his hand. The skin that covered her fingers was hard and cracked like old leather.

"You see that each earring is identical. Feel the weight of them."

"The workmanship is excellent." He lifted one of the crescent, moon-shaped earrings from his hand, and turned it slowly to admire the turquoise set in the metal. "I'm sure that a humble man such as me could not afford such a work of art." He was rushing it a little, but it would be best not to push Koch too far.

"I can see that you are a man of means and surely you would want your wife to have only the best. I like this piece myself, but since you truly appreciate its beauty, I will let you have it for only 200 dinari." She had asked more than twice what Ahmed thought it was worth, but you had to start somewhere.

"Surely they are worth that much, but there would be no money to buy food for the children if I paid that price. My wife would think me foolish indeed to spend every-thing on gold for her ears." He was enjoying this despite himself. It was a ritual and both of them already had an idea what the final price would be.

"I will give you 75 dinari and I will try to keep my wife from learning how much I paid."

"You truly are excellent at negotiating," she said. "But look again at the fine workmanship. If this were only a lump of gold it would bring more than that, and the craftsman has put many, many hours into making them a masterpiece. I could not accept less than 180 dinari for the earrings, and that would be almost giving them away." Her raisin brown eyes smiled at him from above her black, cloth veil.

Ahmed smiled. She was coming down even faster than he had expected. "You are indeed generous, but it is as I expected, I cannot afford these fine earrings. I fear that my wife must go without a present. It is time I go to my work." He stood as if to go. His legs hurt from squatting.

She put her hand on his arm to keep him from rising. "It is I who will do without food, and it breaks my heart, but I will let you have them for 170." She almost sang the words; they fit together so well. As with most Arabs, how the words sounded was as important as the substance. The bargaining was becoming poetic.

Ahmed felt like dancing, he was so excited. She was bargaining against herself. She had made the last two offers and he had not moved from his initial bid of 75. Still, he could not stay here all day.

"I will give you 110 dinari, and nothing more. This is all this poor man can afford. I hope you will take this generous offer, as it is all that I can give."

She smiled. "My husband will beat me for giving them away, but you may have the earrings for 110, and you must know that you are stealing them." Ahmed handed her the amount and put the earrings in his pocket. He had little doubt who was in charge in this woman's house. It wasn't the husband.

It is a fine day! He again started down the street to the factory. Safia would be pleased by the earrings.

A flash of light over the buildings caught his eye, a gleam from the rising sun reflected off metal, as something streaked by over the rooftops. At almost the same time, a sound wave from the roar of a jet engine washed over him, causing the buildings to shake. Ahmed felt his shoulders rise as his head involuntarily tried to retract itself into a more protected position between his shoulder blades.

Ahmed had seen the Libyan Migs at official state functions and he knew their sound, but this object didn't look like them in the brief moment he had it in sight. The aircraft he saw flash by looked more like a metal cylinder with short, stubby wings.

His head pivoted rapidly to his left as another object passed by, from the sound of it, moving from behind him, and somewhere off to the left. It was moving in the same general direction he was traveling. The second one was a little farther away and he couldn't see it over the tops of the low buildings.

Ahmed felt his stomach tighten. These couldn't be Libyan planes, they didn't look like them and if they were, why would they be flying so low?

The ground shook from an explosion. Ahmed leaned against a wall to steady himself against the trembling of the earth as well as the sudden weakness in his legs. Another explosion followed the first, not more than a kilometer ahead. Ahmed started running forward. The explosions were from the direction of the plant.

When Ahmed arrived at the factory, he stopped suddenly and blinked to clear his eyes. He blinked again, but the fertilizer plant was still a pile of rubble, a bad dream that would not go away. What was once the most impressive building in town, was now pieces of concrete, in some cases connected by twisted threads of steel reinforcement, one inch thick. Dust hung over the devastation. The wire mesh fence that once surrounded the plant was twisted, and in several places flattened where pieces of concrete had struck it.

One of the members of the perimeter security force, the officer in charge of the gate guards, sat on the ground, legs stretched straight out in front of him, hand on his head, a blank look on his face. There was a long, jagged tear in the sleeve of his green and gold uniform. Ahmed crouched beside him, putting his hand on the officer's shoulder. The guard seemed unaware of his presence. Ahmed looked around, but didn't see any of the other soldiers who had guarded the gate.

Ahmed coughed as a pungent odor stung his nostrils. It was the same smell that he detected, even through his mask, when Rachmiel disconnected the pipe in the factory and collapsed, coughing out his life and lungs. Ahmed looked at what remained of the factory, and saw a yellow brown cloud hanging over the rubble, as the dust slowly settled out of the air.

He pulled on the arm of the officer. "We must move," he said.

The officer looked at Ahmed's face and said, "What are you saying?"

"We can't stay here. Chemicals have been released, and we will die if we breathe them."

"I can't hear you," the officer said putting his hands over his ears and shaking his head, eyes closed.

Ahmed put his head under the man's arm and pulled him to his feet. The officer didn't resist, but seemed incapable of giving much help either. Ahmed half led, half dragged the guard toward the buildings at the edge of town, only twenty or thirty meters away. Fortunately the breeze, what little there was, seemed to be blowing the cloud of poisonous gas in the other direction, away from the city.

The people in the nearby buildings were peering out of their doors like birds craning their necks out of the nest, to see if it was safe to come out yet. The air smelled of dust, as if the shock from the blast had vibrated the ancient accumulation out of every nook and cranny into the air. At least he no longer detected the pungent odor of gas.

Every sense was alert as Ahmed watched soldiers start to arrive. It was as if his eyes and ears saw and heard things in slow motion and recorded everything perfectly. He watched the soldiers mill about, not sure what to do. The sergeant in charge, feeling he had to do something, ordered his men to form a line between the gathering crowd and the remains of the building, shouting at the soldiers to get them to move faster. It may even have been the right course of action.

The volume of sound picked up as the catastrophe drew people like a magnet. There were no new explosions and their curiosity overcame their fear. Soon there were hundreds of voices asking whoever was next to them what had happened, and then telling that same person their opinion of the cause.

Ahmed felt his stomach churn and his bowels turn to jelly, as he realized that he would have been in the building if he had not stopped to buy earrings for Safia. He stuck his hand into his pocket and clutched the earrings tightly until the sharp, pointed edges dug into his palms. The pain was enough to assure him that he was indeed still alive.

Anger welled up in him, crystallizing the weakness in his belly, as he thought of his crew inside the building. All of his men were gone, even his boss, Koch. It was too much to believe. Maybe there was someone still alive. He wanted very much to believe it, but the pile of rubble was almost flat and the yellow miasma that hung above it precluded the possibility that anyone survived. Something in him held out hope for his men, but the engineer in him knew the truth.

He nearly lost his balance, and grabbed the man next to him to steady himself, as the ground shook from another explosion, this one behind him. Most of the crowd crouched or threw themselves on the ground. Some of the women, and more than a few men, started wailing with fear. Ahmed felt disgust. The last explosion was not anywhere near. It was more than a kilometer away, judging by the ball of dust and smoke rising near the center of the city. If they cried out in fear over a distant explosion, what would they do if they were injured?

Many of the people started running back into the city to see the latest bomb damage, curiosity again overcoming fear. The soldiers didn't seem anxious to let anyone near the factory, so Ahmed followed.

He jogged back toward the center of the city, retracing his steps. He felt a little ashamed of himself for following the crowd, but there was something electric about the feeling of running with the mass of people moving through the city streets. The mob was becoming a herd, driven only by instinct.

"The minaret has been destroyed." He heard snatches of conversation as he drew nearer to the blast sight. "The Americans have bombed the city," someone said.

Those on the edge of the crowd closest to what was left of the building became quiet as they contemplated the rubble that was once the fairy tale like spire that called them to worship. As the crowd swelled, the murmuring started again. "The Americans have bombed the mosque." The mood of the mob became angry as the volume of sound grew.

Ahmed felt himself caught up in the emotion of the crowd, but there was no one to direct the anger against. It was then that he noticed that many of the buildings on the far side of the mosque also had been leveled. His house was on that side. His insides turned to ice as he ran around the edge of the mosque to the buildings on his block.

His apartment was a pile of bricks. He ran to his home. He felt like his lungs were on fire as he started digging at the ruins with his hands. He could not dig fast enough. He clawed at the rubble, not aware that he was ripping pieces of flesh from his hands. Fingernails shattered. He threw bricks wildly behind him.

He lifted a large chunk of mortar and brick and stopped, both hands in the air, time and space suspended. Protruding from the masonry jumble he saw a small hand clutching a colored pencil. The arm that was attached to the hand was bent at an impossible angle. He was completely unconscious of the water flowing out of his eyes and streaking the dust on his face or of the agonized roar that came from his throat as he started tearing at the rubble again.

When he uncovered the little body of his daughter it looked surprisingly natural, almost like she was asleep. Just a small fleck of blood at the corner of her mouth and the arm that dangled unnaturally as he lifted her. She was still warm.

PART THREE

REACTION

CHAPTER TEN

MONTROSE

Craig Jones pulled his car into the driveway of the small, wood shingled house in the Montrose section of Houston. The nondescript, gray building was half the size of his home and little different from the other, nearly identical, one-story houses on the block. The lots this close to the city center were all the size of postage stamps and barely big enough to hold the houses, as small as they were. The homes were occupied mostly by lower income families who couldn't afford the higher price homes in the suburbs, or older people who bought the homes when Montrose had more self-respect.

The neighborhood had a seedy quality to it that varied little from street to street. Although this block was still residential, one of the homes on the next street had been converted to a real estate office. Once the deed restrictions in a neighborhood ran out, there was nothing to prevent a person from turning his or her home into a hair styling salon, and many people did, which created a downward price spiral in property values. The houses were cheap, however, and close to downtown, and suited many people who were not concerned about appearances or the quality of the schools.

Jones checked his watch. It was close to 3:30 PM. He had left work early, as he usually did once a month on Fridays, to get to Navy Reserves on time. He worked through enough lunch hours and put in enough extra time on the weekends that he didn't feel he was cheating, at least not cheating the company. If he added up the hours spent at the office each week it was usually closer to fifty than forty. Baxter collected its pound of flesh and then some.

He raised the door on the rickety, single car garage and drove inside. Having a garage, or at least off street parking, was one of Michelle's prime considerations in picking the place. Actually, approving his choice was the way it had worked. It had taken four tries to please her. Not that she was concerned about vandalism, although that was a problem in parts of Montrose. She wanted to be sure no one saw her car if they drove by. Craig shook his head. She was cautious almost to the point of paranoia. You would think she was a lawyer rather than an engineer.

He took the khaki uniform off the door hook in the back seat, locked the car doors, and closed the garage. The garage door didn't lock, but there was nothing inside to steal, except the car, and that wouldn't be taken during the day while he was there. The garage door wasn't worth locking, some hood was going to kick it in once a month just to make sure the place was still empty. Better to leave it open and let them look.

The first thing he did on entering the small, one bed-room cottage was turn on the air conditioning. Michelle's second criterion was that the house have air conditioning. She would do anything, and had, as long as it was cool. They weren't at the house often enough or on a regular enough schedule to put an automatic timer on the air conditioner. The best thing would be to be able to call from the office and trigger some automatic device to start the air conditioner, so the house would be comfortable by the time he arrived, but that technology had not yet made it to market.

He contented himself with stripping off his jacket, tie, shirt, shoes, and socks, while the temperature came down. It was hard to believe it was still technically winter. Reality was that winter in Houston was one day sometime in January. Two days if you were lucky. It wasn't that summer in Houston was any hotter than anyplace else in the world, it just started sooner and would not go away. He had once heard a passenger getting off a plane at the airport remark on hitting the hot parking lot, that it had to be either Houston or Calcutta. The comment was so appropriate that it stuck like a piece of straw in his mind.

He hung his jacket and shirt on wire hangers in the small bedroom closet. The closet was empty except for a thin, short, silk bathrobe Michelle had brought over. Just like Mother Hubbard's, the cupboard was bare. They had been in the house for a few months, and were both starting to accumulate little things to make the place livable. Michelle had bought curtains and towels. Craig's job had been to purchase the bed, still the only piece of furniture, if you didn't count the single folding metal chair.

He lay down on the small, double bed and propped up the two pillows behind his back. He was looking out the window from his position on the double bed as Michelle's car pulled into the driveway. The driveway was right beside the single bedroom, so the view from the partially opened blinds was essentially unobstructed. She locked the silver Nissan NSX. She liked the powerful little sports car and drove it fast. Fast car, faster lady.

Standing beside the car, she tilted her head forward and ran a brush through her hair, not knowing he was watching her thought the bedroom window. She combed the hair from the nape of her neck forward to give it body, then tossed her head back and gave it a shake to get it right. The blond highlights stood out in the strong sunlight and made him think unexpectedly of a line from a song, "Sister golden hair surprise."

He could hear her shut and lock the front door behind her. She put the chain on. "Hi, there," she said as she came into the bedroom.

"Hello," he said, and stepped up to meet her. He took her in his arms, kissed her. She gave him a perfunctory kiss, walked around him, over to the blinds and cranked them shut. He walked up behind her and ran his hands down over her back, waist, and hips.

"Looks like you're ready," she said, brushing her hand across the bulge in his Jockey shorts. She walked over to the wall switch and turned on the bedroom light. He followed her, put his hands on her shoulder. She let him kiss her on the cheek and then twisted away. She played a game of chase, making him follow her around the room until she let him catch her. He wondered if she was even conscious she did it.

"I've been ready all day. Ever since you told me you could see me. That's twice this week."

"You've been ready all day? It must be difficult getting your trousers on and off," she smiled, running her hand over the front of his body.

She kicked off her shoes. "It's a lot easier to see you on a regular basis now that you have a place that's only five minutes from the office," She said, unbuttoning her blouse. "Besides, you were paying more to rent hotel rooms for me than it cost to rent the house."

"You're right, but I couldn't have made it happen without you paying part of the rent. I'm not sure I could hide that much money from the family budget." He ran his hands up and down her back while she finished with the blouse.

"Here," she said handing it to him. "This has to be hung up. I wouldn't want to go home with my blouse all wrinkled.

"It looks like the Syria trip is on," she said.

"I thought you couldn't get a visa."

"That was last week. I guess the State Department decided they would stop poking U.S. corporations in the eye and let us export some oilfield expertise. The French companies have pretty much sewed up all the near term contracts, but we may still be able to shake some business loose."

"I wish there was some way I could talk my way into going on that trip with you."

"You may just have to make do with Elizabeth for a week."

While he hung up the blouse, she took off her skirt and panty hose. He sat down on the bed beside her as she finished, his hand on her shoulder. He brushed her hair to the side and kissed the nape of her neck. He slid his fingers into her hair, as he tasted her mouth. He tried not to be too eager, but it was hard to hold back. He released her mouth and kissed her neck and shoulders, as he moved in front of her, one knee on the floor. He took her head in his hands and kissed her face, not knowing where to start or stop, wanting all of her at once.

"You still have your clothes on," she said.

"Only my shorts, but we can remedy that."

He stood and started to strip off his shorts. She got down on her knees and took his hands in hers. Slipping his undershorts down to his ankles, she took him in her mouth for a moment, teasing him with her tongue. He held her head against him. Standing she pressed against him and tilted her head back to let him kiss her neck again, inviting him to do it. He slid his hands down her back and over her hips.

She stepped back from him and walked to the end of the bed, putting both hands behind her to release her bra. She tossed it on the gray, folding metal chair. Sliding her panties down to her ankles, she stepped out of them and climbed on to the bed on her hands and knees. She paused, poised on all fours, to make sure that he was watching. How could he not be? She rolled on her back putting her hands behind her head.

Craig watched her a moment more. It was like watching a cat move, grace and beauty, and sensuality all in one. He lay down beside her putting his arms around her, kissing her on the eyes, the neck and the arms, his breathing fast.

"You must have got some last night," she said when he released her mouth.

"Why do you say that?"

"I thought you would have wanted to come inside by now."

"I do, I just wanted to make sure you were ready," he said as he rolled on top of her.

She reached between them to guide him inside her. "Hmmm," she sighed as he thrust deep into her. He gasped and quickened his pace.

"You are excited today. I think you better cover up."

"I think you may be right." He withdrew and reached over the side of the bed to take a prophylactic out of his trouser pocket. He removed the foil, resting awkwardly on one elbow, and fumbled with the rubber, getting it started backward. She laughed. He took it off, turned it around, and rolled it down right side out.

"You don't have to rush," she said, smiling at him and stroking his hair. "I'm not going anywhere." She put her arms straight over her head, grabbing the metal bars of the bedboard, watching him through half closed eyes.

He mounted her again. She gasped and put her arms around him. "Go slower," she said.

"Yes" she said. "That's better. Tell me what you like." Her words came in a rhythm with his thrusts. "Tell me what you're thinking. I want to know what you feel."

They continued a dialogue in short half sentences. So good, tell me, almost there. The bedboard beat a rhythm against the plaster wall. The pace picked up, building to allegro. They finished metzoforte. He lay on top, still inside her. They both panted from their exertions.

"Does Elizabeth let you lay on top like this after making love?"

"With Elizabeth, 'making love' may not be the right term. She isn't into affection, it's a chore. Making love ranks right up there with doing laundry and washing dishes, something that has to be done once a week or so. In fact, I think making love to me ranks after doing laundry."

She gently pushed him back, reached between them and held him to make sure the condom stayed on as he withdrew. He moved to her side. They lay beside each other, sheets at their feet, she on her stomach, he on his side. He put his arms around her, laying one leg over her. Their faces were inches apart, breath against breath.

"So how is Elizabeth?"

"About the same. Still yelling at the children, still yelling at me. She had Abigail in tears yesterday. Abigail is taking more care with her appearance and had fixed her hair for school. She used too much hair spray and her hair looked like it would break if you touched it. Rather than telling her that it would look nicer without all the hair spray, Elizabeth said she looked ugly."

"Elizabeth isn't much on tact, is she," Michelle asked, her voice muffled by the cascades of curls in her face. Craig nuzzled her hair and took in her scent. He thought he would be able to identify her in a dark room merely by sense of smell.

"You got it bad don't you?" she said.

"What do you mean?"

"I think you have a bad case of Michelleitis."

"I think I love you."

"What about Elizabeth?"

"I'm not going to leave her if that's what you mean."

"You haven't got the balls to leave her."

"I owe her some loyalty. She lost her shape having my children. She lost a lot of her job skills staying home and taking care of them."

"Bull!" she said, raising up on her elbows. "You're making excuses for her. She never had any job skills because she married you right after college. As for ruining her shape, if she would take off her bathrobe once in a while and go work out, she would have a better shape, feel better about herself, and stop bitching at you and the children all the time!"

He ran his hand up the groove in her back as she talked, to the hollow at the back of her neck. He traced her spine again to the small of her back, over her bottom, and back up again.

"Can we talk about something else?" he asked. He felt the mellow afterglow of love making and was at peace with the world.

"I told you to get her to join a health spa or take a walk in the evenings or do something. I try to help you, and you just won't learn. I feel like I'm wasting my time. I'm not going to help you if you do not listen to my advice."

"Let's talk about something else," he said, running his hand down her back and between her legs. She jerked as he touched her. She reached down and took him in her hand.

"You're not even hard."

"You could help." He felt himself shrink up even further. Once she got started, she got more worked up as she went along.

"I've heard that before." She got out of bed. "I've got to take a shower. Jim has tickets to the ballet tonight. I need to get home, and you need to get on the road for your Naval Reserves."

He heard the shower go on as he sat on the side of the bed clad only in his used prophylactic. The afternoon started out so nice, but the tryst took a wrong turn and he did not even seen the bend in the road. He wasn't quite sure what he could have said to avoid the argument even if he saw it coming.

When Michelle had one or two hours, they made love twice, sometimes three times, and he would be high for the next several days. But occasionally she got hung up on something, a comment, a question, a phrase, and was not able to turn it loose. Usually it was some form of self-improvement plan for him that he had not completed according to her expectations.

Now, after the argument, he would hurt for the next several days until Michelle forgave him. It was almost like she had an ulterior motive for these confrontations. He just could never figure what it was.

He decided not to join Michelle in the shower this time. He started dressing in his uniform. Now the paint peeling from the bedroom walls looked tawdry. A few minutes ago it was merely plain, almost pleasant. Strike Elizabeth off the acceptable list of pillow talk.

CHAPTER ELEVEN

PREFLIGHT

Otis Edwards checked his reflection in the mirror. He smiled smugly at himself, make that Captain Otis Edwards. He was flying his second run as pilot-in-command for NorthStar Airlines. He was excited and having trouble keeping a lid on his exuberance. He had already patted the head stewardess on the butt, but what the hell, the passengers weren't on board yet and she had smiled. Make that "lead flight attendant," everything was going unisex these days and everyone had to be politically correct. Next the feminists would want men to have babies. Her nametag said she was Betty. He was definitely going to have to get to know Betty better.

Yes sir, he thought, he was about as excited as any pilot ever gets. Not nervous, just experiencing an excess of enthusiasm. The general public thinks pilots are a calm stoic bunch. For the most part they are. The last transmission from many aircraft is the voice of the pilot saying something like, "The left wing just ripped off. I'm declaring an emergency," in the same matter of fact voice that he might use to request permission to land.

The hundreds of hours of boredom that constitute flying routine passenger flights will do that to you, make fanny patting seem exciting. A bus driver of the air. Not at all like landing a jet on the three hundred-foot long, pitching, postcard size deck of an aircraft carrier, in the dark, in the rain, and low on fuel. Now that was exciting.

He straightened his hat in the mirror, and turned his head from side to side to check his teeth. Not bad for a forty-seven year old man. Some gray at the temples, but it blended in with the red hair. The skin was starting to resemble Moroccan leather with fine lines near the eyes, but the stewardess still looked twice.

Of course, every few hundred hours, the boredom that was civil aviation would be punctuated by a few seconds of stark terror. That was why his salary was in the six-figure range, payment for all his years of training and experience. It was an advance against the time when he would save the company a couple of hundred million on airplane, passengers, lawsuits, and publicity by keeping his plane from falling out of the sky. The six figures probably kept the stewardess interested. Nah, they love me for my body.

He flicked a piece of lint off the black shoulder boards that decorated his white short sleeve shirt. The four gold stripes on the boards looked good; hell they even felt good. If he had stayed in the Navy he would have been a Captain by now anyway, maybe even Admiral. But an O-6 in the Navy didn't pay even half what NorthStar did. Of course flying a passenger liner couldn't compare with the thrill of landing an F-14 Tomcat on an aircraft carrier in heavy seas, timing the touchdown so the wheels hit the deck when the carrier rose on a crest rather than when it was falling away in a trough.

Bullshit. The Navy can keep the thrills, give me the money and honeys!

He slid back the latch of the metal lavatory door and swaggered forward to the cockpit. Time to get the troops cracking. The preflight checklist still had to be done if he was going to greet the passengers and get this bird off the ground on time.

"How's it going, Rick?" he said to the co-pilot, his first officer.

"Not bad, you?"

Edwards shrugged. "Could be better." Then he smiled, "But I do not know how."

He slid into the left-hand seat, the pilot in command seat. It felt good, damn good. He picked up his clipboard to review the checklist. The second officer was already in his side seat facing the Engineer's Panel. The preflight was a pain, but with the thousands of things that could go wrong in a modern aircraft, there was really no other way to do it. If the flaps, or trim tabs, or hundreds of other things were not set right the big Boeing 747 wouldn't get off the ground. Or worse, it could get airborne and then fall out of the sky. Now that could ruin your whole day.

Edwards saw that the second officer had already accomplished most of the preflight. He had come aboard the aircraft early and had made an external inspection. Despite the team of mechanics that were responsible for the safe operation of any large, modern aircraft, there was nothing that could substitute for a personal walk around the aircraft by the flight crew. Their lives depended on the aircraft being in good repair. The mechanic's pay might depend on them doing a good job, but if they screwed up, they would still go home that night.

Betty walked into the cockpit. Edwards had trouble keeping his eyes off her body as she moved. Betty is what poetry in motion meant.

"Coffee's ready, Captain," she said. "Would you like some?"

Was it his imagination or had she purposely emphasized, "Would you like some?" Edwards looked at her. She had a faint, enigmatic smile tugging at the corner of her mouth. She had the damnedest eyes, sort of green-yellow. And coffee-colored skin. She looked Egyptian, or maybe Jamaican, or perhaps Creole.

"Well, what will it be?"

"What?" Edwards said.

"Do you want some coffee?"

"Sure, get me a piece."

The first and second officers both turned to look at him. Oh shit.

"I mean a cup," he stammered.

Betty laughed, holding her hand under her nose. "You got it," she said and left.

The first officer continued to look at Edwards as he stared after the stewardess like a puppy that's lost its master. As Edwards turned back around, he caught the first officer's eyes on him.

"What?"

"You might want to reel your tongue back in before you trip on it. Also, I was wondering, Otis. Do you think Betty is a member of the mile high club?"

Edwards looked back at the door. "If she's not, I'm sure it's on her flight qualifications. I'm going to have to check that out."

CHAPTER TWELVE

GATWICK

Khaled Hassan pushed the glasses back into place on his nose. The natural oil on his skin made them slippery and he had trouble keeping them in place. What did people do who wore glasses all the time? They probably had the part that goes around their ears tightened, but the cheap, horn-rimmed, dime store type that Hassan bought would probably break before they bent. They would, however, do for a disguise, and he could put up with the inconvenience a little longer.

The discomfort of the glasses was only minor compared to what he could expect if he was recognized and picked up by the police. His hair was dyed to make it lighter, and it was close cropped on top and trimmed high on the sides to make him look younger. Another dye made his skin lighter, and lifts made him appear taller. He was confident the combination was enough cover to insure he would not be identified. He suspected his picture was not available to the airport security people, but, one never knew for certain what the alphabet people, FBI, CIA, MI5 and so on, knew or did not know. Changing appearance for every operation was a pain, but it insured that no composite description was ever built up. It was best to leave nothing to chance.

He looked around the passenger waiting area. No video cameras, at least none that he detected. Everyone seemed intent on their business, hurrying to or from the gates, dragging their suitcases on fold up trolleys, or groaning under the strain of carrying fully packed bags, like beasts of burden. This was all the exercise that some of them ever got. He would be quite happy to send them all to the slaughterhouse.

His eyes settled at last on Jessie, but he kept the rest of the world in his peripheral vision. Sitting across the table from him, she was chewing gum, as usual, her mouth half open. The resemblance to a cow was uncanny. She looked up from the travel folder on New York City when she felt his eyes on her. Smiling, she reached over and squeezed his hand. She probably thought the smile made her look cute and that she was granting him a favor by flashing it at him. She released his hand, took a sip of her cappuccino and went back to the brochure.

He smiled back at her briefly and looked away to hide his contempt. Not that she was likely to detect his emotions. He knew he was good at acting a part. Good with altering his behavior to match whatever the situation called for. He was a chameleon. But it was wasted on Jessie. Unsophisticated was too kind. Cappuccino and chewing gum, it made his mouth sour thinking about it.

He had chosen her carefully. She was a clerk at Harrods. Twenty years old and doing everything she could to prove her independence. All in all she was rather plain, but that was one reason he chose her. Plain and simple. Her plain, brown hair was pulled back into a one-sided ponytail, like a growth on the side of her head. She would probably have dyed it green if the store allowed it. She wore a short skirt of some awful plaid color, and an off-white blouse. To say she was a little overweight would be exceptionally generous. A comfortable middle class rebel, not ready for punk rock, but timidly daring to be different. And a bit dull. Able to be picked up easily, without competition from a gaggle of other men. She would be a clerk forever and then some. Or at least until she died.

Even the fact that his skin was a little dark, compared to her pasty white complexion, was an incentive for her to see him. He was different. Her parents would disapprove, if she ever gathered the courage to tell them she was seeing him. He knew, however, that knowing he was off limits made him more attractive to her.

Hassan courted her carefully for several weeks. Dressed as a businessman he made purchases from her station, expensive purchases designed to impress her. He always picked an off hour when there wasn't a crowd of customers or other clerks around. He used the time to talk her up. "That's a very pretty blouse you're wearing. Your hair looks nice today. What is that perfume, it's very nice."

After a few visits they were good friends. It was then an easy matter to get her to go out with him. First lunch, then dinner, always at very expensive restaurants. Then he took her to his apartment, again very expensive. She expected him to have sex with her. The things you must do for the *Jihad*. It was part of his cover and he always paid attention to details. This vacation with him to New York for a short business trip was to be more of the same.

And, there were other reasons for choosing her. She took directions without asking too many questions. And she was willing to do what she was told.

"Well, Jessie," he said, patting her arm. "It's time to go. We don't want you to miss your plane."

"Right-o," she said brightly. "I wish you could go over with me Albert." He had told her his name was Albert. She would never have asked for identification, of course, but he had all the right documents to cover the eventuality.

"I wish I could," Hassan said, "but this meeting came up so suddenly that I can't get out of it. I will join you tomorrow in New York and you will have time to sight-see by yourself."

"Are you sure I can't wait the extra day and go over with you?" He hated the way her voice dropped down a half note on the next to the last word and then came back up to pitch at the end. She was so very British.

"No," he said picking up the computer case, as she stood and hooked her purse and carry-on bag over her shoulder. "I bought you a non-refundable ticket that can't be changed. My company issued my ticket and it is a different type that can be rescheduled." They walked through the cavernous terminal to the checkpoint. The crowd swirled around them bumping and jostling.

"Now don't forget how to turn on the computer if they ask you to see it operate when you go through security. Do you want me to go through it again?" They talked loudly to be heard above the din of massed humanity.

"No, I've got it." She sounded cross. "I still don't see why they would want me to turn on the computer, though."

"It is just part of their procedures. You know these bureaucrats. They just have to have something to do to earn their money. Someone told them to follow their checklist and they don't know why they do it, they just do it because it is on the list. It's one more way to prove they're important by holding everyone up a little."

"Right you are. Well here's a kiss for you then." She took her gum out of her mouth and stepped up on her toes to kiss him. He held her briefly by the shoulders and let her press her body against him.

"Remember, don't play with your new computer until I've had a chance to go over all the operating instructions with you tomorrow." He handed her the computer case.

"You've been over that three times already," she said impatiently. "I'll wait until you show me how to operate it."

He watched as she turned and got in the line leading to the security checkpoint. He moved back to a position where he could just see her in the line waiting to go through the metal detectors. She should get through security okay, but in case she didn't, he wanted to be near a door for a quick exit.

The line shuffled forward like cattle into a chute until it was Jesse's turn. Her shoulder bag, purse, and the computer case went through the x-ray machine on the conveyor belt. Jessie walked through the metal detector without sounding any alarms. A security guard took her to a separate table on the far side of the checkpoint. Hassan watched as Jessie opened the computer case and turned on the computer for the guard.

Hassan couldn't see the computer screen from his position, but he knew the procedure. The guard would be satisfied when he saw the computer screen light up and the DOS prompt come on. They had been trained to ensure that a computer was what it appeared to be by having it turned on. A computer was a sophisticated electronic device with a large battery that could be used for some other purpose and was in the category of goods that airports considered dangerous. Hassan knew the computer would work. Or at least the screen would light up. For a little while. The guard waved her on. Jessie closed the cover on the computer and disappeared from view.

CHAPTER THIRTEEN

HOME FRONT

Lieutenant Commander Joshua Clark closed the kitchen door behind him and became a civilian again. He was late getting home again, as usual. It was almost 7:30 PM, which was early by Pentagon standards, but according to the family clock that made wives tick, he was way overdue.

He stopped at the stove and lifted the lid from the pot. He drew a deep breath as he picked up a spoon by the pot. Chicken soup, homemade. Sarah had a way of boiling a chicken down to the bones and adding noodles, which tasted so good words alone couldn't describe it. Almost better than sex. Almost.

Sarah walked up behind him. "Don't you be eating that chicken now," she said, taking the wooden spoon from his hand. She stirred it once and put the lid back on.

"Just checking if it's done," Joshua said, putting his hands on her waist as she turned to face him.

"Of course it's done. It was done at six o'clock." Joshua loved the trace of Jamaican lilt in her voice. The accent was something she could never completely uproot, and he was glad for that.

She put her arms around his neck and kissed him. Joshua felt a small twinge of guilt. He should have left earlier, but there was always one more piece of paper to push and another email message to answer. He should have called to say he was going to be late, but by the time he left, he hated taking even an extra minute to find a phone.

"In that case," Joshua said, running his hands over her hips, "maybe dinner can wait for a little longer."

Joshua looked down as he felt a tugging at his trouser leg. "Daddy," Nicole said, her face barely above the level of his knee. She held up her arms to be hugged. Sarah laughed as Joshua reached down and lifted Nicole off her feet.

"I think you had better have some dinner," Sarah said, her hand hiding her smile. "Nicole and I have already eaten."

"Down, down," Nicole said, done with the hug and struggling in Joshua's arms. He set her down gently and she hit the ground running.

"Where are you off to?" he said.

"The Simpsons are on," she said as she vanished, as if that explained everything.

Sarah set the table as Joshua popped the top on a soda. "What have you been up to today?" he asked.

"Shopping, daycare, and thinking great thoughts. The same old stuff. I did have a call from Elizabeth."

"How is she doing? How is Craig?"

"Elizabeth is okay, Craig's okay, but Craig and Elizabeth are not doing well."

"Oh, what's the problem?" Joshua said, only half interested. It was hard to concentrate with food filling his thoughts. It was funny. He wasn't hungry until he walked through the door each night and smelled the dinner cooking. Then he was ravenous. Pavlov had it right. It must be the sound of the door closing behind him that triggered the response. Maybe I should close the door more softly, he thought.

Sarah ladled the soup into a bowl. She pulled some hot biscuits out of the oven, put them in a basket, and sat down. She watched as he started eating. Joshua knew she was pleased when he enjoyed the meals she fixed.

"It's serious," Sarah said. "She's talking about leaving him."

Now Joshua was concerned. "Tell me about it."

"She said he's just not paying any attention to her. It's as if she doesn't exist. He comes home at night, but that's about all. She thinks he may be seeing another woman."

"That's the first thing women always think," Joshua said. "What's your reading of the situation?" He knew Sarah was a good judge of character, better than he was when it came to nuances and the meaning of pauses in the conversation. "Is it serious or is it just girl talk?"

"It is serious. Elizabeth was depressed. She cried on the phone. I cried. It is real, at least it is real for Elizabeth."

"Should I call Craig and talk to him?

"I don't know," Sarah said. "He might think you're interfering. It might make the situation worse if he thought Elizabeth was talking behind his back.

"Maybe you could call," Sarah said thoughtfully. "Give him the opportunity to tell you there is a problem. Draw it out of him, rather than putting him on the defensive. After all, they're our friends. Maybe there is something we can do to help. We should at least try."

Joshua nodded his head as he ladled soup into his mouth, spoon in one hand, roll in the other. Craig was his friend, perhaps his best friend. They roomed together at the Academy until Joshua had decided marrying Sarah was more important than graduating from Annapolis, even knowing he would have to serve out his obligation as an enlisted man. Craig had helped him through those difficult times.

Joshua wiped his mouth with a napkin and pushed the bowl back from his place. He picked up the phone from the kitchen wall mount while Sarah picked up the dirty dishes.

"Craig, here," Joshua heard when the call went through. Joshua couldn't help smiling. It was amazing how he could recognize someone's voice after months, weeks, and years. Craig still sounded the same as when Joshua first met him plebe year at the Academy.

"Earth to Craig, Earth to Craig, come in Craig."

"Joshua Clark, how the hell are you?"

"Doing good, man. This Pentagon job is tough, but we're doing some interesting stuff. Learning a lot, working hard, but enjoying it. Even this twelve hour day stuff is not as tough as being at sea. That was eighteen hours a day and then we got woke up in the middle of a night for a drill."

"You got that right," Craig said. "Civilian land is even easier than shore duty, but not much. I only have to work ten hours a day for my corporation."

"Is that right," Joshua said. "I thought you corporate lawyerly types only went into the office to pick up your check and cash in your stock options." They laughed together.

"If lawyers were only as rich as everyone thinks we are, I wouldn't be doing this Naval Reserve stuff on my weekends.

"I hear you," Joshua said, "But I know you enjoy it. You still have some saltwater in your veins.

"So tell me, how are you doing?" Joshua emphasized the "you" a little more than he intended. Silence hung on the line as light as a feather. Joshua suspected by the brief pause that Craig knew that there was more to the question than words implied. They had thought on the same wavelength since they met and could tell from overtones and inflection what the other was thinking.

"Okay, I guess," Craig said. "Well, not so okay," he added. "But we'll work it out."

"We'll work it out? Problems with Liz?"

Craig's silence said more than words. "Sort of," he answered reluctantly.

"Anything I can do to help?" Joshua met Sarah's eyes as she cleared the table. He knew she was tracking the conversation.

"No, I don't think so," Craig said. "Look, I need to go, but thanks for your offer, really."

"If you want someone to listen to you," Joshua said, "just let me know. I know talking it out with you back at the Academy helped me a lot. There was still some discrimination against blacks back then. There was lip service about equality, but you can't change the way people think by making a regulation. You helped me get through all that by just listening."

There was a moment of silence then Craig said, "You're black?" Joshua laughed until tears ran down his face. He heard his laughter echoed on the other end of the line.

Craig said again, "Got to go. We will talk later."

Joshua hung up the phone. "Something's wrong, but he wouldn't talk about it."

Sarah shook her head. "Well, you can't help if he won't let you. Wait a week and try him again. Why don't you catch the news while I clean up in here? You will have to use the small TV in the study, however, "The Simpsons" take priority over the news while Nicole is up, and she has the big screen."

"I might watch TV with Nicole," Joshua said. "I do not get to spend nearly enough time with her."

"Good plan, man" Sarah said. "I will finish the dishes and join you. You might want to check the news later; however, there was something on CNN about pieces of the Tomahawk missiles that destroyed the mosque in Libya. You might find that interesting."

"What? There wasn't any Tomahawk missile attack on a mosque in Libya. That's just some PR stuff Libya is doing to make us look bad. Only two Tomahawks were launched and they were on target."

"Hey," Sarah said. "I'm just a telling you what's on TV. Don't get defensive with me. The Arabs have a piece of a tail section from a Tomahawk missile that they dragged out of the rubble from the mosque."

Joshua went into the study and turned on the news, thoughts of "The Simpsons" forgotten. Two televisions might seem like an extravagance, he thought, but only to those without children. Tearing Nicole from her programs before bedtime was something Sarah could manage, but it was well beyond his capabilities.

The Arabs had been claiming for several days that a U.S. missile destroyed the mosque and apartments during the raid on the chemical factory, but Joshua knew it wasn't so. He was on the inside. He knew how many missiles were launched, what their targets were, even what their effect had been. It didn't happen.

The view on the screen switched from a man with a microphone to rubble that was once a building. A big earthmover rumbled in the background. A group of men were gathered around what looked like winglet or elevator. A section of a fuselage was in the foreground. The camera zoomed and a "4D," and a part of a "3" were clearly visible on the fuselage.

"The minister of the interior stated" the announcer said, "that sections of a Tomahawk missile were recovered during removal of debris from the mosque and a nearby apartment building."

The camera switched to an obviously Arabic man with a mike held in his face by an off screen arm. "We recovered the sections of Tomahawk during excavation of the rubble."

Joshua felt his face flush with frustration. The announcer always told you what the person was going to say and then the person said the exact same thing. They could skip the middleman.

The Arab added, "We were looking for the bodies of women and children."

Joshua was angry. He flipped off the TV with the back of his hand. Oh, bullshit, he thought. It didn't happen. The missiles were accurate, the satellite photos showed where they landed, and he knew exactly how many were launched. It didn't happen.

CHAPTER FOURTEEN

MIDAIR

Craig Jones carefully pulled the hang glider out of its protective wing bag. The folds of the fabric whispered against itself like the sound of silk, or the zipper on one of Michelle's dresses as it slid from the nape of her neck to her hips to the floor. He handled the hang glider lovingly as he coaxed the disparate parts into an entity almost alive in its beauty.

Michelle would be surprised he had actually done something dangerous. He was still smarting from the tongue-lashing she gave him several weeks ago, before his Naval Reserve drill. It would be nice to see her eyes grow wide when he told her he was hang gliding after she returned from her trip.

The glider wasn't the best available or the most high tech, but it was good. The new double surface, advanced gliders were harder to fly and took a lot more concentration. It was difficult to have fun if you were thinking about the mechanics of staying aloft all the time.

He caressed the magenta colored dacron as he unfurled the sail. The trailing edge was a deep red with dark red circles in the middle of each wing. It resembled a moth in the air. He called it The Gypsy.

Working at a steady pace, he assembled the aluminum tubing into an isosceles shaped, triangular frame. The morning sun was hot on the back of his neck. Each of the legs extended past the base and a third leg bisected the two. He tightened the self-locking nuts and checked that there was no slack in the stainless steel cables. He skinned a knuckle as his finger slipped on a wing nut. He put the bruised knuckle in his mouth tasting the salty blood. Illogically, it eased the pain, as it always did. Mothers may know best after all, kissing the bruise made the hurting stop.

When he talked about taking up hang gliding, Michelle said "We'll see." He knew from her look and the way she said it she did not think he would ever do it. Just like when they first became lovers, he said off hand that he would never leave Elizabeth. She said, "We'll see," so softly she may have thought he hadn't heard it.

Looking down at his hands, he realized he had stopped working. He attached the control bar, another triangle of tubular steel beneath the glider. It hung below the wing and would hold his harness. Tinker toys for big boys. The harness would suspend him inside the control bar like a pendulum.

He looked at his chronometer, a present from Michelle. Not a watch, but a chronometer. Michelle had insisted that for flying, if he ever actually did it, he would needed a chronometer. She could be so contradictory. She as much as said he would never get the courage to go hang gliding and then gave him a chronometer.

Michelle demanded a lot, but was very generous. When he first started pursuing her, she told him in her straightforward manner that she expected flowers and jewelry. It was easy to give her presents, she was that kind of beautiful, but she was insatiable. Nothing is free.

The chronometer showed it took ten minutes to assemble his aircraft, even with Michelle dancing through his thoughts. Slower than the instructions promised, but it was better to be slow than fall to earth because your wing fell apart over your head.

He walked to the edge of the rock outcrop. The wind was already warming, a prelude to the hot, blast furnace that blows over central Texas in the summer. He pushed his damp, brown hair back from his forehead. The dry, warm air sucked the moisture from his face, built up from the mild exertion of assembling the glider.

He looked at the rugged flat land hundreds of feet below. The tan colored rocks cast sharp shadows in the morning sun. Not quite nine o'clock. The thermals should be starting soon, as the sun warmed the rocks and sand.

Zipping his gray, surplus, army flight suit over his jeans and shirt, he began sweating again. The ground temperature was nearly eighty degrees, and the desert shimmered in the distance. It was hot here, but it would be icy aloft. He put on sunglasses, helmet, and gloves to complete his outfit. Strapping the harness over the flight suit, he checked the anemometer, altimeter, and variometer strapped to the trapeze. He was ready. Preflight complete.

Craig stepped to the edge of the cliff, the triangle of dacron balanced above his head with its aluminum tubes and wires of steel. The wind snapped the trailing edge of the glider like a flag flapping in a stiff breeze. The rugged, rubber soles on his hiking boots gripped the rock as he braced against the steady, southerly wind. He looked at his anemometer. Twenty miles per hour. Perfect soaring conditions.

He stepped over the edge of the precipice. The rush of wind and adrenaline carried him up and away from the cliff. The breeze blowing across the flat land below struck the rock outcropping and was deflected upward, much like the ocean rushing against a cliff at the seashore. Craig rode the crest of the wave of air washing over the steep face of the rock below.

He pulled the control bar to his hips, shifting his center of gravity forward. This brought the nose down and increased his air speed to nearly thirty miles per hour. He pushed the bar forward and moved it left, shifting his weight to the right and back. The nose of the hang glider moved up and right, turning Craig forty-five degrees to the cliff in a banked turn. Now the vertical wind had lifted him higher than his starting point above the edge of the cliff.

He adjusted position again. Pull back to send the glider into a dive and build up speed; push out, much like a swan dive from his prone position beneath the glide, to gain altitude; and push the bar right to bring the nose up and left, banking the craft to the left. Hang gliding was still new enough that he had to consciously think through each maneuver. Soon the memory would be built into his muscles and he would think left and his body and the wing would react as a single entity, turning in the new direction.

He tried to soar motionless relative to the cliff wall below him. Sea gulls made it look so easy at the seashore, hanging in the air as if nailed to the sky, floating rather than flying. He adjusted the nose up and down periodically to change his forward air speed and sink rate. The glider moved forward and backward, shifting relative position as it hovered forty feet above a small shrub he had picked to mark his position. He was never quite motionless, but he was getting good at it.

Soon tiring of the game and the concentration it required, Jones pulled the bar back, feeling, not for the first time like he was on a trapeze. He gathered speed as the nose dropped, and he flew out and away from the cliff.

The wind whispered in his ears, as soft and gentle as Michelle's breath as she slept in his arms. It was a clear blue day and he had the sky to himself. He was squandering a vacation day for the price of being alone, but it was worth it. On a weekend the sky would be full of people with their gaudy colored hang gliders. Then it was more like flying in a flock than soaring like an eagle.

He drifted along the rocky trail that passed for a road. He had driven his four wheeler up the tortuous path in the early morning hours. With a sink rate of two hundred thirty feet per minute, it would not take long to glide all the way down to that road if he did not find a thermal soon. Then he would have to drag his kite, all seventy pounds of it, back up the hill for another ride.

He felt a bump in mid-air, like the sensation you get when an elevator starts up the shaft. He didn't need his variometer to tell that he had just passed through a thermal updraft. He turned tightly to the left to stay in the rising column of air. The variometer now registered more than five hundred feet per minute. Like an elevator going up, after the first starting jolt, it felt like you were motionless, but the variometer showed a steady upward climb. A freight train to the sky, now moving at six hundred feet per minute.

He looked at his altimeter. He was several thousand feet above his starting point and still climbing, turning in a tight circle to stay in the thermal. Elation was rising in him as the rocky terrain shrunk to picture postcard size. The reds and yellows of the desert were in perfect contrast to the crystal blue of the sky, too beautiful to be real.

He felt a smug sense of self-satisfaction. Michelle would be surprised to learn that he had actually done it. He had complained about Elizabeth once too often and Michelle had told him if he had any balls he would leave her. She never tired of castigating him on his lack of daring. We will see who has balls. Of all the many things Michelle had done, hang gliding wasn't one.

The sky really was blue out away from the city. He was so accustomed to the milky white, auto-exhaust haze that passed for sky in Houston, that he forgot what a pure, pretty color the sky really was. Even the anvil shaped cloud to the west might have been painted as a counterpoint to a too perfect picture.

The variometer showed that he was no longer climbing. The thermal had topped out at more than eleven thousand feet. Eleven thousand feet meant something, but he couldn't remember what it was. He was filled with euphoria. He shivered with the thrill of being so far above the mundane world below.

He shivered again. This wasn't excitement, it was cold. No wonder. At eleven thousand feet the air temperature must be in the teens. Even the flight suit couldn't keep him completely warm.

He was feeling good. And sleepy. His head snapped up. Of course. He was getting spaced out on lack of oxygen. How can you tell if you are suffering from oxygen deprivation if the first thing that happens is that your mind stops working? He gave himself a mental slap for being so stupid. He bit his lip to wake his brain up.

He dipped the nose to get the glider down to where the air was denser, to give himself some breathing room, which in this case was literally true. Pulling off a glove, he flexed his hand. It had a slight blue tinge to it, not just from the cold, he realized, but from lack of oxygen.

Craig grabbed the control bar again as he was buffeted by a gust of wind. The glider shook as it was rattled by another blast, like a toy in the teeth of a dog. The variometer showed he was moving rapidly upward again, with the nose down in what should have been a steep dive. Not good.

He noticed for the first time that the thunderhead had advanced on him while he was giddy on lack of oxygen. It now filled half the sky and was bearing down on him like a bull. Adrenaline raced through his body. The comments his instructor made in an off-hand manner now came back to him. A steady wind is what you want, but don't fly on a gusty day. And there were stories, vaguely remembered, about parachutists, and hang glider pilots, that were turned into popsicles when they were sucked into thunder clouds and carried tens of thousands of feet into the air.

His stomach churned as his body became weightless. He looked at his variometer. Eight hundred feet per minute sink rate! He was caught in a down draft. A sheet of lightning flashed in the thunderhead, illuminating it from the inside. The cloud had an angry look.

Michelle could be angry at a moment's notice, mercurial. He sometimes thought she was angry with him just to see what he would do, to get a reaction from him. Just like he was doing with Elizabeth he had to admit. Pushing her away, finding fault with her when there was none. Magnifying her failings in Michelle's reflection.

Craig pushed Michelle from his mind as he turned the glider at right angles to the line of advance of the thunderhead, trying to fly out of the fierce, descending current of air. Drops of rain spattered his face, a precursor to the torrents to come.

The altimeter indicated he was only two thousand feet above the ground when the buffeting stopped. He released his breath in a long sigh and loosened his death grip on the control bar. But, his respite was short lived.

He felt himself go weightless again and discovered he was upside down looking at the now gray sky, the glider strapped to his back below him. Thoughts of Elizabeth and the children went flying through his mind and he was engulfed in guilt. What would the children think of him if he died and they found out about Michelle? Would Michelle come to the funeral? Would she miss him at all?

His thoughts moved in slow motion as he looked up at the sky. He heard an echo of his instructor's voice in his head. *The center of gravity of a hang glider and pilot is located approximately with the pilot, since his weight comprised eighty percent of the total weight of the craft.* Gravity pulled him back to his proper place below the wing with a bone jarring snap.

As the earth and heaven reoriented themselves to their correct position he noticed in a detached fashion that the left trailing edge of the glider frame was bent up at an awkward angle like the broken wing of a bird. The airflow over the damaged wing was no longer aerodynamic. It had stopped flying. With the left wing stalled and the right wing flying fine he was starting to turn in ever tighter spirals to the left. He knew the tight turn would soon become an uncontrolled spin, ending abruptly on impact with the earth. He tugged frantically at the control bar but was unable to correct. The glider was spinning faster and losing altitude rapidly.

The ground below was in focus only at the center of his probable point of impact. The rest of the world was a circle, blurred by his spin, and approaching rapidly. He grabbed the deployment handle of his back-up reserve chute and gave it a sharp tug. The rocket deployed parachute opened with a sharp crack. The parachute lines jerked him to what felt like a complete stop in midair. He hung suspended between earth and sky, drifting slowly down to the desert. He climbed on to the control bar. The metal frame would absorb part of the shock as he hit.

As he landed, another gust of wind dragged him across the rock strewn ground. He tugged at the shroud lines to deflate the chute but quickly gave it up and pulled his knife from the sheath strapped to his leg. He cut the straps. The chute, shorn of it burden, raced away ahead of the rain. He felt like a heavy load had been lifted from his shoulders.

The deluge, which seemingly had only waited his return to earth, washed over him.

CHAPTER FIFTEEN

ONBOARD

Craig Jones parked in the lot at the end of the pier. He was careful not to bump his hip, which was still bruised from the glider crash. His joy in bragging to Michelle about his hang gliding was subdued by his admission that he crashed. It made her laugh, however, and he could not help being happy when he heard her laugh.

He put his white combination hat on his head, checked the angle of the bill with two fingers over his nose. Straightening his back and shoulders, he completed his transformation from merely Craig Jones, to Lieutenant Jones, USNR. On the drive down from Houston, along the long and lonely highway, a metamorphosis took place. Perhaps the change was not as complete as Clark Kent becoming Superman or Elizabeth becoming the lady he would like her to be, but it was significant none the less.

Craig Jones, lawyer, to Lt. Jones, U.S. Naval Reserves, was more a mental make-over than anything physical. The change from suit and tie to Summer White uniform helped, but what was in his mind mattered the most. As a lawyer, his job was to make sure that all the pieces of paper fit together, all the options were considered, and all the paragraphs were cross referenced one to another. All the details done right. As a Naval Officer, even a weekend warrior, he was a leader of men. No longer in charge of only one secretary, shared at that, he now supervised a division of twenty, at least for this two week active duty period.

Straightening his shoulders, he pulled the military creased shirt straight across his shoulders. He marched to the head of the pier, shoulders back, head high. Self-important? No, confident. How you felt about yourself was often how the men, or women, for that matter, thought about you. They could sense your attitude. They could smell fear. On the other hand, it was a two-way flow. How they reacted to you determined how you acted.

The river lay slack at the base of the pier, given pause by the high tide. Flotsam and jetsam hesitated on their journey to the sea, ripening in the setting sun. The smell of the brackish water filled him with a sense of the familiar. It was not quite salty, but certainly not fresh. Neither sweet, nor sour, it gave off a tang of fish and fuel oil.

The smells and nearness to the sea always brought a sense of excitement, expectation. It had been the same since the early days of childhood, outings to the beach with his family, holidays from a landlocked home. The car was always packed with towels and eager, sweaty children. But the smell of the sea, the salt in the air seasoned with seaweed, dominated and flavored the memory. Long before you saw the sea you smelled it.

The gangway in front of Jones rose at a steep angle from the pier to the ship. The USS *Stephen W. Groves* rode high on the full tide. Jones shifted his briefcase to his left hand and held the rail in his right. His footsteps had a hollow echo on the sheet metal ramp, as he marched upward toward the haze gray ship. The angle of the gangway and the ache in his muscles from auguring his hang glider into the ground made him feel old. Actually, it made him feel his age, although he did not like to admit it.

He stopped short of the brow of the ship, faced the flag at the stern, and saluted. The quarterdeck watch, a young, petty officer third class, came to attention and returned the salute.

"Permission to come aboard," Jones said.

"Permission granted, Sir."

Jones stepped aboard. Transformation complete. The small ceremony made him feel good. He was once again a part of history, part of the fraternity of the military who defended their country, at least for the weekend.

"The captain wants to see you, sir," the third class said.

"See the captain, aye. Any idea what it's about?"

"No, Sir." The sailor was everything the recruiting posters promised, but seldom delivered. Handsome, wholesome, young and fresh in his pressed uniform. Capt. Bennett ran a tight ship, including putting his best people on the quarterdeck.

"We are getting underway tonight. Maybe that has something to do with it, Sir," the sailor said.

"That certainly is a high profile evolution. Are you checking briefcases tonight?"

"No, sir. I've seen your lunch before."

"Hey. I've got important Naval Reserve paperwork in this briefcase."

"Yes, sir. Also two undershirts, undershorts, socks, and gym gear. I have checked your briefcase before."

Jones shook his head. He was becoming too predictable. He exchanged salutes with the quarterdeck watch and headed forward. Winding his way through several watertight doors and up metal ladders, he reached the 0-1 level. The captain's cabin on Navy ships was always near the bridge so he could be there quickly if an emergency arose, for example, when ships go bump in the night.

As maneuvering watch OOD (officer of the deck) Jones hoped fervently that no ship, especially the *Groves*, would crash into another ship, lighthouse, or rock, in the night, or even in the day. A collision at sea could ruin your whole day, not to mention your career. The collision might not be the captain's fault, but he would get relieved and a letter of reprimand would be placed in his service record. The navigator and the officer of the deck would also get mangled at the Board of Inquiry and it would probably be the end of their careers. All this was in addition, of course, to possibly sinking the ship and drowning the men on board, a not so coincidental consequence. And Jones could not forget that he would be officer of the deck, responsible for guiding the ship out of the channel tonight.

The door to the captain's cabin was open and he was seated at his desk reviewing paperwork. The twentieth century warrior up to his elbows in bureaucracy. Most likely the weighty subject of the moment was another regulation on sexual awareness, or racial awareness, or twenty questions you never thought of asking a homosexual, or any other human being, but are now not allowed to anyway.

Jones reached inside the room and rapped his knuckles on the metal door as he entered.

"Good evening, Captain."

"Hey, Craig. Come on in." Capt. Bennett motioned to a chair by his desk. "Have you heard that we will be getting underway tonight?"

"Yes, sir. Just heard when I came aboard."

"Have you ever conned the ship down the ship channel at night?" Bennett sounded concerned. He turned away from the paperwork and gave Jones his full attention. Forty-five years old, heavy set, he looked more like someone's father, which he was, than a naval captain. But Bennett could be hell on wheels when he wanted. When one of the enlisted men or junior officers did something stupid, his voice would drop an octave and increase three decibels in volume. You didn't want to be on the receiving end of a blast from Bennett. Other than that, which fortunately comprised only about ten percent or less of his available time, he was a caring, sincere, likeable person. However, the troops respected him, which is an important attribute in a military organization.

"No, sir. This will be my first night transit. I have, however, been OOD for more than ten daytime transits."

"I know you have, that's why you're maneuvering OOD on my ship. But nights are different. You're not going to have the big picture. You won't get the visual perspective you get during the day. You're going to have to rely heavily on radar and the navigator's recommendations."

Jones was feeling a little nervous about being in charge of getting underway at night, but the captain actually seemed more worried than he was. Had the captain ever made a night transit of the ship channel?

"We probably should have done a night underway as a training evolution before now," the captain said. "But now is as good a time as any. You'll do okay." Jones wondered if the captain was trying to convince himself.

"Get up to your stateroom, stow your gear, and change into Khakis. Go over the charts with the navigator and set the underway watch when you're ready. I want to be out of here by 2000 hours. Any questions?"

Jones knew the Captain was very serious about training. That was most of the reason for the existence of Naval Reserve Force ships. They were staffed with a skeleton crew of active duty personnel who provided practical training to the reserves assigned to the ship. That was Captain Bennett's job, training, and he was good at it. The captain would let him conn the ship, but he would hover over him the whole time.

"Yes, sir. Why the rush? We could do some detailed planning for the evolution and get underway tomorrow night."

"We could, Craig. But we are directed to get underway tonight. This is mission support, not just training. We will be searching for ships trying to bring contraband weapons into the United States."

"Contraband weapons? Are we going to be boarding ships? We don't have any experience in that, sir."

The captain's face flushed red. Jones knew he had hit a hot button before the first word came out of the other man's mouth.

"Damn it, Jones, leave the details to me! The first lieutenant will be in charge of the boarding party and a Coast Guard officer will be aboard to insure we do it right. You just make sure we get underway properly.

"Dismissed!"

Jones brought his lower jaw back to battery position in time to mutter a hurried "Aye, aye, sir." When the captain started calling the officers by their last name, it was time to run for cover. He came within inches of tripping over his chair as he hurried to leave the room.

"Jones," the captain called, as Jones was halfway out the door.

"Yes, sir?"

"Don't forget. Red right returning." The captain smiled.

Jones smiled back through force of habit. What the hell did he mean by that? He was halfway to his room before he realized the captain was making a joke. Rules of the road dictated the color of the navigational buoys in the channel. If you were returning from the sea, keep the red buoys on your right, and the green on your left, and you would be in the safe, you would be in the channel. That was vintage Bennett. Chew your ass and then expect you to laugh at his jokes. Go figure.

CHAPTER SIXTEEN

IN-FLIGHT

Jessie entered the jumbo jet at the midship door. The passengers swirled around her like minnows in a rushing river, in their eagerness to board the plane. It was a lot like being swallowed by a whale, she thought, as she gawked at the interior of the huge plane.

A flight attendant directed her through the galley to the aisle on the far side of the aircraft. Jessie's head swiveled like her neck was made of rubber, tilting at impossible angles as she tried to take in everything at once. It was all so big. The oval shape of the fuselage arched above her head. Seats marched in rows to the rear of the cabin, ten abreast.

Carried along by the crowd, she found her seat, 32I. It was an outboard seat on the right side by the window. Good, that would give her a chance to look outside as the plane took off. The problem was that a man was in her seat, and he took it all up.

"Excuse me," she said. Her voice rose in pitch in a hump at the middle and fell off at the end. Her jaws worked her gum furiously. "You're in my seat." Her voice was plaintive. She held her boarding pass in his face as if there could be no argument with something so official.

The man slowly put his newspaper down and adjusted his glasses, tilting them down on his nose to peer at her pass. He slowly and methodically stuck his hand into his shirt pocket. His hand dug around without success while his other hand expanded the search to his trouser pockets. The shirt pocket hand started on the back pockets as he leaned forward in his seat. Jessie rolled her eyes upward, chewing her gum furiously.

"Ah, yes," he said. Even his voice was slow. The Second Coming will have come and gone by the time he's done, Jessie thought.

"Here it is." He pulled a stub out of the shirt pocket where he had started. "It seems that I'm assigned seat 32I also." He compared stubs with Jessie, looking at her over his glasses.

"I suppose you could sit in my lap." His smile showed a mouthful of yellow teeth.

"Oh, please," Jessie said, and did her eye roll again. He was old enough to be a grandfather. And he was probably married. She shrugged her shoulders and fought her way upstream against the dwindling trickle of inflowing passengers. She found a flight attendant in the galley. Her name tag said she was Betty.

"There's a man in my seat," Jessie said.

"Sorry about that." The flight attendant's smile was bright, overly cheerful. She looked like there wasn't any problem she couldn't solve today, a regular superwoman. Jessie smiled back. She needed help.

"We're not going to be a full flight today. Why don't you take any empty seat."

Jessie shrugged her shoulders and worked her gum with great vigor. Betty was no help after all. Well, no big deal. Jessie headed back toward the rear. A few of the passengers were still flopping around stowing their bags. Jessie looked around in frustration. The only window seat open was one next to a large, fat man whose enormous gut was spilling over the armrest into the next seat. No thank you.

"You're going to have to take your seat now," a stewardess said coming up behind Jessie. It was Betty again. "We can't move the aircraft until all passengers are seated." Betty was no longer so patently friendly.

"I'd like a window seat, please," Jessie said. This was her first flight and she wanted to make the most of it.

"They all seem to be taken." Jessie recognized the no nonsense tone in Betty's voice. Her parents often used it. "Sit here for now and you can move after we're airborne." She pointed at a seat in the center section.

The young man in the aisle seat looked interesting. With his uncombed hair and rumpled gray tweed jacket, he looked well, cuddly. He might make for a bit of conversation during the flight. No ring on his hand that she could see, but she had heard that some men hid them on business trips.

"Excuse me," she said. She gave him her best smile and pointed to the empty seat next to him.

He looked up without smiling, moved his knees to the side, and quickly went back to his book.

Jessie struggled to squeeze between the seat in front and his knees. Her ample, jean-clad bottom squeezed by his face with inches to spare. She was disappointed to see he did not seem to check her out.

She deployed her bags, magazines, and the computer around her feet and under the seat. She had brought enough material to keep her distracted for days.

"How long is the flight?" She was unwilling to let him escape back into his book so easily.

"Eight hours." He put his finger in his book to mark the place as he looked over at her. His eyes were such a pale blue they were almost gray. The faded color of prewashed dungarees. They were intelligent eyes, caring, loving, innocent eyes. Jessie imbued them with all the characteristics that popped into her head from her diligent reading of romance novels.

Not like Albert's eyes, she thought. If his name was really Albert. Albert Brown was just too British for someone with his dark cast. He had probably changed his name to fit in. Albert's eyes were watchful. They examined you. The face sometimes smiled but never the eyes.

Jessie was silent, lost in her new friend's eyes. He turned his head and dove back into his book. Jessie groaned inwardly, but kept the watery smile on her face as she turned away and tunneled into her bag for a magazine. He had eluded her for the moment, but she would loosen him up before the flight was over. In eight hours, she could move mountains.

~ ~ ~

Otis Edwards checked the instrument panel. He looked over at the first officer and second officer checking their instruments. They were young, but they knew their job. Hell, he thought, everyone around him was young and getting younger.

The Big Bird was ready to go. Blowers brought the engines up to speed. Fuel was added, igniters energized, and the whine of the turbine changed to a muted roar.

"Ground to cockpit, are you ready for the pushback?" The voice came over Edwards' earphones.

"The flight attendants are seated. I guess you can shove it," Edwards said. The motorized tug attached itself to the nose wheel and rolled the 747 away from the gate like an ant pushing an elephant.

It would have been fun to powerback, Edwards thought. Crank up the engines and cut in the thrust reversers. But no, NorthStar was run by bean counters, not pilots and a powerback would have used more gas. Therefore, there would be less profit. Also, he grudgingly admitted it might not be good for the engines.

The tug finished the pushback and disconnected. The ground jockey said, "Was it good for you?"

"Hey, I'll make the jokes, here." Edwards taxied the plane out to take off position on three engines. The bean counters again. The procedure used less fuel than all burners lit, but it felt like hobbling around with a broken wing. And it was slow.

"Do you know that a guy once rolled a 707?" Edwards asked the first officer.

"I heard that, but it's just a rumor."

"No, it's true. A test pilot for Boeing named Tex Johnston. I talked to an engineer that knew him. It was before an air show and the pilot did it as a promotional stunt. A one gee roll. They got pictures. Damn, it would be fun to do something like that. Just once."

"I bet the pilot lost his license," the second officer said.

"Damn right," Edwards said. "But it sold a hell of a lot of planes. They fired him, but I bet they gave him a fantastic severance check."

"You're not thinking of doing any stunt flying, are you Cowboy?" the first officer asked.

"Not me, hoss. I just get tired of flying low and slow. A bus driver of the air."

"I hear you," the first officer said. "In the meantime, I think its time to get us off the ground."

"Start number three," Edwards said. "How did you know my call sign is Cowboy?"

"Starting number three," the first officer said. "Just heard it around." A high pitched whine began, going up scale as the turbine spun faster.

They swung onto the runway, all checks complete. Edwards advanced the throttles to the pre-computed power setting and kept his right hand on them. The first officer followed the throttle movement with his hands and made the final adjustments. The engines spooled up with increasing power until the plane shuddered with eagerness to be off.

The big plane started forward, slowly at first, but with increasing speed. At 155 knots Edwards pulled back on the yoke and the nose wheel rose off the ground. The plane continued to tilt upward as the main wheels lifted off. A gust lifted the right wing and Edwards smoothly rotated the yoke to the right. The first officer toggled the landing gear to the up position. The plane was now at a fifty-degree up angle and gaining altitude at 1,000 feet per minute.

~ ~ ~

In the passenger cabin, the acceleration pushed Jessie back into her seat. She couldn't see anything out of the windows but blue sky. Bummer, she thought.

The bags stowed under the seat in front of her began sliding out around her feet. The computer slid about a foot, gaining momentum before it struck her on the ankle.

"Yiiip!" She put her hand to her mouth. She sounded like a puppy that had been stepped on. She had yelled louder than she intended, but damn it, she was startled. What a way to impress a guy. Heads craned around to look at her from several rows. At least her bookish neighbor looked up, she noticed.

"Are you okay?" he asked.

"I think so." Actually the ankle wasn't that bad, but she winced and rubbed it for effect.

"The computer banged into me." She released her seat belt and bent to retrieve it.

"The seat belt sign is still on," he said. He pointed at the illuminated words below the baggage compartment. He probably never disobeyed a sign in his life, Jessie thought. At least he looked concerned.

"It's okay," she said. "We're airborne now." Let him think she was an experienced traveler. Jessie pulled the computer out from under the seat. "I hope the computer didn't get damaged."

"What kind is it?" He put his book away. He seemed interested.

"I'm not sure. It's a present." She unzipped the canvas carrying case.

He leaned over her shoulder. "That's an Apple PowerBook. It's got a Motorola chip in it. They are supposed to be fast."

"Would you like to try it?" Jessie asked. The admonition from Albert about not playing with the computer gave her only a moment's pause. Screw it, if he had to delay his flight that's his problem.

Jessie pressed her shoulder against him as he flipped the cover open and clicked the power switch. He didn't seem to notice. She could feel the warmth of his body against her arm.

Numbers counted upward in the left-hand corner like a mad odometer, checking available memory. It stopped at the DOS prompt. "That's strange," he said. He typed "DIR/W", but no letters appeared on the screen. He hit several keys at random, but got no response on the screen.

"Your computer doesn't seem to be working."

"Well, it's brand new, it should be." She leaned over and pressed a key, careful to brush her breast on his arm.

"Do you mind if I take a look under the hood? I'm a bit of a hacker."

"No. Please do," she said. He seemed so accomplished. The flight might be interesting after all. "My name is Jessie," she said, sticking out her hand.

"Oh, hi." He held her hand briefly then pulled a wallet sized, miniature tool kit out of his coat pocket. He selected a small screwdriver.

"Well, what's your name?"

"Oh, sorry. Rick Dirani." He concentrated on loosening screws to open the cover.

Rick would have been surprised to see the inside of the computer. A small battery powered the screen. A logic circuit connected to the screen generated a series of numbers similar to the system check of RAM memory in a DOS based computer. Other than that, the resemblance to a computer was superficial.

The heavy, plastic battery pack contained two pounds of plastic explosives. The disk drive was also plastic explosives sculpted to resemble a drive. Pieces of metal hardware were attached to the pseudo-drive, with just enough wire to fool an attendant watching the airport x-ray machine. The circuit board was an electric tuner and detonator. An internal timer on the circuit board was set for three hours. Hassan set the timer shortly before placing Jessie on the plane.

Rick would have been surprised if he saw the inside of the computer, however, Hassan left little to chance. Hassan was confident that the computer would pass the x-ray inspection, but there was the possibility that it would be opened by an inspector prior to Jessie boarding the plane. An anti-tamper device would then detonate the bomb. The number of people killed at the airport would be in the tens rather than hundreds, but the operation would still be a modest success.

As Rick lifted the top of the computer an electrical connection was broken. This caused an electrical discharge into the detonators. The detonators ignited the explosive charge. The case holding the explosives contained the rapidly expanding gases for a fraction of a second.

The blast ripped Rick and Jessie to pieces. Fingers, arms and legs flew like little missiles about the plane. The explosion blew downward into the cargo compartment taking several seats and part of the floor with it. The outboard fuselage near them was breached. The rapid rush of wind lifted a flight attendant off her feet and plugged the hole in the fuselage temporarily with her body. Pressure inside the plane and the shock of the stewardess hitting the hull, ripped the skin of the aircraft further and the woman was gone. The 480 knot wind peeled back the fuselage like a tin can, tearing out tubes, wires, seats and people.

The man with yellow teeth who had occupied Jessie's seat rose into the air like he was levitating and was sucked out through the widening gap. Betty fell on the downward-tilted deck and slid on her face along the aisle, wedging at last under a seat. Breathing masks popped out of the overhead and danced on plastic tubes as they dangled in front of the frightened passengers. A chorus of screams could be heard above the roar of the wind. Papers, purses, books, baggage, flew through the air like a flock of crows in a hurry to get out the hole.

~ ~ ~

In the cockpit, the explosion was more felt than heard. A deep-throated boom rippled through the deck, muffled by the 200 feet that separated the flight crew from the rear of the plane. The 747 veered sharply to the right from the blast on the starboard side. It shuddered like a wounded animal as the jagged hole in its side dragged down the air speed.

Edwards pushed hard on the left rudder and grabbed the control yoke already held fast by the first officer. Vibrations shook their hands and forearms, and were transferred up into their chests.

"Hold the controls!" Edwards shouted over the roar of escaping air. He pulled on his oxygen mask.

"I got it." Edwards said as he finished putting on his mask and grabbed the yoke. The first officer already had his oxygen mask on.

"Nearest airfield," Edwards yelled putting the craft into a shallow dive. "I'll shed some altitude and get the air pressure back up in the cabin for the passengers.

"There's an abandoned military field twenty miles north," the second officer said.

"Damage assessment?" Edwards asked.

"No hydraulic pressure to the tail surfaces, number three engine is out," the second officer replied.

"The hell you say. Those systems are triple redundant!" Edwards pulled the yoke backward and forward to lift the nose of the aircraft. Nothing, the big plane lumbered along slowly losing altitude. He pushed the foot pedals trying to steer the plane without result.

"Captain, I'm just telling you what the gauges say. I didn't design the system."

"Second, get back there and find out what happened." Edwards had a sinking feeling in his stomach as he thought for the first time about casualties. Please, not on my plane, he thought.

"First, get on the horn and declare an emergency," Edwards said. He had taken care of his first responsibility, flying the plane, now there was finally time to call for help.

The first officer set the radio to the emergency frequency. "Mayday, Mayday, Mayday, NorthStar 2 heavy, 40 miles west of Gatwick, declaring an emergency. Main cabin depressurized, tail control surfaces inoperative."

Edwards waited until the first officer finished with the transmission. "We're heading West and we need to go North to get back to that runway," he said. "Any suggestions?"

"You bet," the first officer said. "We can steer by changing the power settings on the left and right engines. With the number three engine out, however, we are limited to right turns."

"Good plan," Edwards said. "We should also be able to use the ailerons. Let's give it a go. We'll try a turn to the right."

Edwards increased the power to the port engines while the first officer decreased the power to the remaining starboard engine. The large plane turned sluggishly to the right, sliding sideways as the nose came around.

"Banking right," Edwards said as he rotated the control yoke clockwise. The big plane fishtailed and tilted to the right. Edwards took part of the bank off and the plane steadied.

"I better get on the speaker to the passengers," Edwards said. "If they haven't already soiled their shorts, that last maneuver will have done it."

Edwards switched the mike over to intercom. "Ladies and gentlemen. As you may have noticed we are experiencing slight mechanical difficulties." He smiled at the first officer. Most of the initial terror had worn off, but not the euphoria from the adrenaline. He hated to admit it, but he was starting to enjoy the challenge. It was the most fun he had since his last carrier launch seven years ago in the Naval Reserves.

"The bad news is that we are not going to be able to get you to Houston on time. The good news is that we are going to get you down safely. We are checking for alternate landing sites now. The stewardess will instruct you on emergency landing procedures."

Edwards clicked the intercom off. "How are we doing, First?"

"We are coming around to the North okay, but we are losing a lot of altitude. We have twenty miles to the emergency airport, and we are down to 7,000 feet. We need to pick someplace else to land. We're not going to make it to the military field."

"Give me some alternate landing sites. I've got the controls."

The second officer stepped back into the cockpit. The roar from the hole in the cabin was cut off as he closed the door behind him. "There is one hell of a big hole in the right side aft, close to the tail section. It looks like a bomb. We're just lucky that it wasn't further aft or it might have blown the tail off."

"Casualties?" Edwards asked. Suddenly it wasn't fun anymore.

"Yes, sir, I'm afraid there are. There may be as many as thirty or forty people dead. It looks like a war zone back there."

"Thanks, Second," Edwards said. He pushed the dead to the back of his head. For the present he had to concentrate on saving the rest.

"Captain, there is no place else around that is big enough to land this baby. Looks like it's going to have to be a pasture."

"Not on your life. Find me a motorway. Any idea what the wind direction is?"

The second officer checked his clipboard as strapped in. "The wind was from 010 degrees at fifteen when we departed Gatwick."

"Good, let's assume it's the same here. Find us something going north and south, First. Then get on the radio and have the civilian authorities shut down the road, ASAP."

The first officer released his seatbelt and leaned forward to look over the control console, checking the terrain for a suitable landing spot.

"Altitude 3,000 feet, First," Edwards said, impatience straining his voice. "Give me what you've got."

"Looks like a motorway about a quarter mile to the east," the first officer said. He craned his head out of his side of the window.

"Second, dump as much fuel as you can," Edwards said.

Edwards raised up in his seat to see past his copilot. "I see it," he said. "Right turns we can do." He added power to the left engines as the first officer cut back on power to the right. "We'll skip the bank. That doesn't buy us much and we lose a lot of altitude."

Edwards leveled the plane out over the large divided highway. The second officer lowered the landing gear and the first officer lowered the flaps. The plane bucked violently as the large, metal flaps extended to the rear of the wings.

"Enough of that. Get those flaps up to half," Edwards said.

The shaking eased as the flaps came back to fifty percent. Edwards lined up the plane on the right hand side of the motorway. The cars zipping by underneath the aircraft were clearly visible.

"Second. Turn on the strobe lights and anything else you have. We'll give the auto drivers a chance to get out of the way if we can. If they don't move, we are going to have to land on top of them."

Edwards kept one hand on the yoke, the other on the throttles. At least the road was flat and relatively straight. The 747 came down quickly. As it neared the motorway it hesitated, held up by the ground effect. It floated, wheels reaching delicately for the earth like a fat lady testing the water with her toes. Finally, she touched down on the concrete road in a gentle anticlimax. The big wheels smoked as they came up to speed.

"Thrust reversers," Edwards said.

The first officer engaged the thrust reversers. Cowlings on the engines popped open, directing the jet exhaust forward, rapidly slowing the plane.

A Volvo came over a low rise headed directly toward the 747. Edwards steered the nosewheel to the right. The main wheels crunched on the gravel shoulder of the road. The Volvo swerved in the same direction as the plane, quickly veered back to the left, spun out and rolled over the grassy embankment as the car slipped beneath the left wing.

"Can you imagine how the driver will explain this to his insurance company?" Edwards asked no one in particular.

"Shut down the engines," he said.

The large plane shuddered as it came to a complete halt. The silence was awesome, the absence of sound unearthly, almost frightening after the roar of the jet engines. Edwards let out his breath unaware until now he had been holding it. "Well that was fun. Not as exciting as night carrier landings, but it will do." He picked up the intercom mike.

"Ladies and gentlemen. Welcome to Cotswold Motorway. We hope your stay in England is a pleasant one."

PART FOUR

REVENGE

CHAPTER SEVENTEEN

ANALYSIS

Lieutenant Commander Joshua Clark twirled the ballpoint pen around in his fingers like a baton. Smoking was prohibited in the conference room, so he couldn't light up his pipe, he wasn't about to buy a set of worry beads, so the only acceptable alternative was to make do with the writing placebo. The digital distraction required a modicum of concentration and was not as relaxing as a pipe, but with the world on the way to being a smoke free zone, this might be as good as it gets.

Clark looked at his watch. General Armstrong was late again, irritating him once more, this time with his absence. You shouldn't have to wait more than fifteen minutes, even for a general. Even for the chairman of the Joint Chiefs of Staff, although Armstrong lacked a few steps of being that. Clark felt that old anxious feeling in the pit of his stomach he got when he had more to do than he could possibly get done, even if he worked twenty-four hours a day. And here he sat waiting on General Armstrong.

General George C. Armstrong made his entrance. "Entrance" fit the way he entered the room. Staff officers followed in his wake like a convoy of auxiliary ships tending a battleship. Armstrong was Army, so the Navy analogy might not be appropriate. Perhaps courtiers would be better, lesser lights who attached themselves to his rising star. He was a tall, handsome man on a horse, and being related to the president did not hurt.

Clark kept himself from shaking his head only with great effort, which would be too obviously judgmental. Banging his head on the table would be more satisfying, but that would be too self-indulgent. Armstrong had to be doing this on purpose. Make sure everyone else was assembled in the room waiting for him before he put in an appearance. Armstrong had pulled the same trick at every single meeting Clark attended. Armstrong might be a busy man, but so were all the twenty or more captains, colonels, and commanders gathered around the table waiting for him.

"Gentlemen," Armstrong said. Clark glanced at the female lieutenant colonel across the table. Clark knew what it was like to be excluded, even by something as little as a general salutation.

"Thank you for coming," Armstrong continued. Did we have any choice, Clark thought.

"What have we got on the NorthStar crash?"

An Air Force colonel lead off. "General. The Brits have some preliminary data on the NorthStar bombing. There is very little left of the bomb mechanism itself, but fortunately the plane landed intact so the analysis is a lot easier than it would have been with pieces strewn over the countryside.

Parts of the mechanism were embedded in the fuselage, seats, and people. What has been recovered so far gives us a pretty good idea of what happened. We were able to trace the bomb to a specific seat."

"Can you identify the individual sitting in the seat?" Armstrong asked.

"The manifest shows that the individual in that seat was a Rick Dirani. He's a Director of Engineering, for ... ".

"Wait a minute," Armstrong interrupted. "Isn't that an Arab name?"

Clark felt uneasy. He had a suspicion where Armstrong was headed and didn't like it.

The colonel flipped through his briefing papers. "There isn't anything in the preliminary check about his ethnic background. The name does sound Arabic, but I will make a note to get it checked out."

Armstrong nodded. "Good. Go on."

"Dirani is director of engineering for a small U.S. oil company. He has no known terrorist involvement, no political activities out of the ordinary, and doesn't fit any of our profiles for terrorists. None of the security personnel at the airport noticed anything unusual about him or any of the other passengers.

"It will take awhile to analyze the bomb fragments. I'll get back with that information as soon as I have something."

"You do that." Armstrong waved the back of his hand at the colonel as if brushing a crumb off the edge of the table.

"Gentlemen. I think what we have here is an attempt by the ragheads to up the ante. They did not learn the lesson we gave them when we bombed Libya. I think it's time to give it to them again. I want some target recommendations for a strike. And this time I want some ground troops involved. If this is going to be a joint operation, we need to have some U.S. Army units involved on the ground."

Clark noticed his fingers marching of their own volition in sequence, in a drum roll on the edge of the table. There was something about General Armstrong that rubbed him the wrong way. "Excuse me, General," Clark said, "but some of our Arab allies might find it disparaging to call them 'ragheads'. Not all Arabs are our enemies."

Armstrong's face changed slowly from tan to pink to deep red, a silent metamorphosis. He seemed at a loss for words for a moment. "Lieutenant Commander." He emphasized the words. "At my confidential, secret, private staff meetings, I will damn well call Arabs 'ragheads' if I want! You got that, LIEUTENANT COMMANDER?"

Clark was suddenly aware that he was the junior officer present. In the Pentagon, captains and colonels made coffee, and Clark was two steps below that. Clark had long ago accepted the fact that he would never make admiral. Starting out as an enlisted man, the ladder was too long to climb to the top from his present age and position. Still, he knew when discretion was the better part of valor. The notoriety in the news about his heroics onboard the USS *Martin Luther King* would only protect him so far, but damn, this guy made him mad. "Yes, sir," he said quietly.

Armstrong tugged at his collar, mollified for the moment, collecting his thoughts. "Now how about some ideas on a retaliatory raid. Something with ground forces."

A Marine Corps general motioned with his hand. "How about snatching a high level Arab official involved with the bombing and putting him on trial? Syria may be implicated and their leader would be a good candidate. We have not done anything that bold for quite some time."

Armstrong smiled. "I like it. Panama redux. Now that was a good, solid, joint exercise. In and out quick, a lot of good publicity, arrest the bastard in his own country and put him on trial in the United States. The president of Panama is still serving time in an American jail, if I remember right."

From his position halfway down the long mahogany table, Joshua could see heads nodding like apples bobbing in a washtub full of water, with about as much intelligence. The officers, all bespangled in their uniforms, were nothing more than yes men. The female lieutenant colonel met his eye for a moment and then dropped her gaze to the table. They were going to go along with General Armstrong on this one. No one was going to tell the king he had no clothes.

"Excuse me, General," Joshua said. "But that sounds an awful lot like kidnapping."

Joshua could see the other officers out of his peripheral vision. They were keeping their heads down. He couldn't tell if they were studying their papers or admiring the wood grain on the expensive conference table.

General Armstrong gave Joshua the cold and silent treatment, staring at him with those steel blue eyes. This time ice rather than fire. Joshua locked looks with the general. He would be damned if he would back down. In old England a man might not look at a king, but this was America and General Armstrong was no king despite his airs.

"Nations can do with equanimity what men cannot individually do." The general's voice was cold and flat, but had a timbre that carried easily throughout the room. "If you abducted Bashar al-Assad, Mr. Clark, it would be kidnapping. But if the United States captures the President of Syria and brings him to trial for crimes against humanity, it will be justice. Besides what use is power if you do not exercise it periodically?"

"I know we can do it, General, but should we do it? What will world opinion be if we go in and kidnap, excuse me, arrest, the president of another sovereign nation?"

"Let's leave politics to the politicians. The Arabs have stuck a stick in our eye. Our assignment is to extract an eye for an eye and a tooth for a tooth. This operation will do that and I think I can sell it to the president. We have a man of action in the White House for a change, and he will act."

Clark grudgingly nodded his head. He was starting to believe that General Armstrong could sell ice to the Eskimos. Of course, it helped that General Armstrong was the president's nephew. The press once tried to play up the nepotism aspect, but Armstrong had clearly earned his way up long before his uncle was elected president.

"Since you have such a keen interest in the operation, I want you intimately involved in all aspects of planning for this raid. You will do your part to insure it is a rousing success. Do you understand, Mr. Clark?"

"Yes, sir," Clark said.

Now he too was a yes man. It was the military way. Once the boss made up his mind, everyone marched in line and made sure it happened. At least he had expressed his opinion; not that it made a difference.

CHAPTER EIGHTEEN

PLANNING

The makeshift, glass panel in the door rattled as Clark slammed it shut behind him. Damn Armstrong for making me angry, and shame on me for letting him do it.

Clark looked back at the door to make sure he hadn't broken the glass. He shook his head as he walked to his desk. The glass was another one of the Navy's half-assed solutions to an edict the bureaucrats mandated. The Navy perceived soft sailors, females, as problems looking for a place to happen. If the Navy reduced the privacy of offices by putting windows in doors, there was less likelihood that one Navy person might hug or kiss another Navy person while on duty.

And public display of affection was only half the problem. If it was determined to be unwanted sexual attention, then it was sexual harassment. If the affection was agree-able to both parties, it was fraternization providing it was between an officer and an enlisted person. Worst of all, it was subjective. Fraternization, harassment, romance, it was entirely in the mind of the beholder, or beholdee. Either way, it was against regulations and too frivolous to be con-doned by the United States Navy. Clark realized he was pissed at the Navy because he was still angry with General Armstrong for making him angry, but logic did not lessen the emotion.

Mrs. Porter leaned over her desk in the open bullpen area outside Clark's office and looked in through the door. She stood, picked up a pad from her desk, and walked into Clark's office, closing the door silently behind her.

Clark had a scowl on his face as he watched her enter. If she was not careful she would also get a blast. Noticing his attention, Mrs. Porter put a finger to her lip and drawled, "We have some secretaries out there be doing some mighty important work, Boss."

Clark smiled in spite of himself. "Don't be 'dissing' me girl." It was hard to be angry with Mrs. Porter when she was giving him her southern black routine. The incongru-ity of this genteel white southern lady calling him "boss" in an Afro-American dialect never ceased to amuse him.

"You do not have to call me 'boss'," Clark said. "We have worked together for several months and I anticipate, look forward to, working with you the rest of my tour. Can we be a little less formal?"

"Well now," Mrs. Porter said, sitting in the chair across from Clark's desk. "You are my direct reporting senior, you prepare my annual evaluation, and you recommend and approve my pay increases."

Mrs. Porter had switched to a formal, college educated, Bryn Mawr patois. She enunciated every word so distinctly and concisely it would have made an Englishman's chest swell with pride. "It is of course," she said, "quite proper for a subordinate to call her superior 'boss' under these circumstances. However, in deference to your wishes, I shall be quite happy to call you 'master,' if you so desire."

Mrs. Porter crossed one leg over the other and stretched the edge of her straight skirt toward her knees. Clark tried not to look at her legs. He actually would not have noticed at all if she had not drawn his attention to her legs by tugging at her skirt. Not that she was not pretty. She was on the high side of forty and her short blond hair had traces of silver, but she was still very sexually attractive. Clark made a mental note not to mention her to Sarah too often.

"No, thank you, Mrs. Porter. Joshua will do fine."

"Joshua may be more than I can manage, but I think we can settle on Lieutenant Commander Clark."

"Good enough," Clark said. "And I am sorry I slammed the door. Now what can I do for you?"

"Actually, I was wondering what I can do for you. You are back from a meeting with General Armstrong and obviously angry about something. Which probably means you have something on your mind. So what is bothering you? Out with it."

Clark considered. Mrs. Porter thrived on information. She knew who was doing what to whom, both socially and professionally, all over the Pentagon. She was also cleared for top secret information and he had already learned there was no way to get his job done without her help.

"Here is the deal, Mrs. Porter. I have got to prove that Syria bombed the NorthStar flight. That is my assignment from General Armstrong himself."

"That is one good assignment. It is an important piece of work."

"Is it? Armstrong merely wants to justify a retaliatory raid against Syria. It would enhance his career militarily and politically."

"There is nothing wrong with that, Mr. Clark. So long as he gets the job done, he deserves the credit. Have you considered that Syria may actually be responsible for the NorthStar bombing?"

Clark leaned back in his chair and looked carefully at Mrs. Porter. She held his gaze. There was a sharp mind behind those wire rimmed glasses and steel blue eyes. Was it possible that Syria might be responsible for the bombings? He had been so caught up in his attitude toward General Armstrong and the general's desire to kick ass that he had not really considered that Syria could actually be backing the terrorists. There was a scary thought — General Armstrong right about something.

"Mrs. Porter, it is possible. Anything is possible. The British could have bombed the NorthStar flight, after all we dumped a ton of their tea in Boston Harbor. Maybe they have been holding a grudge all of these years. The flight did originate in Gatwick. Syria is, of course, a more probable location of a state sponsored terrorist operation. Why do you think Syria is the source of the bomber?"

"You remember the Lockerbie, Scotland bombing in 1988? The Pan Am flight?

Clark nodded his head.

"Libya took the blame for that," Mrs. Porter continued. "But, there was scuttlebutt at the time, mind you just rumors, that the terrorists responsible were operating out of Syria. We were encouraging Mideast peace between Israel and her neighbors, so we did not want to stir that pot, but there was no reason to be nice to Libya. Syria may or may not have been responsible, but any leads in that direction were not followed up."

"Go on," Clark said. "So far, so good. It sounds logical."

"It is a different administration. The world situation has changed. The Gulf war is over. Israel is kissing up to any Arab nation that so much as winks at her.

"Let's find out if it is really Syria," Mrs. Clark continued. "If it is Syria, it is. If it is not, we can find that out too. Even generals are sometimes right."

Clark could see the laugh lines around Mrs. Porter's eyes behind the gold rimmed glasses. But right now, she was keeping her face very straight. Clark laughed. He tried to hold it in, but it spilled out anyway. It burst forth full and hearty. Holding it back momentarily only made it stronger when it broke loose. Now Mrs. Porter smiled, watching him hold his hand to his stomach.

"Right you are, Mrs. Porter. Now tell me how we get started. You know the ropes around here."

"Let's talk about the results of the physical investigation of the bombing. We will tell each other what we saw and what stood out and why."

"You read the file?" Clark asked.

"Of course I read the file. I am your assistant. I am also cleared for top secret. How can I assist you unless I know what is going on? So, tell me what you know."

Clark tilted his head back and scratched his neck under his chin. His five o'clock shadow roughened his fingers even though it was only 4 PM. "Shards of plastic were dispersed in the fuselage in a roughly spherical pattern around the probable location of the bomb."

"Why probable location?" Mrs. Porter prodded.

"Damage to the seats in front and back. The seats in front were pushed forward, the seats in back were pushed farther to the rear and ripped off their foundations. Seats to the side were flattened. Sections of the fuselage on the right side of the plane were punched out."

"I will buy that," Mrs. Porter said.

"How about you, Mrs. Porter? Tell me about the accident."

"The dispersal of the plastic shards indicates the bomb was probably enclosed in a plastic case. Chemical analysis shows that it is a high impact type of plastic, a type that is commonly used for a variety of appliances, including electronic equipment such as computers and stereos. I think we can rule out computers. Spectrographic analysis is still ongoing to try to determine the manufacturer of the plastic. Eventually we should even be able to determine the particular batch the plastic pieces came from and when it was produced."

Clark held up his hand to interrupt. "Why are you ruling out computers?

"When you take a computer through an airport security station, you have to turn it on after it has been x-rayed. That is the method that is used to check that the computer is operational and that it is not just a laptop shell full of high explosives."

"Good point, but now it's your turn to play the 'What If' game, Mrs. Porter. What if you were a terrorist, you knew airport security procedures and you wanted to smuggle high explosives aboard an aircraft. What would you do to smuggle those explosives in a decent size laptop computer case?" Clark watched Mrs. Porter's face as her mind worried at the problem. Her eyebrows pulled together in a frown as she concentrated and then her eyes widened with surprise.

"I did take one of the laptops with me on a trip once. When they check the computer to see if it's operational, all they do is have you turn it on and watch as the numbers count upward in the upper left hand corner, telling you whether the random access memory checks out okay. I bet it would be possible to put in a small electronic counter in a computer case just to run through a fake random access memory check. The numbers would roll up on screen, but nothing else would happen. A terrorist could still have the rest of the computer stuffed with explosives."

"I bet you're right, Mrs. Porter," Joshua said.

"Had you already thought of that?"

"No, but your suggestion about batting around ideas was a good one. When you said a bomb could not be smuggled aboard an aircraft in a computer case, it made me start thinking about how it could be done. Laptop computers are ubiquitous, and that would be a great way to smuggle several pounds of high explosives aboard an aircraft.

"Anything else?" Clark said.

"The clunky older model computers have large batteries. If it wasn't really a computer and you don't need the battery to power up the hard drive, you could replace the battery with a good size block of plastic explosives." She was sitting forward in her chair, obviously excited about the possibilities. "You could use a smaller battery just to run the counter. What was nominally a big, bulky battery could be a block of plastic explosive. Doing it that way you could still have all the standard computer parts in there, circuit board, disk drive, they would just be inoperative. The circuit board could be used as a timer."

"Good point, Mrs. Porter. You get an A on espionage on this one. I did notice that the report on the timer showed it was a type that was used by Stazi operatives in the former East Germany."

"I noticed that too. That means it's the same group that bombed the Kit Kat Club in Italy." Mrs. Porter said. "But the Libyans were responsible for that. Weren't they?"

"It may be more appropriate to say the Libyans were blamed for that, Mrs. Porter. Whether they were responsible is another question."

"Another question for you," Clark said, "is how do I follow up on the NorthStar bombing? I have a strike-planning meeting in an hour. We can worry about whether or not Libya was responsible for the Kit Kat Club bombing another time. We may never know the answer to that question, but I do need to know more about the bomber." Joshua knew that Mrs. Porter didn't mind giving advice and had the knowledge and experience to make it good advice.

"I will set up a meeting for you with the CIA section that's conducting the review. Will tomorrow be okay, Lt. Cdr. Clark?"

"Yes, Mrs. Porter." He resisted the temptation to emphasis "Mrs." She did such a good job on everything else that there was no way he was going to antagonize her by making her call him Josh. She could call him whatever she wanted. He was just grateful to have her helping him.

CHAPTER NINETEEN

IN TRAINING

Ahmed woke in panic, ripped from the complete sleep known only by the deeply exhausted or near dead. The staccato rattle of an AK-47 tore through the pre-dawn silence. His pulse raced in time to the beat. Fear was an acid in his belly and his loins as he rolled out of bed onto the canvas covered floor. Shadowy shapes ran through the rows of cots, shouting, illuminated by the muzzle flashes from their guns. The smell of gun smoke filled his nostrils. Bullets hissed over his head.

Ahmed crawled like a crab on forearms and shins, belly only inches from the floor, moving at what would have seemed a lightening fast pace to one of those crustaceans. The canvas floor chaffed the skin from his arms and legs unnoticed. Moving fast, his only thought, more instinct than any rational or coherent process, was to get clear of the tent.

The pale outline of the entrance was in front of him. He scuttled toward it, the cold, desert, night air in his nostrils. He hadn't stopped or even slowed since the first shot.

A boot caught him in his ribs as he crossed the last row of cots. Ahmed rolled onto his back with the kick, catching the boot in both of his hands. A dark figure fell forward, past him. Ahmed completed his roll onto the top of the fallen figure.

The fear that filled him turned to rage. The Israelis must have found the camp. His fists found a target. He pummeled his adversary, head, face, back, and kidneys as the man struggled beneath him. Whatever he could reach in the near darkness he hit as he straddled his opponent.

The butt end of a rifle was a blur in his peripheral vision. He started to turn his head, but was too late. The heavy end of the gun followed through, snapping his head to the left like a tetherball. From inside his head it sounded like a brass knocker hitting a heavy wooden door. His body followed his head to the floor.

When he woke, Ahmed was looking up into the barrel of an AK-47. Several seconds of time had disappeared. Between the stroke of the rifle butt and the gun in his face, nothing. The man holding the gun had a foot on his throat. The barrel of the rifle was pressed against his cheek, squeezing the skin on his face against his eye. In the dim glow of a lantern someone had lit, Ahmed saw his comrades being bound. Forced to kneel, face on the floor, their hands were being taped behind their back. The black clad figures moved in pairs, quickly and efficiently, one standing guard with his rifle, the other binding the hands of Ahmed's comrades.

The soldier Ahmed had beaten lay unconscious beside him. A black clad soldier grabbed Ahmed and pulled roughly at his arm and rolled him face down. The other man, the one holding the gun on Ahmed, pulled the rifle away from Ahmed's face to give his comrade room. Ahmed continued the roll and drew his feet under him. The anger was still in him, dormant for only a moment while he was unconscious. Rising quickly to his feet, Ahmed struck the man with the tape with the back of his fists, the fingers of both hands laced together. The black clad figure's head snapped back with the force of the blow.

Ahmed stepped to the gun-toting soldier, his movements a seamless blur of motion. He stiff-armed the man bringing the open end of his palm up under the chin of the startled gunner as he was taught in class. Everything around him seemed to move in slow motion. Ahmed saw the man's startled eyes widen, the pupils circled with white as his body lifted off the floor with the force of the blow, his eyes rolling back, his lids falling closed.

Ahmed's hands closed on the rifle as it fell from slack fingers. He whipped the gun around as heads turned toward him. His new friends on the ground, clad only in shorts, looked up, their faces pale circles in the light of the lamp. The soldiers in black shirts and slacks were frozen in place, a tableau in silence as Ahmed's finger tightened on the trigger. He could not kill them all, but he would try.

The whole scene lasted only a second or two, but it seemed infinitely longer. A shrill whistle from the front of the tent unfroze them all. Ahmed turned with the others to look, keeping the black clad men in view from the corner of his eye, the rifle never wavering from their direction. The commander of the training camp stood near the front of the tent, whistle in his hand.

"The exercise has ended," he yelled in his gravelly voice.

The camp commander turned to look up at the man beside him. Tall and thin with graying hair, the man looked little like the Kit Kat Club bomber. But Ahmed would not have recognized Hassan even without the three days worth of stubble on his face and the gray hair.

Hassan walked slowly toward the center of the tent. All eyes followed him. He stepped up to Ahmed. Ahmed was unsure what to do with the gun, point it at Hassan or point it at the floor. The presence of the training camp commander indicated that this was not a commando raid by Israeli troops, which was Ahmed's first coherent thought. The gun barrel wavered with his indecision, but he pulled it back against his chest as Hassan drew closer.

Hassan stopped toe to toe in front of Ahmed. Ahmed looked up at the taller man and stood his ground. There was a strong urge to step back a pace. Hassan stood only inches away from him, and Ahmed could feel the warmth of the man's body, the heat of his breath in his face. Ahmed shivered, feeling for the first time the chill of the desert air, the shaky sensation of adrenaline draining from his body. He remembered he was dressed only in shorts. Hassan challenged Ahmed with his eyes, but Ahmed would not look away. Hassan nodded slightly as if satisfied with something he saw there, and turned his back.

Ahmed let his breath go, not realizing he had been holding it. The man had a magnetism about him, a powerful aura. Dangerous. The eyes held you like a snake.

"This was a test," Hassan said. His voice was quiet, but carried clearly. "You have failed. If these men were American commandos, or Israeli, you would be dead. Where are your sentries? Where are your trip wires?"

There were no answers from the men kneeling on the floor. We are only soldiers in training, Ahmed thought, but he knew that it was not the right answer.

"Do not ever put your trust in someone else. You must protect yourself. Pick sentries from among yourselves.

Learn from this lesson." Hassan looked slowly around the room. "Or you will die."

Hassan turned to face Ahmed. "You. Put on some clothes and join me in the commander's tent." He turned on his heel and left. The black clad soldiers followed him.

Ahmed stood watching the door after Hassan left. The overdose of adrenaline caused him to shiver again. He put the safety on the rifle and laid it on the nearest cot. He removed the tape from the hands of the nearest prisoner. He pointed toward the rest of his comrades and said, "Untie them."

Ahmed pulled on coarse, green trousers and shirt. He put on his boots and drew the laces tight. His anger gathered about him again as he dressed. Who was this person running a live fire exercise on trainees at night? Someone could have been killed.

He was close to running when he entered the commander's tent. The commander and Hassan were sitting in canvas chairs when Ahmed entered.

"What do you mean shooting at us!" Ahmed shouted at Hassan. The commander stood and started to speak. Hassan silenced him with a gesture.

"Whose side are you on?" Ahmed continued.

"Leave us," Hassan said to the commander, his voice calm and steady. Hassan never took his eyes off Ahmed as the commander left the tent.

Hassan let the silence linger. "You are right to be angry." His voice was slow and methodical. "But you must use your anger. Make it work for you. Direct it. It can give you strength or it can rob you of reason."

"But you could have killed us."

"Of course. But we do not play games here. We do not play by the rules here. We break the rules. When the American commandos come in the night they will not have blanks in their guns. They will not try you and find you guilty. They will kill you. They will not play by any rules.

"Live ammo focuses one's concentration," Hassan said. "When you practice your crab crawl under the barbed wire here at training camp, the machine guns use real ammunition. It is much more effective than having a sergeant yelling to keep your head down.

"But enough of this," Hassan said. He waved his hand to dismiss the discussion. "Sit. Save your anger for the Americans and the Israelis." Hassan motioned to the commander's chair. Ahmed struggled with himself, but finally sat.

"You have technical expertise." Hassan didn't ask it as a question, but he clearly wanted some answers.

"Yes. I have experience working at a chemical factory. I was a maintenance supervisor."

"Why are you here?"

"I want to kill Americans." Ahmed's eyes sparked when he said it. He would not think of the death of his wife and children, that brought sadness and weakness. He would only think of revenge, that was his strength.

"Good. We shall certainly do that. I have need of someone with mechanical knowledge for a mission I am organizing. These other trainees are good foot soldiers. But I have need of someone with intelligence. Someone who is brave enough, or angry enough, to stand his ground when arming a bomb. I think you will do.

"Work hard at completion of training," Hassan said. "You already have good hand-to-hand combat skills, but there is more for you to learn.

"You will soon be killing many Americans, more than you can imagine. I will send for you when I am ready."

CHAPTER TWENTY

CONTINGENCY PLANNING

Joshua Clark took his place near the end of the short table with the majors and other lieutenant commanders assigned to the planning team. The team had arranged itself around the map table, without any formal planning, in a pecking order determined by rank. The head planner, General Armstrong's chief of staff, Colonel Morgan, was at the head of the table.

"Gentlemen," the colonel said. "Let's get started." He rapped his knuckles on the map table. A detailed map of Damascus was taped to the top of the table.

"In broad outline, the purpose of this mission is to conduct a swift, tactical raid on Syria, apprehend Bashar al-Assad, President of Syria, and bring him out of the country for transport to the United States to stand trial for terrorism.

173

"This must be done," the colonel continued, "in a fashion, which minimizes casualties. There will be no accidental bombing of embassies, orphanages, or anything else that might adversely affect public opinion. Speed is essential to the operation. We should be in and out before the Syrian forces know that a raid is in progress, let alone determine the purpose of the operation. Ideally, we will be in and out even before CNN can broadcast it on the nightly news."

The colonel looked around the table holding each officer's eyes in turn. Clark felt Colonel Morgan was speaking directly to him, which was undoubtedly what the colonel intended. The colonel stared at them through eyes ringed with gray circles from too many nights spent planning ways to kill the enemies of the United States. They were tired eyes that had a film of hardness to them.

"Suppression strikes will be the responsibility of the Navy." The colonel nodded to a Navy commander on the left side of the table.

"Plan on hitting all radar stations and antiaircraft batteries in the vicinity of Damascus. Also plan on cratering all runways, both military and commercial, to keep aircraft on the ground." The Navy commander nodded his head as he took notes.

"Air Force," the colonel looked at an Air Force lieutenant colonel to Clark's right. "You are responsible for destruction of Syrian troop barracks. I want the Syrian troops keeping their heads down during the operation. Do you have stealth fighters in the area that can be used?"

"Yes sir," the lieutenant colonel said. "We can bring down a squadron from Germany and stage them out of air bases in Turkey. That should be well within their operational range."

"Good. Intelligence, most probable location for Bashar al-Assad?" The colonel looked around the table.

"Here, sir." An Army major raised his hand. "Assad's home is in the Malki neighborhood. Assuming we plan a night operation, it is most likely Bashar al-Assad will be at his residence." He indicated a position on the map.

Clark bent his head for a closer look as the Major touched a point on the map of Damascus with his finger. "The location has been confirmed by Mossad," the major said. "Assad's routine is known with a moderately high level of accuracy."

"Troop strength at the compound, Major?"

"The opposition is company strength, Colonel. No more than one-third of the company will be on duty at any one time. Walled compound with medium caliber gun emplacements at the corners according to our Israeli contacts."

"Estimation of the caliber of the troops?"

"There have been no major military confrontations, internal or external, in Syria for a number of years. Syrian military units have little combat experience. Some units have seen action in Lebanon, but those were more on the order of peace keeping operations, guard duty. According to Israeli operatives, there are no combat veterans in the Presidential Guard Company."

"Good. The most important part of the raid is up to you." The chief of staff looked at another Army colonel beside him. "Plan on using a Delta Force unit to make the strike. Time on the ground should be approximately 0200. The psycho war people have picked that time as optimum for decreased level of alertness of defending troops.

"The planning should include using Apache helicopters to hose the strong points with miniguns and to breach the walls with rockets. As for timing, the Apaches should arrive immediately after the Stealth fighter strike against the barracks. Plan your flight path routing to avoid the inbound trajectories for Tomahawk and Stealth aircraft both inbound and outbound. We do not need any self-inflicted causalities.

"Can the troop helicopters land inside the compound?" The Army Ranger colonel asked.

"No sir," the Intelligence major answered. "But the set back from other buildings in the neighborhood is several hundred yards. There is plenty of room to land outside the walls of the compound."

"Outstanding," the chief of staff continued. "From start of operation to finish, I want no more than two hours total time. The window for the Tomahawks will be ten minutes on target. For the Stealth fighters, fifteen minutes over target. The Apache operation also has a fifteen-minute window. The rest of the time is for ground operation including search of the compound."

"Gentlemen, I want detailed portions of your strike plan by 0800 tomorrow. It should not be a difficult plan to prepare. The guts of the operation were laid out in the War College Plan and war-gamed. You will brief me on the coordinated plan at 1000 with a formal briefing for General Armstrong scheduled at 1200 hours. Any questions?"

Clark raised his hand.

The colonel looked at Clark and thrust his chin out. He obviously had not expected and probably did not want any questions, and certainly not any from Clark. The colonel had been at the earlier meeting and watched General Armstrong chew Clark's butt. From the set of Colonel Morgan's chin, Clark could tell he expected to have to do some ass chewing himself.

"Sir, what if Bashar al-Assad is not at his compound?"

"What?" the colonel twisted his head to the side.

"What if President Bashar al-Assad is not in his compound?" Clark let the silence draw out for a few seconds.

It was obvious Colonel Morgan didn't understand the question or didn't know the answer. "Colonel, there are reports that Bashar al-Assad's health is not good. He may be getting medical treatment at some location other than his compound."

"What makes you say that, Lieutenant Commander?" The colonel's eyes were suspicious.

Clark noticed his emphasis on lieutenant commander. Colonel Morgan had been hanging around General Armstrong so long, he was picking up his characteristics. Did his emphasis on Clark's rank mean that an 0-4 Navy officer couldn't possibly have information that an Army 0-6 colonel didn't have?

"*Time* Magazine ran an article on Bashar al-Assad recently. It is well known that his father had cardiovascular problems and had heart bypass surgery. That's pretty well documented. The article also had a one-liner speculating on Assad's current health, his recent cancellation of public appearances, and it was rumored that he might be receiving medical treatment."

"So what are you suggesting, Lt. Cdr. Clark?"

"Let's do some contingency planning. Use our human intelligence contacts, Israeli agents if we do not have our own operatives in country, and find out the location of the hospital that Assad might be using if he is sick. We can put a squad of Delta Rangers at the hospital before the primary raid starts. That way we have covered both bases. If Assad is at the hospital, then there is no need to go with the primary raid and we can minimize casualties on both sides. After all we're not teaching the people of Syria a lesson, we are teaching terrorists a lesson. It is Bashar al-Assad we want to put on trial for backing terrorism. Let us make sure we grab him if we are going to do this."

The door to the briefing room opened, flooding the dimly lit room with light. General Armstrong walked in.

"Attention," Colonel Morgan ordered. The officers around the map table came to attention, looking straight ahead.

"Carry on, gentlemen," Armstrong ordered. "I merely wanted to check on the status of planning the Syrian raid. How's it going, Colonel Morgan?"

"Very straightforward, sir. We're following the basic outlines of the War College plan as you suggested. However, Lt. Cdr. Clark wants to modify the plan." Colonel Morgan smiled as he gestured with his thumb at Clark, not bothering to look in his direction.

"Oh," General Armstrong said and slowly turned to look at Clark. Clark swallowed as Armstrong focused his full attention on him. The look on Armstrong's face reminded Clark of a wolf he had once seen. The wolf was in the zoo watching the spectators, savoring their scents, watching them warily, obviously wishing they would come just a little closer.

"So, Commander, you had some ideas for improving on my plan?"

Clark noticed that the War College plan was now General Armstrong's plan. The sarcasm in Armstrong's voice was thick enough to stick a spoon in. Clark felt his face flushing.

"General, I have some suggestions for improving the canned plan to cover the facts of this particular situation." As soon as he said canned plan, he regretted it. It would have been diplomatic to say "the general's plan" and let it go at that. He rushed ahead. "Bashar al-Assad may not be in his compound. There have been media reports that he is ill. It would be logical to have a unit raid the hospital prior to commencement of the suppression strikes to cover all our bases."

Clark took a deep breath and made himself talk slower. Rushing the words as he had made it seem like he was pleading rather than persuading. "It would be politically inappropriate to go in, kick ass, and come away empty handed."

"Would it?" Armstrong said. "No one knows that the object of the strike is to kidnap, excuse me, arrest, Bashar al-Assad. If we don't get Assad out at least we've torn up his military runways and killed a few companies of troops. That's still a successful retaliatory raid and Assad and Syria are both punished. No one knows the real purpose of the mission, except me, the president, and the planning group. Therefore, we can have a success either way."

Clark looked at the rest of the officers. They were keeping their heads down which was probably the smart thing to do.

"Yes, Sir, but if you get Assad out and try him, that would be more effective politically for..." He caught himself before he said *you*. "For the United States," he said. "If the purpose of the mission is to arrest Assad, we should take actions necessary to insure the success of the mission. If we get Assad out from a medical treatment facility before the main raid, we can save a few million dollars on ordinance and minimize casualties all around."

"Money is the least of my worries," General Armstrong said. "We pull this off and those bastards in Congress will have no choice but to vote us another couple hundred million dollars to replace the ordinance." General Armstrong tapped his teeth with his thumbnail as he considered.

"Still, you've got a point. However, if we go in before the main attack, the unit we assign to the hospital raid will be more exposed, and they will be subject to a higher risk of casualties. Are you willing to accept that risk, Mr. Clark?"

"The hospital is less likely to be as heavily defended as Assad's residence compound, General. I think we can expect minimum casualties from a raid on a medical compound. Most of the rest of the operation, except for the Apache helicopters, is for suppression purposes only, to keep everyone's head down. Going for the hospital first, the total body count, both us and them, may be less."

"I do not care about the body count we inflict on them. Then you're willing to accept some minimum risk of casualties for U.S. personnel assigned to target the hospital, Commander Clark?"

"Yes, sir."

"Good. Work with the Rangers and make it happen. I personally believe that the chance of finding Assad at the hospital is small. You can not believe everything you read in the press, Mr. Clark. But we will cover that contingency."

General Armstrong turned to go, paused and turned toward Clark. "By the way, Mr. Clark, you will be going in with the team assigned to the medical facilities. You may provide a small measure of quality control. A planner should be willing to go in with the operational people if he has confidence in his plan. Right, Mr. Clark?" General Armstrong said. Colonel Morgan was now smiling broadly.

"Yes, sir." Clark worked hard to keep from swallowing.

"That's the right answer. Who knows, this time you may *earn* a combat decoration."

CHAPTER TWENTY-ONE

EVIDENCE

Joshua Clark came to a complete stop at the gate. The gate guard stepped to the side of the car and bent down as Clark lowered his tinted window, letting in the crisp D. C. air, and a slice of spring sunshine. Clark wore his uniform and had a military sticker on the front bumper, but just being military wasn't good enough to get through the gates at Langley. I suppose it wouldn't be the CIA headquarters if just anyone could drive in, he thought.

"May I help you, sir?"

"Lt. Cdr. Joshua Clark to meet with Mr. Dallas."

The guard was giving Clark a visual strip search and checking all the corners of the car while he talked. "Identification, sir."

Clark showed him his green, military I.D. card. The guard checked the printed list.

"Very good, sir. Drive straight through to parking area A. Someone will meet you there."

Clark pulled through and wound around to the parking area. This was his first visit to Langley and he wasn't sure what to expect. The gate security was good enough, better than most military bases where you were allowed to drive on base if the vehicle you were in had a government decal. But still, the guard did not search the trunk, look under the car, or x-ray him and his briefcase. Maybe they had hidden cameras that checked the bottom of the car while it was stopped at the gate. Yeah, that had to be it.

Clark pulled into the parking lot and stepped out of the car. A nondescript man waited patiently at the curb, hands clasped behind his back. He stepped over to the car and thrust his hand out.

Clark checked him over as he reached for his hand. Medium height, medium build, brown hair, glasses. He had been expecting someone more formidable, if not Sean Connery, at least Kevin Costner or Jean Claude Van Dam. A human lethal weapon trained in all the martial arts, who could kill you with a look if you let your guard down. Instead, this guy would blend in with the wallpaper if he didn't move for more than a minute. He might have been an accountant or lawyer, except for that brown suit. No one wore brown suits anymore.

"Hi, I'm Jim Dallas," he said in a surprisingly strong voice. "I understand you want to look at some of the physical evidence from the NorthStar bombing."

"Joshua Clark." Clark's breath was a frosty cloud in front of his face as he shook Dallas' hand. "Yes. I've read some of the reports and summaries, but I wanted to see as much as I can for myself. Get my hands around the problem, if you will."

Clark remembered making a report to his engineer officer once about plans to repair a ventilation fan while on his second submarine assignment. He had just reported aboard and the Blue Crew auxiliary division chief had gone over the repair package. Clark went forward to brief the engineer on repair work for the upkeep and the engineer asked how much time it would take to complete the fan motor change out. Clark did a quick calculation in his mind, which included rigging the old motor out and off the ship, and estimated ten man-hours. "How about removal of the other equipment? You cannot get the fan out without pulling other motors."

"There isn't any interference, sir," Clark said. "The fan sits on the bulkhead of the torpedo room, straight bolt and unbolt job."

The engineer threw the A Division package in his face. "Get the fuck out of here and come back when you know what the hell you're talking about," was the rather eloquent way he put it.

Clark found out later that the fan motor on his new boat was in the fan room, not in the torpedo room where it was on his old boat. Removal of other equipment to provide access to the defective motor would take three times the amount of time he estimated. The engineer officer was an ass, but Clark had learned a lesson. Never, never make your report without looking at the equipment yourself. An executive officer later put it more succinctly. "When you 'assume' you make an ass out of you and me."

"Good," Dallas said. "We'll help you all we can and we can definitely get you some hands-on experience. Come with me." Dallas took Clark in through the double doors into the building. Clark was pleased to see that they had a metal detector for him and an x-ray machine for his briefcase. The CIA was living up to his expectations on the physical security side. He was issued a clip-on visitor's badge and advised to wear it conspicuously while in the building.

"What would you like to see first?" Dallas asked, hands clasped behind his back again. Clark couldn't help wondering if his name really was Dallas. Didn't the CIA give all their employees false names and identifications?

"Let's look at the bomb material and fragments from the container," Clark said.

"You got it." They continued to a large laboratory-like workspace lined with long tables.

"You realize, of course," Dallas said, "that we don't have everything here. When an air accident occurs on an airplane in British airspace, even a U.S. flag carrier, the Brits have primary authority. There is a lot of cooperation, however, and they allow our Federal Aviation Administration folks, FAA, to help with the investigation. The CIA and sometimes the FBI get assigned part of the investigation, as is the case here.

"The piece of the action that we were able to cut out," Dallas said, "is bomb analysis. The CIA, and all the other organizations, are working on identification of the terrorist group involved, but the bomb is our baby. There is some duplication, actually a lot of duplication and overlap, but the process seems to work pretty well.

"We've got the plastic shards from the casing laid out on these tables." Dallas walked along the tables as he talked. "Near each piece of plastic is a photograph of the location showing where it was recovered, in the fuselage, from the bodies, or removed from the seats."

"There aren't many pieces," Clark observed, looking back along the length of the table.

"No, some of them probably blew out the side of the fuselage. Others may be too small to identify. And there are probably some that were pulled out of survivor's bodies by the medical team and discarded, or may even still be in the bodies. In a major medical emergency like the NorthStar bombing, the medical team's first priority is saving survivors. They're not concerned about saving physical evidence and probably shouldn't be."

Clark started working his way back looking at the pieces of gray plastic shards in clear plastic baggies.

"How about some coffee?" Dallas asked.

"Sounds good. Black, if you don't mind." Clark put his briefcase down.

"May I take some of these pieces out and look at them?"

"Sure. I'll be right back. Just make sure they go back into the proper bags."

Clark pulled a piece of plastic from one of the bags and rotated it in his hand. It was dark gray. Slick and shiny on what must have been the fracture line and mat gray on what was probably the outside surface. He looked at the diagram near the shard on the table and read the legend next to it.

Removed from white Caucasian female, cranial area, in seat adjacent to bomb blast. Seat listed as unoccupied on airline manifest. No positive identification. Believed to be one of three passengers not accounted for.

Clark turned the piece of plastic in his fingers as he read. He rubbed at a rust colored stain at the sharp end of the sliver with his thumb. He pulled his hand away as he realized it must be dried blood. He transferred the piece to his other hand and rubbed his fingers on his trousers. Looking again at the plastic, he noticed a thin line of color at the edge, half-blue, half-purple. Now that seemed familiar. Why?

Dallas handed him a cup of coffee as he walked up. "Find anything interesting?" Dallas asked as he blew the steam from his coffee and sipped from the cup edge.

"Not really. I have some questions though."

"Shoot."

"Why can't you make an identification of the passenger seated in the seat adjacent to the bomb blast?"

"There are several reasons." Clark noticed that Dallas didn't seem to mind answering questions that must seem obvious to him. "The blast pretty much blew her apart. Her seatbelt wasn't attached and we're only about 80% sure she was sitting in that seat, whoever she was. We made the determination that she was probably sitting in the seat adjacent to the blast based on bloodstains on the seat matched against her blood type and blood splattered on other seats in the row.

"But you narrowed her identity to one of three individuals?"

"Yes. It was a process of elimination. First of all, a large number of people survived. Bingo. That eliminates two-thirds of the individuals on the manifest. A number of those who didn't survive were strapped in their seat. Enough was left for the relatives to easily identify the remains.

"However, there were some that were up and walking about. They got sucked out of the cabin. Some were sitting in the seats adjacent to the breach in the fuselage and they also deplaned in a hurry. Some were sitting in their seats and didn't have their seatbelts on, some people never learn, and wind surfed out of the aircraft when the cabin depressurized. A hard way to learn a lesson, but they won't do that again."

"How about dental records, passport photographs?"

"That may come eventually. Sometimes these investigations go on for a very long time. And believe me, we're still looking. We'll be looking as long as the case is unsolved. But some of these people haven't been to dentists. Also, foreign dental records are not as accurate as ours. Remember this was an international flight.

"What about passport photos?" Clark asked.

Dallas shrugged. "We check them when people board the aircraft. We don't make copies of them."

"But doesn't the Passport Office keep a copy of the photograph when they issue a passport?"

"Of course," Dallas said. "Would you like to see them? I'll get those."

Dallas set his coffee on the table and walked to the file cabinet at the end of the room. Clark liked him. He wasn't James Bond, but he was good at what he did and he made no apologies for not having solved the case immediately. And he didn't pretend to have all the answers.

"These are the three possibilities," Dallas said, handing Clark three slim file folders.

The photograph of a dark skinned Pakistani lady looked out at him from the file. Clark flipped the page and looked at the information summary. He flipped back to the picture. Middle-aged, dark curly hair, going to gray. Thin, gold rimmed spectacles. The information sheet identified her as a doctor.

He put the folder on the bottom and flipped open the next one. He looked up at Dallas. "There's no photograph in this one."

"That one is Hungarian. We'll eventually get a photograph, but we don't have it yet. The Hungarians would probably like to cooperate with us, but they are badly disorganized. There is only so much we can do to push them along. This project is a high priority for you and me, but not necessarily at the top of the list for the State Department. They're the ones who have to lean on the Hungarians."

"Why doesn't the airport make a photocopy of passports when people check in?"

"Beats me," Dallas said. "One more expensive piece of equipment for the airlines to buy. They won't do it until someone beats them over the head." Dallas smiled.

Clark could tell by the way Dallas added a smile at the end of the sentence that it wasn't a criticism or a complaint. It was just the way things were.

Clark closed the folder and opened the next file. A chubby faced British girl stared back at him. She was a full-faced, wide eyed, exceedingly plain-looking girl. Clark flipped to the information page. Her name was Jessie Foster. He scanned the passport data and flipped to the next page. She had been assigned a seat farther back, near the fuselage. The information sheet showed she was employed by Harrods. A note indicated that her parents didn't know she was taking a trip to the United States. The parents held conservative political views. She was unlikely to have been involved in any of the lunatic fringe organizations. This record was significantly more complete than the others. God bless the British. They were nothing, if not efficient.

"How about airport security photographs, monitoring systems, video cameras?"

"There are some videos. Gatwick does a good job and we have copies of all the videotapes they had. But we've looked at all that. A lot of people have looked at that."

Clark said nothing.

Dallas shrugged his shoulders and said, "OK, I know. You've got to see it for yourself. Let's take a look. You might see something from a different angle."

Dallas took Clark to an adjacent room. The room was filled with television monitors, computers and electronic equipment. It looked like a cross between a techno-junkies' nightmare and a computer hacker's wet dream.

"Sit here," Dallas said, pulling out a chair for Clark near a large-screen monitor. Clark sat down as Dallas pulled videotapes from a cabinet. "We've got the tapes from two hours before flight time at the airport security check point. No video monitors were at the gate itself so you're going to see thousands of people pass through the checkpoint going to all the flights that left during that time period.

"Using this equipment," Dallas said with pride in his voice, "we can zoom in on any frame and pull up as much detail as you like. There is a computer enhancement program loaded so the frames don't get too fuzzy as you magnify them. If you see something you really like, we'll send it to the video lab and they will get the rest of the fuzz out of the picture, only it will take a lot longer."

"You're being pretty helpful," Clark said as Dallas loaded the first tape into a VCR. "Is there always this much interagency cooperation?"

"Sometimes, but not always. But my full-time assignment is solving this case and I know I'm not going to do it all by myself. If you can add anything to it, I'd love to hear it. Even if you solve the case, I still get part of the credit. Besides, rehashing the information we have, answering your questions helps me refocus. And last, but not least, the director personally told me to give you full cooperation and any help you needed. The director is ex-Army and my guess is your boss, General Armstrong, gave him a personal call."

Clark nodded his head. That sounded like Armstrong. He knew all the important people in Washington, D.C. or at least thought he did, and would call them every time he had an opportunity, for networking if nothing else. But he did seem to get the job done.

Dallas hit the play button. "Here are the standard controls, Play, Stop, Reverse, Fast Forward, Freeze Frame. Use the cursor here to move the on screen box to pick up more details."

Dallas demonstrated freezing the video as a man walked through the metal detector. He moved the box to the man's face and hit the keys to enlarge the picture. The man's head filled the screen. Each time the frame was enlarged, there was a brief delay as the computer enhanced the image. Dallas moved the box again, this time to the man's ear and enlarged that. In the enlarged picture, you could see that he was wearing an earring.

"Isn't he pretty," Dallas said. Clark could tell by his tone that he didn't really think so. The man in question had a close-shaved head of black hair, looked like he was in his early twenties and had a terminal case of acne. Clark looked at Dallas who was smiling at him broadly.

"Maybe not exactly pretty," Dallas said. "But certainly happy. Or maybe just gay." Clark shook his head and pressed "Play." Dallas pulled another chair over and sat next to him. Clark ran through the first tape quickly. Fast forwarding when there was no traffic through the checkpoint, switching to play or slow motion when the traffic got heavy. He stopped to zoom in on the face of each person passing through the checkpoint. Dallas stopped him near the end of the tape.

"This is the individual that had the bomb, Rick Dirani." Dallas took over and zoomed in on the face and enhanced the picture, switched to slow motion and let it advance through several frames for different views of the face.

"Nothing spectacular about the guy, one way or the other. His file shows that his mother is Syrian. That's where he got most of his features. His father is American. No known political activity by anyone in his family. Notice his only carry on item is a book." Dallas zoomed in on the man's hands as he placed a book on the conveyor.

"Go ahead," Dallas said, hitting the play button. "You have command of the control key, lieutenant commander, or as they say in the Navy, you have the conn. We have run through freeze frame photos from the video of everyone we could. Tried to tie them to a passport and to files of known terrorists. So far, we have not been able to attach names and identifications to all the faces that we've seen. But I think we will eventually. As you can see, it is going to take some time. Spy work is ninety-nine percent checking out boring details."

Clark popped the tape out and went to the next one in the sequence. He fast-forwarded the tape, stopping occasionally. He focused in on a dark-skinned lady passing through the metal detector.

"Good. You've found her," Dallas said. "That's our Pakistani doctor. Of course we don't know what the Hungarian looks like and we haven't matched up the British girl with anybody on video yet, but she had to go through the security checkpoints to get on the plane."

Clark continued as Dallas leaned back in his chair, fingers laced behind his head. Going forward again, Clark stopped suddenly and put the VCR into reverse. He enlarged a section near the edge of the screen. It showed a pair of hands opening a black, canvas carrying bag for a security officer.

"What's happening here?" Clark asked.

"Any electronic equipment carried through the checkpoint has to be turned on even though it's x-rayed. This allows the security personnel to determine if the equipment is operational."

"That looks like a computer they're checking," Clark said.

"For a computer you're required to turn it on to show it's operational. The screen lights up and that's about it."

"Do you have them load a program?" Clark asked, looking at Dallas.

"No. I don't think so. It probably takes too long when they're busy. It takes what, a minute, two minutes to energize the computer, get it to speed, and have it load a program? I don't think they've got that much time per person."

"Maybe they should take the time," Clark said. Clark zoomed in again, and enlarged and enhanced the computer and the gloves holding the case open. The gloves had a logo on them he couldn't identify, but they looked expensive. The computer had a multicolored symbol on it. Clark couldn't see it distinctly, but he thought he knew what it was.

"Look at this," Clark said pointing to the fuzzy multicolored symbol on the screen.

"Looks like an Apple to me," said Dallas.

"Could be one of the MacIntosh lap-tops. A PowerBook maybe?"

"So what does that tell you?" Dallas asked.

Clark went to slow motion through another couple of frames and zoomed in on the screen on the computer. "Look at these numbers on the top. The computer is counting available RAM as it goes through the boot up process."

"So what? I don't get it."

"So that's what a DOS based computer does when it's energized. Apple computer products don't operate like that. It may mean that what's inside the computer is something other than a computer. A number generator perhaps, attached to the screen with the guts replaced with explosives.

"Let's back up and see who's carrying the PowerBook." Clark said. He ran the videotape backwards until he saw a woman waiting in line with a carrying case similar to the one holding the computer. He zoomed in on the gloves.

"Bingo," Clark said. "Same gloves." He zoomed back out to a look at her face. Her face was half hidden by a man being frisked with a hand-held metal detector. He zoomed in on a partial view of her face. The man's outstretched hand blocked one-quarter of her face. "Think that might be the British lady?" Clark asked.

"It's kind of fuzzy," Dallas said. "And the ponytail is pulled off to a side, but she may have had her hair different for the passport photo. I'll get a computer enhanced photograph and we'll double check it against the passport."

Clark backed the tape up again, following the woman as she walked backward into the crowd. He enhanced the view several times until she backed up next to a man in the waiting area and stood next to him. Clark enhanced the frame several times and studied the blurred details.

"We definitely need a computer enhancement of this frame," Clark said. "Some guy is giving her a send off when neither of her parents knew she was flying. I'll bet this is the lady with the bomb. You have a plastic shard with a purple-blue section on it that came out of a woman's head. I bet it came right out of the Apple logo we were looking at a few minutes ago."

CHAPTER TWENTY-TWO

DELTA

The CH-3 helicopter was not built for comfort. It did not even have a seat belt, but that was the least of Joshua Clark's worries. He gritted his teeth, or tried to. The vibration from the helicopter blades rotating overhead was enough to shake his bicuspids, incisors, and everything else in his mouth, right out of his head. If his teeth didn't fall out, his organs would surely disintegrate. What a way to go. Perhaps not go, ever again, would be more correct. He had no doubt that his kidneys were being homogenized by the helicopter ride. Worse, it had continued so long, at so strong a level, that it set up vibrations in his very soul and threatened to detach it from its fleshy husk. Clark hung on to his seat, knuckles stiff from gripping. Maybe that was what General Armstrong had planned all along. That was one sure way to get rid of a wise ass pain-in-the-ass junior officer.

"It's your plan," Armstrong had said. "Don't you have confidence in it? Besides, there might be unexpected contingencies. It might even give you another opportunity for 'exemplary and incisive action in the face of an extreme emergency.'" The quote from his Navy Cross commendation and the hint, not even subtle, that it might have been more than he deserved, pissed him off, as the general had probably intended. You can never trust those political types; they always have a hidden agenda. The hidden agenda in this case might be the permanent elimination of a thorn in Armstrong's side. Nah. Even politicians and generals, or even a political general in this case, weren't that crass — or were they?

Focusing on Armstrong brought Clark a quick flash of anger, which pushed the discomfort back, but only a little. Armstrong was leading from the rear again. Typical. Of course, it was logical for the flag officer commanding the operation to be offshore running the show, but logic didn't help much when you were angry. Make that angry and sick.

Clark looked around at the other men on the chopper. Delta Force. Scary mothers. It was more than a little intimidating to be part of their team. If half of what you read was true, these guys were not the kind of people you wanted to bump into in a dark alley. He suspected they ate nails for breakfast and spit rust all day.

Their helmets were covered with camouflage material, which blended in with the paint covering their faces. Black on the cheekbones and other prominent parts, light in the hollow part of their face. In the dim light of the cabin it was hard to tell where their camouflage fatigues left off and their faces began, even with night vision goggles.

He was the outsider and felt like it. An observer. He was dressed right for the "party," but had not been invited. He was forced on the Delta Force by General Armstrong.

The Delta guys didn't like having him on board. He didn't blame them. They were a precision team, and he did not know the tune to which they were marching. He was an unknown quantity. They would have to do their job, which was tough enough, and be careful not to trip over him while they were doing it. Joint operations sounded good in principle. In practice, it was something quite different. You plunked a Navy lieutenant commander down in the middle of a squad of Army Rangers or Delta Force, whatever the latest buzzword was, and the well-trained squad was going to operate like an engine with a transmission full of sand.

The helicopter crested a hill and followed the slope down the other side. Terrain following. Staying below the radar horizon. "Roller coasting" would have been a better phrase for it. When the chopper made that last dip his stomach stayed at the higher altitude.

"If you grip that seat support any tighter, Commander, you're going to bend the metal." The sergeant sitting next to him yelled above the engine noise.

Clark looked at the man. He felt like he should make a pithy reply, but at this point, all he could do was nod. He swallowed hard trying to get his stomach back in place. He wasn't going to chuck his cookies in front of these guys. At least not if he could help it. He burped, tasting the salami sandwich that was in the box lunch he ate several hours before. No one else seemed bothered by the greasy meat or the bumpy ride.

Clark was introduced to the squad at the briefing the day before. Sergeant O'Rourk, the squad sergeant, waited until the briefing officer had finished, then took Clark aside.

"With all due respect, sir, you don't belong here."

"I was ordered to be here, Sergeant. Whether I like it or not, or whether you like it or not, that's the way it is."

The big sergeant put up his hand. "That's not the point, Sir. I just wanted to let you know that no one here has time to look after you. You stick close and when I say jump, you do it. Do you understand, sir?"

Clark had understood. Sergeant O'Rourk was right, he didn't belong here. He was excess. Expendable. Baggage. The sergeant was also clearly letting him know who would be in charge once they got on the ground, "with all due respect."

Clark turned his head to scan the group crammed into the chopper again. He noticed a corporal smiling at his obvious discomfort. The soldier quickly turned his head away when Clark looked at him. The corporal's teeth were the only part of him clearly visible in the dark. At least they weren't filed to sharp points. Maybe these guys weren't so tough after all. Clark clamped his jaw shut. He wasn't going to be sick.

The whine of the rotors changed pitch as the pilot cut back on the throttles and the helicopter descended. The noise level in the compartment went from mind numbing to merely piercing. And this was the stealth version of the bird? Anyone on the ground would have to be deaf or dead not to hear them coming. The change in the noise levels was only a matter of degree. Its significance would be lost on any OSHA inspector who checked the decibel reading in the passenger cabin. Did it make any difference if you were deaf or very deaf? But the military wasn't subject to such trivial concerns as Occupational Safety and Health Administration inspections. The lead level they would encounter in just a few minutes would also be above OSHA standards and of more immediate concern than noise pollution. Dead people were not concerned about being deaf or about the level of lead in the bullet that killed them.

The helicopter flared as it reached the landing point, tilting up at a forty-five degree angle and blowing sand outward at hurricane velocity. Even before they touched down the first members of the squad jumped out of the open door. Clark grabbed his rifle and scrambled toward the opening with the rest of the troops. He kept his head down, crabbing toward the exit in a half crouch. The sergeant had placed him in the forward section of the craft so he would be last out. If he fell he would not hinder the rest of the men disembarking; they wouldn't trip over him. Embarrassing, but on the bright side he wouldn't get trampled.

Clark jumped the several feet from the open door to the soft sand and managed to keep his feet under him. He ran after the shadowy shapes disappearing into the darkness. Modern day Ninja warriors. It wouldn't do to get separated from the rest of the squad and get lost. Getting stranded in Syria after this operation was not the way to reach retirement. A U.S. attempt to capture Syrian President Bashar al-Assad and try him for terrorism was one of the craziest things General Armstrong had conceived. And he had sold it to the president of the United States. Of course being his nephew helped, but it was still one wild idea.

The chopper lifted off as Clark hit the sand. The wind buffeted him from behind and hurried him along. The flying sand was a pain in the ass, literally. It would, however, also blind any Syrian soldiers that were close enough to be a problem and who were aiming their rifles toward them.

Distant gunfire could be heard above the noise of the helicopter as Clark ran after the last of the squad. The short death rattle burst of weapons on automatic. The sounds came from another part of the city. Probably from one of the other squads that was checking other locations for President Assad. Clark listened for the deep-throated roar of heavier weapons. There was none. That meant that there were no pitched battles. So far so good. Reconnaissance had indicated no heavy opposition. The only chance to bring off this operation was surprise and they might have actually achieved it.

Once they reached the urban area, a short sprint, but one which left Clark winded, the squad ran from building to building. In the green light of the night vision goggles, the landscape was like a scene from a science fiction movie. The city looked normal, but there were no people, only the dreamlike shapes of Nintendo soldiers.

They advanced, building to building, using a sprint-and-wait technique. One member would run to the next building while the squad covered him. He would check the area and give an all-clear sign with his hand. Another "grunt" would then dash to the next building on the other side of the street. Then the whole squad moved up. One man hung behind to cover the rear until it was his turn to move up. The procedure was more like a well rehearsed dance routine than an army exercise. Clark was determined to stay in step.

Clark stopped in front of a shop window after a short sprint. His ragged breath caught in his throat and the hair on his neck rose as he realized someone was watching him through the window. He turned slowly. A poster of Bashar al-Assad looked out at him. A large, red heart was underneath the implacable face of the leader of the country ranked number one on the U.S. list of countries sanctioning terrorism. Clark shook his head and raced forward with the squad when his turn came.

Clark hung back with the young lieutenant leading the squad. He expected to feel fear. They were in enemy territory after all, and could be killed or captured at any instant. But his only emotion was an excited sense of unreality. It was like watching a movie with someone else in the lead role.

Clark pulled up short with the lieutenant at the edge of the next building, a short two-story hospital. He leaned against the wall to catch his breath. The thousands of hours he had spent in the Pentagon gym, sweating and groaning did not prepare him for a sprint with a helmet, rifle, and goggles. Fortunately, his pack carried only extra ammo and communications gear.

Clark ducked his head as bullets pocked the wall in front of him, sharp chips of stone flying in his face. The pattern of bullets continued forward, shredding the lieutenant. The squad turned as one and fired at an adjacent building. An individual crouching at the corner of a building across the street was clearly visible in the dim green glow of the night vision goggles. He did a brief jerky dance, arms akimbo, as the squad played a rapid rhythm on his body with their guns. He fell forward on his face and lay still.

Clark realized that he had not fired his rifle. Too late for that now, the bad guy was dead. No one seemed to notice that he had not held up his end. Now he felt fear, a hot sensation at the bottom of his abdomen.

"Jenkins," Sergeant O'Roark's voice whispered in Clark's ear over the squad net. "I thought you secured that building?"

No answer. "Roberts, check it out," the sergeant said as he bent down and felt for a pulse at the lieutenant's neck. Clark could tell by the lieutenant's open, staring eyes and the mangled mess that had been the back of his head, that the soldier would not find one. This was no longer life at a distance, this was up close and personal. The copper smell of fresh blood was real.

Roberts ran to the building. The other squad members watched the building, weapons ready, looking for anyone else that might like a piece of the action. There were no takers. If there was anyone else in the area he was keeping his head down. Roberts disappeared into the darkened doorway.

"Sarge, Roberts here. Jenkins is dead. Building is secure. I repeat, building is secure."

"Acknowledged. Hold your position," the sergeant said into the mike attached to his earpiece. "Johnson, Peterson, around the corner. Move it!"

The two soldiers ran to the corner of the building. Peterson paused, then rolled past the edge of the building into a prone firing position. Johnson stepped around the corner and dropped to his knee. Johnson jumped to his feet and ran forward out of Clark's sight.

"No action at the entrance, Sarge," Johnson's voice whispered through the earphones.

"Roger. Johnson, Peterson hold position. Henandez, Black, check out the entrance."

Two more squad members disappeared around the corner of the building. The city was quiet, in sharp contrast to the earlier echo of gunfire. The night looked normal, one street light lit, halfway down the block. The well kept lawn that surrounded the small hospital was surrealistic in the night vision goggles. Except for the accelerated beating of his heart, it could have been Anytown, USA, Clark thought. And, except for the blood on the wall where the lieutenant had stood.

Clark jumped as a burst of automatic weapons fire and the crystal sound of glass on concrete broke the quiet. Two more bursts of gunfire followed. The sergeant had his head around the corner of the building, his hand out to motion

Clark to keep his head down. Clark did not need any encouragement.

"Report!" the sergeant said into his throat mike. "Do not make me guess what is going on."

"Sergeant," Hernandez voice came over the earphones. "Black is down with a leg wound. I am inside the door. Only one guard and I have taken him out."

"Peterson, move up. Johnson, Hernandez hold position. Mr. Clark, follow me."

At this point, Clark would have followed the big sergeant anywhere. The quality of command in his voice booked no argument. He did not have to think, only do what the sergeant told him to do. Clark sprinted after the sergeant, running in a crouch, holding his rifle in front of him with both hands. He was glad to have the broad bulk of the sergeant's back between him and the last burst of fire. The universe had contracted. Getting to the next objective was all that mattered. There was only now. No time for thought, only for action.

The sergeant stopped next to Johnson at the base of broad concrete steps leading up to the hospital entrance. Clark collected his breath for a heartbeat and ran up the stairs as Sergeant O'Rourk took off again. The sergeant's shoulder bounced the door off the wall as he bulled his way into the building.

Hernandez stood inside the door, back to the wall. Corporal Black sat on the floor next to the body of a Syrian soldier. He gave a thumbs up sign as he finished knotting a piece of bloody cloth around a section of his thigh. Clark watched as Black's lips pulled back in what was probably meant to be a grin. He was obviously trying to reassure his friends. Hey, what's a little bullet through the thigh? Clark thought the answer might be that a bullet through a body part is the difference between a grimace and a grin.

The sergeant looked at Hernandez and pointed down the hall. Hernandez nodded his head. Black gave a thumbs up again and edged into position to cover the hall, keeping his leg straight. It was almost a form of telepathy. This time Clark understood the conversation. He followed their lead and pointed his gun down the hall to cover Hernandez.

Sergeant O'Rourk looked at Clark. Clark could tell he was considering whether Clark would be more dangerous to the Syrians or to Hernandez. The sergeant shook his head and looked back down the hall.

Hernandez sprinted down the passageway, stopping outside the first door. He slowly twisted the knob and abruptly pushed the door open. He stood with his back to the wall as the door swung completely open. He disappeared from sight as he dove into the room. Hernandez appeared a minute later and gave the safe signal with a wave of his hand.

Hernandez stopped at the only other door in the short hall. He tried the knob, his back to the wall. He glanced down the hall at the sergeant and shook his head. The Sergeant held his rifle at waist level and motioned at the door. Hernandez nodded again. He turned to the door and fired a burst at the knob at an oblique angle. The wood around the knob ripped and splintered. The noise was deafening in the small hall.

Hernandez kicked the door open and leaned back against the side of the door. Clark ducked his head as bullets ripped pieces of plaster out of the wall halfway down the hall on his left.

"Hernandez," the sergeant said into the mike. "He is to the right of the door, probably standing. Lights going out in the hall." The sergeant shattered the hall light with a single bullet.

Hernandez dove through the door firing his rifle. Flashes from a gun firing inside the room moved in an upward arc.

"Stay put," the sergeant said pointing at Clark. He ran to the end of the hall and took a position outside the door.

"Hernandez, coming in." The sergeant rolled through the door on the side opposite the direction Hernandez had taken. He was surprisingly agile for such a bear of a man.

"Clear here," the sergeant's voice whispered in Clark's earphone. "Black, you cover the entrance. Mr. Clark, please join us." It seemed more of an order than a request. Clark sprinted down the hall.

Clark stopped just inside the door, rifle at the ready. The hospital room was more crowded than he expected. The sergeant and Hernandez covered several people dressed in green coveralls and white cotton coats. They crouched in a corner, hands behind their heads. A Syrian soldier slumped against the wall, arms and legs splayed. He had more holes in his body than Clark could count at a glance. Hernandez had the Syrian's rifle over his shoulder.

"We struck pay dirt, Commander Clark," the sergeant said, nodding to the man in the bed.

Clark stepped to the bed and checked the patient's face. "Looks like a positive ID to me, Sarge." Bashar al-Assad, President of Syria, did not look so impressive with tubes in his nose and arms, and wires worming their way out of his hospital gown. This squad had drawn the right location all right.

"Call the chopper, Sarge and let's get the hell out of here." Clark was trying to keep his voice under control, but could hear it hitting the high notes in the middle of the measures.

"It's not that simple, Commander." The sergeant nodded to one of the medical people with a stethoscope around his neck.

"He has had heart surgery," the doctor said in heavily accented English. "He cannot be moved. It might kill him."

All eyes fixed on Clark. It was his decision, or at least no one else wanted to make it. Should he call back to base and let them make a decision? They would all be old men before the buck stopped being passed up the chain. Or worse, some civilian defense weenie might decide to pull out, like Desert One in Iran, and fly aircraft into each other in the hurry to be gone. No, the decision was his, and right or wrong, he was going to make it.

"Sergeant, arrest that man." Clark pointed to al-Assad.

"Yes, sir!"

"No, please. He will die," the doctor said.

"Doctor, if you want to keep him alive, you can come with us. Otherwise, shut up and stand back." Clark's voice was stronger now.

The doctor hesitated only a moment. "I will come," he said. He stood and started unhooking monitors. The sergeant finished on the com phone.

"Chopper inbound, Mr. Clark. ETA five minutes."

The sergeant stepped to the bed and gently hoisted the unconscious Assad on his shoulder. The doctor fluttered around the big sergeant, but could find nothing productive to do except wring his hands.

The sergeant looked at Clark with something that looked like respect. At least it was a level up from the tolerance Clark had seen before. So this was a contingency, Clark thought. Now he was in charge. Something out of the ordinary. Something that could not be planned for.

"Let's move out, Sergeant," Clark said with authority.

PART FIVE

RETALIATION

CHAPTER TWENTY-THREE

UNDERWAY

Ahmed Mohammed watched from the pier as the crane swung the cargo container from the dock to the ship. The large, corrugated metal container looked like a toy suspended by a metal thread above the deck of the freighter. The overhead crane set the container down on the aft end of the ship next to the other container, which belonged to Ahmed's new organization. The access doors were facing aft as had been agreed on with the ship's Captain.

As expected everything had gone smoothly. The two containers were the last ones on board the ship. Khaled Hassan called it babysitting the cargo when he gave Ahmed his instructions. Nothing should go wrong with the loading, but if it did, Ahmed was to ensure that it was fixed, and he was given a large wad of cash to do it. If the containers were oriented in the wrong direction, there would be no way to correct it at sea.

The second container was Ahmed's idea. When Hassan briefed him on the secret negotiations to buy an Exocet missile, he said price was no object. They were bargaining for the sake of form so that they would not be taken advantage of next time. It was expected. Ahmed suggested buying a second Exocet since money was no concern. If there was a malfunction in the first missile, the second would be ready and available. Hassan liked the idea and the deal proceeded.

Training on the equipment was a part of the package. Ahmed remembered the long hours of learning with a sense of satisfaction. The speed with which he grasped the subject surprised the Russian technicians, but the chance to take revenge on the United States was a strong incentive. The United States would pay for the death of his family. He looked down at his hands. As they started to shake he clenched them into a fist. Thoughts of his Safia still brought rage so strong it was a physical pain.

He forced his thoughts away from his family as the container landed on deck with a hollow bang. Stuffing his hands into his pockets, he walked to the metal stairs leading to the crane operator's enclosed cab. He looked up the rusting steps until he had the man's attention then gestured with his hand for him to come down. The man locked the controls and climbed down from his glass-enclosed box.

"Well done, my friend," Ahmed said, handing the operator a wad of Euros.

"Your television sets are safe, and they will be the first off the boat when it arrives in Houston."

"You have done well. My uncle will be pleased with how I've handled his business. If this shipment goes well, we will bring more merchandise through this port."

Ahmed turned and climbed the gangway to the deck of the ship. The man had been told that most of the family money had been invested in the shipment of two cargo containers of television sets. Damage to the cargo would be a catastrophe. It was a believable story, but Ahmed wondered if the crane operator really believed it.

The crane operator was an Algerian and a Muslim, one of the few on the Marseilles docks. Still, he could not be trusted with the information that each container carried a cruise missile. Hassan made it clear that the only way to run a successful operation was to limit the number of people who knew the details.

Ahmed had pieced together details from around the training camp about Hassan. He learned that Hassan liked to work alone. Ahmed also knew that he was here only because of his technical expertise. Hassan could carry a bomb anywhere and he was reputed to be fearless, but Ahmed knew that Hassan had doubts about his own electrical technical competence. Ahmed tried to show him how the panel operated, but his eyes always glazed over as the layers of technical detail built upon each other. Ahmed attempted to persuade him to train a second operator, but Hassan again refused. Secrecy was Hassan's obsession.

Working his way aft, Ahmed turned sideways to walk between the containers. He stepped carefully over the thick metal cables that tied them to the ship. Arriving at the aft end, he watched as the cargo handlers used a ratchet mechanism to tighten the cables holding the last container. When they finished, he walked to each cable and pulled at it to assure it was taut. No need to pay these men extra. They were doing their job and had done it well. Distributing too much money would only call unwanted attention. Another lesson from Hassan.

Ahmed walked to the rail of the ship and waved his arm at a Volvo waiting on the dock. He could not see the occupant through the dark tinted window from this distance, but he knew Hassan was watching. The door opened on the passenger side and a man stepped out wearing a dark trenchcoat, gloves, and dark glasses. Ahmed recognized Hassan even from afar. Despite the beret, Ahmed could see that Hassan's hair was cropped so short he appeared to be bald. He saw him yesterday to finalize details and check out the equipment. Before that he had not seen Hassan since they negotiated for the cruise missiles, a month earlier. Hassan's appearance changed so frequently that Ahmed wondered if Hassan knew who Hassan was.

Ahmed walked forward to meet his mentor as he came up the gangway. Hassan stopped as he boarded. "All is secure," Ahmed said. "I checked the Bill of Lading before the cargo was loaded. The cargo is listed as Procar television sets. Both containers are securely attached to the deck."

"Good," said Hassan. He spoke with his head half turned away, dark, wrap-around glasses, impenetrable. "I'll be in my cabin. Have the captain get underway immediately. Watch until the gangway is removed, then come to my cabin."

Ahmed climbed to the bridge, the metal stairs echoing under his heels. "Captain, all is in order. We desire to get underway immediately."

"Very well, Monsieur Smith." The captain replied.

Ahmed knew his passport said Smith, but it still felt very much like a game, this changing identities and appearances, and watching the gangway to make sure no one came aboard at the last minute. He let his anger rise up in him as he clamped his throat shut. A game perhaps, but a deadly serious one. The United States would wish they had not made him a player before the match was finished.

The gangway was being removed as he climbed down the outside ladder from the bridge. Taking one last look at the gray Marseilles sky, he ducked his head and followed the passageway to Hassan's cabin. He knocked on the metal door. An inside bolt audibly slid back and the door opened. Ahmed stepped inside. Hassan looked up and down the corridor before bolting the door behind him.

"Is the gangway up?"

"The gangway has been removed and a tug is made up alongside. They have already started swinging the aft end of the ship out."

Hassan nodded his head. Ahmed waited. Hassan appeared to be listening. Then he heard it too. The deep throated rumble of the ship's engines as the big vessel pulled at the water behind the stern, shuddering as it backed away from the pier.

"Very good. We are underway." Hassan appeared to relax. He took off his glasses and overcoat. "I will show you the rest of the plan. This information is for you and me only. The crew on this vessel is Muslim, but they are not to be trusted any more than anyone else. You understand?"

Ahmed nodded his head. Hassan's cold direct stare was enough to make anyone serious, even without the Uzi that Ahmed knew was tucked under the other man's arm by a shoulder strap.

"The person responsible for this latest insult to Islam is the president of the United States," Hassan continued. "He personally ordered the death of Bashar al-Assad and now he must pay."

Hassan unrolled a large map on his bunk. The legend said Houston, Texas. Ahmed looked up at Hassan and back down at the map. The pieces were falling into place already in his mind. He had been reading what he could from the English language newspapers and watching the English language television. He learned Arabic, of course, as a child. He picked up some German working for Herr Koch in the factory. But he decided learning English was the best way to find out as much as he could about this enemy of his, the United States. The information from the newspapers and the destination, which Hassan had now provided, pointed in only one direction.

He also learned from watching Hassan. Hassan spoke French, English, and Arabic, and perhaps many more languages. Hassan kept silent about what he knew unless it was useful for him to tell you something. Ahmed now saw where this trail led, but decided to let Hassan explain it to him. It may be better not to let Hassan realize how much he knew.

"Here is the George R. Brown Convention Center." Hassan placed his finger on the map near the downtown area. "There will be a Governors Conference and the leaders of all fifty states of the United States will attend."

"And the president?" Ahmed asked.

"The president does not advertise his travel plans in advance. The United States has a good security system as far as it goes. But the president has been recently elected and is looking for support for his new programs. He will be there. He also has strong ties to Texas."

Hassan moved his finger to the edge of the map. "This is the Houston Ship Channel. Ships proceed from the Gulf of Mexico, to Galveston Bay, and up the Houston Ship Channel almost into downtown Houston. I have timed our arrival so we will be near Houston at the start of the conference. The American television news station, CNN, will provide live coverage. When we see the president speaking on the television from the Convention Center, when we hear him on the radio, we will launch the missiles. He will not escape."

"A good plan, Mr. Jones," Ahmed said. Hassan insisted on being called by his cover name at all times even when they were alone. Ahmed might not have known his real identity except for having seen him once long ago, before he became the man of many faces.

It had bothered Ahmed ever since the first meeting at the training camp in Syria. He finally fit the different pieces of the face together that Hassan wore. After seeing several disguises, Ahmed knew that Mr. Jones, by any of his many other names, was Khaled Hassan. Ahmed had seen him at a family gathering, older than the myriad of other children. Always standing silent and alone. Ahmed knew instinctively to keep this knowledge to himself.

"You will plot the position of the Convention Center on the guidance system. The coordinates of the Convention Center are well known. Our position in the ship channel will be well known. The solution should be very easy.

"You must be prepared to launch anytime we come in range of the city. If the president comes early, we will be ready. If he comes late, the ship will go slow. If necessary, we will have mechanical problems after we dock to delay off-loading the cargo. The captain has been well paid to accommodate his passengers. Do you have any questions?"

"No, Mr. Jones."

"The Great Satan will not escape us." Hassan said. His voice was level and calm, but Ahmed saw that he crushed the map in his hand.

CHAPTER TWENTY-FOUR

FULL COURT PRESS

News reporters filled the room. Their chatter raised the noise level to that usually reserved for sporting events. The louder it got, the louder they got, with each one raising his or her voice to be heard above the din.

Joshua Clark watched them warily, standing to the side of the platform. I would not want to be talking to this mob, he thought. Mob was a good description of the group. If they smelled blood or sensed fear, they would tear a man apart, figuratively, of course, or perhaps editorially, but they were hungry for a story and used to having their way.

"Ladies and gentleman, the secretary of defense," a public relations specialist announced on the podium microphone. This brought a moment of quiet to the press corps as the secretary of defense strode into the room, followed by General George C. Armstrong.

"Good evening." The secretary barely had a chance to get the words out before individuals in the audience began yelling 'Mr. Secretary' and raising their hand. There was usually a pecking order on who got the first question, but with an explosive story like this, no one would wait. The noise level rose rapidly to its previous levels as most of the reporters vied for attention by yelling louder.

"Janet, you have a question?" The secretary looked at a UP reporter in the first row.

Clark did not allow himself to be impressed that the secretary knew the name of an individual reporter. The secretary of defense had not played politics all his adult life like many of the political appointees, but he was well educated and knew many of the reporters by name from the nightly news if nothing else. Those he did not know personally, his staffers probably briefed him on prior to the meeting.

Clark was rapidly losing his illusions. If he worked in D.C. long enough, he was sure he would doubt whether up was up and down was down. Promotions depended on whom you knew rather than how you did, and how impressive you *appeared* rather than any quantifiable measure of your work. The reporters the secretary would call on were those who gave him the best write-up in other conferences and could be expected to give him good press in the future.

"Mr. Secretary, did the United States achieve all its objectives in the Syrian raid?" Once a member of the press corps had been chosen, the rest of the gallery became quiet in order to hear the question and the response. The reporter took her seat.

"I believe we did, Janet. As you know, it is this government's policy that acts of terrorism will not go unpunished. Once we determined that Syria was responsible for the NorthStar bombing, we proceeded expeditiously to retaliate for the deaths caused by these anarchists."

Clark felt his attention start to wander. His focus was getting fuzzy despite the excitement of being at a nationally televised press conference. By the time the television news crew finished culling the secretary's remarks down to a ten-second sound bite and synopsis, it might actually be interesting, but the man's speaking voice would put a hyperactive teenager to sleep. He was obviously well educated — he was a Harvard graduate and a former college professor — but lacked dynamic delivery. He droned on and on in a monotone. His students must have graduated well-rested from the noon day naps he presented.

"Mr. Secretary," another reporter asked loudly, standing to be recognized. "How many causalities were sustained by our forces during the raid?"

"Well, I believe," the secretary stopped to cough into his hand, "there were some U.S. casualties."

Clark realized the secretary was stalling for time. How could he not know the answer? This was an obvious question, one that should have been expected. Of course, being well-educated did not necessarily translate into being quick on your feet. The secretary had worked hard in the presidential campaign, contributed financially of course, received this post as his reward, but he was not a good front man. He was foundering after only the second question.

Looking over at General Armstrong the secretary said, "I believe five men were killed during the operation. But let's let General Armstrong discuss the details."

General Armstrong stepped up to the podium. "Yes, Mr. Secretary, it is unfortunate that five U.S. servicemen were killed during the course of the operation." Clark doubted that Armstrong would say otherwise. He was one of those people who always tried to make his boss look good. So long as it suited his purpose.

"It's always a tragedy," General Armstrong continued, "when people die. These people, however, these brave U.S. soldiers, died in the service of their country. Their actions made the world safer for all of us.

"I believe we have seen the last of these terrorists for a while. The president's policy of extracting an eye for an eye is the only one these terrorists understand. The two recent U.S. operations should teach terrorists that they cannot have their way with the United States of America."

But have we had any lasting effect, thought Clark. The terrorist attack that blew up the nightclub in Italy was supposed to be Libyan based. Teaching Libya a lesson had merely moved the terrorist base of operations to Syria. If General Armstrong's theory was correct, and that was still up in the air, would teaching Syria a lesson merely move the terrorists to another home base? Or would they operate independently? Did they really need a fixed location? Were they operating independently all along?

General Armstrong scanned the room as he talked making eye contact with individuals around the room. Clark felt General Armstrong's eyes on him as he continued speaking. Clark suddenly stopped; he realized he had been shaking his head.

"It's unlikely any Arab government would support terrorist activities after this last military operation against Syria." Clark realized he was shaking his head again. He looked at Armstrong and held his eyes momentarily. Clark froze in mid-headshake. General Armstrong was right about one thing, never disagree publicly with the boss. Privately, maybe, if you had the balls, but never publicly. Never.

"General Armstrong," a TV reporter asked, standing, "What about Syrian casualties?" The reporter's face looked familiar. Clark wished he could keep them straight, but maybe that's why he wasn't a politician.

"There were, of course, a number of Syrian casualties. We have no way of knowing the exact count since Syria is a dictatorship and their government only releases what they want us to know. However, Mr. Brown, your station, CNN, reports the total at more than 800. I guess that's as close to an official report as we can get." That drew a number of laughs. Clark felt himself smiling.

General Armstrong was a consummate politician even though he wore a uniform. He may be even more, Clark grudgingly admitted. He might even be a leader. Armstrong's strong suit was crowd control. It was obvious he loved the smell of the greasepaint or whatever makeup they used prior to TV appearances, and of course, the roar of the crowd. With bright lights of the television cameras on him, he showed he was capable of taking the heat, literally. Clark knew that his own jacket had dark circles under his arms from the body heat of the packed room. The general must be wearing Maxi Pads under his arms not to have sweat through his dress uniform by now.

"The important thing," the general continued, "is that the purpose of the raid was to disable Syria's offensive capabilities and military intelligence operations." Clark saw General Armstrong casually glance his way, but there was no way he was going to shake his head again. One mistake like that was more than enough. One more inappropriate headshake and he would be beheaded.

"We cratered the runways, destroyed a number of military aircraft, and leveled the military intelligence complex that we believe directs terrorist operations. These are significant accomplishments. When conducting military operations on this scale, it's expected that you will inflict casualties on your enemy. You cannot make mayonnaise without breaking some eggs."

This time the general's humor fell flat. It was nice to see that even General Armstrong could strike out occasionally. Clark was embarrassed at the small stab of pleasure he felt as the general's joke failed. Both emotions dissipated quickly as Clark noticed that the press corps passed right over the attempt at humor. They were not even embarrassed by the clumsy attempt, if they noticed it at all. They rushed on, mesmerized by this man on a horse, and their own rush to get in the next question.

"General Armstrong, General Armstrong." A number of the reporters were vying for attention simultaneously. The secretary of defense was still on stage, but he had faded into the background. General Armstrong pointed at a woman with oriental features. "Ms. Casey," he said. Her red dress made her stand out in the sea of somber business suits worn by her drab, male contemporaries. General Armstrong didn't appear to be opposed to picking one of the prettiest members of the press corp.

"General Armstrong, there are reports that President Bashar al-Assad was killed during the raid. Was taking out the President of Syria also one of the objectives?" She remained standing.

"The United States does not engage in political assassination," General Armstrong said loudly. The self-righteous indignation was obvious. Clark felt his pucker string tighten even though the general's anger was not directed at him. Armstrong was using the type of command voice that would cause any enlisted man or junior officer to jump and run for cover. Ms. Casey, to her credit, stood her ground waiting for his answer.

"Ms. Casey," the General continued, his face returning to a normal shade of pink, "I have stated the mission's objectives. There has been no official announcement from the Syrian government that President Assad is dead. It's possible that he may have been killed if he was at one of the military installations that were targeted."

When President al-Assad died on the helicopter shortly after lift-off, Clark had called General Armstrong on the command and control link. It was a political decision at that point whether to go forward and bring out a dead man or take President Assad back to the hospital. Clark recommended taking the body back and for once General Armstrong agreed. He had said essentially, what do I need a body for. You cannot put a dead man on trial. The general also added a long string of expletives, but for once they also were not directed at Clark.

General Armstrong continued, "I can state quite emphatically that the mission objective was not to kill Bashar al-Assad."

"If there are no more questions," General Armstrong said brusquely, "I believe that concludes the press conference. Thank you."

Clark noticed Armstrong did not even ask the secretary of defense for permission to end the session, although he did wave the secretary in front of him as they left the podium. Clark followed General Armstrong and the secretary of defense out of the room along with the other staff planners. Just outside the conference room, the general's chief of staff stopped Clark in the passageway, putting his hand to Clark's chest.

"The General wants to see you in his office. Right now. You will stand by until he gets there."

Clark was not sure what the general wanted, but he was sure he would leave with a big bite out of his butt. A visit with the general was becoming a down right disagreeable experience.

CHAPTER TWENTY-FIVE

DRESSING DOWN

Joshua Clark waited with trepidation for the general in his secretary's office. He shifted uneasily on the over-soft sofa. He had decided on the way to the meeting with the general that he was definitely going to get another ass chewing for some infraction, real or imagined. It was getting to be a habit, a bad habit. It might also be the only way he could take a few pounds off his fat butt. Now that he was assigned to the general's staff, he had no time for a workout in the Pentagon gym. Zero, zip, none.

Clark looked at General Armstrong's secretary, a pretty brunette in her mid-twenties. She smiled as she looked up and saw Clark's eyes on her. Clark gave her a smile in reply, but it was difficult to be enthusiastic about social amenities with his head stuck in a nimbus cloud anticipating another encounter with Armstrong. Clark stood and paced.

"Can I get you some coffee?" Armstrong's secretary said. "The general might be awhile."

"No, thanks. One more cup of coffee today and I might jump out of my skin."

She laughed. "Don't do that."

Clark was pleased that she did not add that the general would be skinning him soon enough. He really should not pace, but he was pleased that he was not climbing the walls. It was hard to sit still knowing he was about to be hammered for something.

The speaker on the secretary's desk barked, "Send Clark in."

"Yes, sir.

"The general will see you now," she said. Her smile was genuine and friendly, as if she did not know she was announcing to Daniel that the lion would see him in his den. Clark could not help smiling back at her. She was so enthusiastic, it was contagious. There were worse things for a condemned man to do than share a smile with a pretty girl.

Joshua closed the door behind him, stepped to the front of the general's desk, and stood at attention. "Lieutenant Commander Clark, reporting as ordered, sir."

"How about a salute, Mr. Clark."

Clark hesitated. "Sir, the Navy does not salute when uncovered." Is that what this was about? Had he failed to salute some Army colonel?

Armstrong stood suddenly, leaned over and put both fists on the blotter. "This is my office," he shouted. "I am in the Army and you are reporting to me. You will damn well salute me when you are in my office."

"Yes, sir," Clark said, and brought his hand sharply to his right eyebrow. Armstrong made him stand there holding his salute several seconds before returning it.

Armstrong slowly walked around the large desk to stand in front of Clark. He leaned down until his face was inches from Clark's face. "How dare you shake your head at me when I am in the middle of a news conference. How dare you!" he said again, thumping Clark on the chest with his fingers.

Clark was speechless. He was not sure if General Armstrong wanted a reply, but he could think of nothing to say.

"I will not tolerate insubordination from a junior officer," Armstrong continued. "In particular, public insubordination. Do you understand me, Mister?"

"Yes, sir," Clark said. This time he did understand, at least that Armstrong wanted a reply.

"What in the hell were you thinking about?" Armstrong continued. "I am telling the world one thing and a member of my staff is standing off to the side shaking his head. On national television, no less. What on God's green earth were you thinking about?"

Clark was still at attention, eyes straight ahead. He focused on General Armstrong's Adam's apple, which was all that was visible at this close range, and which bobbed furiously.

"Sir, request permission to speak, Sir," Clark said.

Armstrong slowly marched to his side of the desk, sat down and pulled a cigar out of a mahogany box. He clipped off one end, lit up and leaned back in his chair. "Okay, so tell me what you were thinking about," he said in a normal tone of voice. "If you were thinking at all."

Clark was glad the general had quieted down. He was sure the secretary just outside General Armstrong's wood paneled office had heard him being chewed out. It was bad enough being berated, but it was worse having to have it done in front of a woman.

"Sir," Clark said. "I am not sure we have seen the last of this terrorist organization. No one has positively identified the individual or organization responsible for the bombing, either of the NorthStar flight or the nightclub in Italy."

Clark watched General Armstrong, gauging his reaction. There was none. Armstrong leaned back in his chair, smoking his cigar, eyes burning into Clark. "Retaliation is a fine idea, general, and I know it is the president's policy, but retaliation against Libya did not work to stop the terrorists and retaliation against Syria may not work.'

Clark rushed on. "The timing mechanism used in the Italian nightclub bomb was the type the East Germans provided to the terrorist group Abu Nidal. Organizations like Abu Nidal are not controlled by any Arab government, or any other government for that matter. Bombing Libya and Syria may not have any affect other than to cause the terrorists to move their base of operations. You, or we, are sticking our necks way out by essentially promising the public that it is over."

General Armstrong leaned over and put his elbows on his desk. He looked interested now, or at least calm. "Go on, Mr. Clark."

"Each time the terrorists have struck, it has turned out to be tit for tat. The terrorists are aggressively retaliating against the United States each time we take retribution against them, and they are upping the ante each time. In the Italian nightclub attack, twenty-three people were killed. In the U.S. airstrike against Libya, we do not have an exact body count, but we estimate thirty or forty were killed in the chemical factory. In the NorthStar bombing, the terrorists killed fifty-six people and we were lucky it was not more. It could have been much more, hundreds more."

Clark waited in vain for some reply, but Armstrong merely let cigar smoke trickle out of his mouth and collected it with his nose. "The next round was when we took action against Syria, and you..." Clark stopped himself. He had been about to comment sarcastically about the general's decision to shoot up the Syrian Army barracks, but he was not going to allow himself to be disrespectful to a senior officer no matter how he felt.

"Sir, when we initiated the suppression strikes against the Syrian army barracks, we killed more than 800 Syrian soldiers."

Armstrong smiled as Clark said 'we.' He looked at his cigar and then looked at Clark. "So what is your point, Mr. Clark?"

"Sir, if the terrorists follow the same pattern, the next step should be another escalation. They will try to kill a greater number of U.S. citizens. Also, the terrorist operations have been hitting closer to home. The first one was the bar in Italy, the next one against a U.S. airliner. It is logical that the next one will be against a target in the United States. I would like to follow up on this line."

Armstrong rolled the cigar between his thumb and his fingers. He put the cigar back in his mouth and looked at Clark. "You do that. You follow up on that and keep me informed.

"And do not ever, ever disagree with me in public again. You got that?"

"Yes, sir."

"Dismissed."

Clark, still at attention, started to execute an about face. He stopped and brought his hand up in a salute. General Armstrong smiled and returned the salute. Clark took one step backward, turned and marched out of the room. He could feel Armstrong's smug smile on his back even after he closed the door.

CHAPTER TWENTY-SIX

COCKTAIL CONTINGENCY

The lazy fans circling overhead stirred the barroom air into murky eddying currents. The dimly lit Georgetown bar could have been anywhere in the world, almost any where, Joshua Clark thought. The dim light softened the features of the patrons; the alcohol numbed their brains, and eased their pain. Some things never change.

Clark stood as Mrs. Porter walked over to his table. She was prim, but also sexy in a mature sort of way. Not beautiful, but definitely attractive. It was her air of self-assurance that made the difference.

Mrs. Porter gave him a smile as he held the chair for her. She smoothed her skirt under her as she sat. "Why thank you, sir." Today she was accentuating her southern belle voice. Clark never quite knew what to expect from her, but was always pleasantly surprised.

"What would you like," Joshua said as he sat down.

"What are you having?"

His put his finger to his lips. "I'm drinking ginger ale, but don't let that get out."

"Of course not," she said. "I'm cleared for Top Secret. Your personal peccadilloes are safe with me. Only those with a need to know will ever find out. Of course, if they pull my fingernails out with pliers, I will have to tell. But why would anyone care?"

"I hope it won't be necessary to sacrifice your nails," Clark said. "As for the why, real men don't drink soda."

"Real men do what they think is right and do not worry what others think."

Now it was Clark's turn to smile. "But what are you having?"

She took her purse off her shoulder and hung it over the back of the chair while she considered the question. Clark looked around and caught the eye of the waitress.

"Hi," the waitress said. She pressed her thighs against their table. "What will you have?" Her voice squeaked on the end of each sentence, no doubt due to an overdose of exuberance, Clark thought, or perhaps an overabundance of estrogen. He let his eye linger, surreptitiously, on her well-packed short shorts. Twenty-five, brunette and very, well perky was the best he could come up with. His shipmates on the USS *Martin Luther King* would have said anyone that happy does not understand the situation. They would have also used a word other than "perky" to describe this buxom young woman. He pushed the *King* out of his thoughts. It was still hard to believe they were all dead. Thoughts of them still caused pain.

"The lady will have a …" Clark looked at Mrs. Porter.

"White wine," she said. Mrs. Porter was looking at him over her glasses, one eyebrow arched.

"Thank you," the waitress said, her voice squeaky happy. It was hard to imagine her any more exuberant if someone had given her 100 shares of Amazon stock as a tip. Clark let his eyes linger a moment longer and looked back to Mrs. Porter. She still had an eyebrow cocked.

"What?" he said.

"Does your wife know where you are?"

Clark felt a flash of irritation, sharp and irrational. "Why do you ask that, Mrs. Porter?"

"We work together, Mr. Clark. I'm curious. I would like to know you a little better. When you stop for a drink after work with a female colleague, what do you tell your wife?"

Clark ran his hand over his face. It was five o'clock and his shadow was showing. Mrs. Porter was one of the few people he had ever known who would ask such a direct question. And one of the few that he would answer. "I told my wife I was meeting you after work. I told her we were both busy in meetings today and there were several things we needed to discuss. I also told her I would be home at 7:00 p.m." He leaned his arms on the table, cocking his eyebrow, matching her gaze.

"That sounds reasonable," she said.

"Thank you." Clark instantly regretted how stilted his reply sounded. He valued Mrs. Porter's inquisitiveness even when it was directed at him.

"I saw you checking out the waitress and I wondered."

Clark leaned back, sipped his soda. "God made women beautiful so men would enjoy looking at them. I'm just doing my job. Being married is not the same as being blind."

"So some men say," Mrs. Porter said.

"Sarah doesn't have any problem with me meeting you after work for a drink," Clark said. "She is relatively reasonable. Now if we were having dinner, going dancing, and I got home after midnight, that would be another story. Even Sarah has her limits."

"Tell me, Mr. Clark, you always seem so confident. What does bother you? What gets under your skin?" Mrs. Porter pushed back her glasses as the waitress brought her drink. She took a long sip of her wine. "Does it bother you that they're staring at us?"

"Who is staring at us?" Joshua asked. He resisted the temptation to swivel his head around and look at the other men in the sparsely filled bar.

"Really," she said, "Sometimes men are smart in so many ways and other times I'm surprised they do not walk into doors. There is a man at the table near the door that has been positively drilling holes in your back with his eyes. Another man at the bar is a little more cautious, but keeps checking us out also."

Joshua watched the bar with a corner of his eye. The long mahogany stretched into the dim recesses of the room. A casually clad man sat on a stool, elbows on the bar. Sure enough, he was stealing furtive glances at them between sips of his drink. He would look away for a moment, but quickly look back at them.

"But why would someone be watching us, Mrs. Porter?"

"Because we are a mixed couple, Mr. Clark."

Joshua tilted his head in a question. "You mean heterosexual? I know this is Georgetown, but surely it is not that unusual to see a man and a woman together."

"Oh, please. You are black and I'm white," she explained.

Joshua leaned back from the table. "I'm not black," he said.

Mrs. Porter leaned forward, put her hand on his arm and said, "You don't need to be defensive with me."

"I'm not black," he said again. Then he smiled. "I'm mahogany." They both laughed.

"I do not have much preference about what people call me," Clark said, "as long as they are respectful when they say it. If you are comfortable with calling me black, Negro, or Afro-American, I will accept that. You may even call me colored if that is the respectful term you were raised with, but that is somewhat dated. There is only one pejorative term that everyone knows is a means of disparaging gentlemen of color, and that one I will not accept. I do not want to say it, I find it so distasteful.

"But enough of that." Clark said. "We should do some business. You had something you wanted to discuss with me."

"I was checking weapons purchases on the black market." Mrs. Porter paused. "Should I call that the mahogany market?" She looked at Clark over her glasses, smiling. "Anyway, I found that two Exocet missiles were purchased in France and shipped out of Marseilles."

"You did this on your own?"

Mrs. Porter nodded her head. She nibbled her lower lip. Surely she didn't think he would criticize her for taking some initiative, Clark thought. "That's great," he said. "I admire your initiative. Where do you think this is leading? You must have had some reason for looking at weapons purchases."

"I did," she said. "You told me you thought the terrorists would escalate their response each time we retaliated. You also said the conflict was moving closer to the United

States." She was speaking rapidly now, as if she couldn't get the words out quickly enough, perhaps afraid he might stop her.

"Yes, go on," Joshua said. The way her mind worked was fascinating. He prided himself on imagining alternate outcomes, keeping one step ahead, but she was two steps beyond him.

"It's obvious," she said. "The next step has to be to bomb something in the United States. The terrorists do not have airplanes, so that eliminates actual aerial bombing. They could smuggle in a ton of explosives like they did at the first World Trade Center bombing, but security is getting tight and you would have to get past Customs. Airplanes are out after September eleventh. But how about a missile? You bring it in by ship, set it up, and fire it. You do not have to smuggle the explosives into a building or hijack an airplane."

"Look," Mrs. Porter pulled a magazine article out of her purse. "This is what gave me the idea. The article says that the most plentiful missile on Earth is the Exocet. Everyone has them. They're everywhere. They can be fired from any platform, truck, train, plane." Clark glanced at the article.

"Good thinking. Excellent. It sounds right to me. What's the next step?"

She shrugged her shoulders. "I have not got that far yet."

"Good. You've left something for me to do. We need to check possible ports of entry. How long is the transit time from Marseilles?"

"Five days?" she said. "I suppose it would depend on which port in the United States you were going to arrive at."

"Do you know the exact date of departure? I don't suppose you know the name of the ship, do you?"

"I'm good, but not that good. I do not have the name of the ship or the exact date of departure. The sources indicate the vessel left Marseilles one or two days ago."

"OK," Clark said. "See if you can get a more exact date and the names of all ships leaving Marseilles in that time window. I'll work on ports of entry and possible targets. What do you think would make a good target, Mrs. Porter?"

"Something that would make a big splash," she said. "This terrorist seems to like publicity, although General Armstrong seems to be outdoing him. Something in the hundreds or thousands of people range, perhaps."

"We killed a lot of their people during the raid on Syria," Clark nodded his head. "But keep in mind the objective of the mission was to actually kidnap the President of Syria, not to achieve a large body count."

There was silence for a moment and then their eyes locked. They both said at the same time, "The President of the United States."

Clark paused for a minute. "No way."

Mrs. Porter said, "As they say on the street Mr. Clark, 'way.'"

CHAPTER TWENTY-SEVEN

HOT PURSUIT

The bridge of the USS *Stephen W. Groves* looked more like a high-tech control room for a nuclear power plant than a ship. It was not at all like the conventional destroyer Clark took his Midshipman Cruise on at the beginning of his Third Class year.

Joshua Clark held onto a handrail as the ship swayed back and forth, rolling over the smooth glass-like swells. With the *Groves* traveling at an angle to the seas, the motion was more like a slow roll as the ship climbed the front side of the wave, followed by a sharp pitch in the other direction as it crested the swell.

Clark shifted his weight from foot to foot to keep himself upright against the rocking of the destroyer. Already the fried eggs he had for breakfast felt uneasy in his stomach. This slow motion seasickness reminded him why he

239

chose submarines. Even the beautiful burnt orange sunrise tagged with streamers of purple colored clouds could not compensate for the queasy feeling in his belly.

"Best course to close target, zero-three-zero degrees at twenty-five knots," the Quartermaster said.

"Zero-three-zero, twenty-five knots, aye," Lt. Craig Jones said.

Clark watched with a mixture of pride and jealousy as Jones carried out his duties as OOD with efficiency and authority. When they were classmates at the Academy they both were more concerned with passing the academic courses than being leaders of men. The midshipman's uniform they wore was almost coincidental, especially for Jones. Joshua Clark often had to remind Jones to brush the lint off his uniform. Now Jones was officer of the deck running a 3,700 ton ship manned by 140 people. As a staff weenie, Clark got to go home every night, but he missed being on the operational end of the business. There was much to be said for the smell of salt air and commanding a ship.

"Helmsman, left ten degrees rudder. Come left to course zero-three-zero," Jones said. "All ahead full, make your speed twenty-five knots."

"Left ten degree rudder, come left to zero-three-zero," the helmsman repeated. "Make my speed twenty-five knots, aye."

The helmsman moved the throttles forward and turned the small wheel on the control panel. Not like the old Navy, Clark thought. It just did not seem the same without a large ships wheel and engine order telegraph. Hell, the helmsman was even sitting down. Not "standing" his watch at all. Granted, the Navy had to change with technological advances, but what happened to tradition?

Craig Jones picked up the bridge phone and dialed the Captain. "Captain, officer of the deck. The estimated time for closest approach to contact Sierra 7 is ten minutes." Jones listened intently, and said "Yes, Sir," and hung up the phone.

Jones walked over to Clark. "The captain is coming to the bridge, so don't embarrass me. Try not to spill coffee on yourself."

Clark smiled. "We both know he's coming to the bridge to check on you. I don't know how he can sleep at night knowing you're up here driving his ship."

Jones laughed. "Let's go outside and take a look."

They walked to the bridge wing. The twenty-five knot relative wind flattened their khaki uniforms against their bodies. Even at this time of year and with the warm Gulf of Mexico waters, the stiff breeze was chilly.

Clark leaned into the wind as he adjusted the focus on his binoculars. The contact was a nondescript looking merchant ship carrying a cargo of containers. He hoped this was the one, but there were five others inbound that fit the profile he developed. The initial excitement of the helicopter ride to the ship was wearing off and the job winding down to a routine. It would definitely be hard work if they had to check all five ships that were inbound today. And the next day and the day after that.

Clark grabbed the rail as the ship lurched over the top of a wave. At twenty-five knots and now running crosswise to the waves, the ride was rough.

"Hang on there, Sailor," Jones said, a gleeful look in his eye. "I don't want your butt falling over the side on my watch. I haven't practiced my Williamson turn since I left the Naval Academy and I'd hate to have to go back and dip you out of the water while we're in hot pursuit.

"At least you wouldn't have to worry about me sinking." Clark patted his stomach. "The way General

Armstrong keeps me running around I don't get much exercise. He keeps taking big bites out of my butt and I just keep getting fatter."

"What's he like to work for."

"He is a tough old bear, but he knows what he's doing." Clark was surprised to hear himself say something almost nice about Armstrong. He quickly added, "That doesn't mean I always agree with him. He can be hell on wheels if you cross him in the slightest. Just when I start thinking he's okay, he does something to make me realize I wouldn't want to drop the soap in the shower when he's around."

Jones put his arm around Clark's shoulder. "I understand," he said. "But wait 'til you see someone spin up my commanding officer," he added in a whisper.

"Let's get back inside," Jones said.

"Hold up a minute. We haven't had a chance to catch up since I came aboard. I've been meaning to ask you about Elizabeth. How is she? Is everything going well?"

Jones stopped at the door to the bridge and turned to look at Clark. "Elizabeth is well. The children are healthy. Why do you ask?"

"I could tell you it was a casual remark, but Sarah said Elizabeth seemed upset the last time they talked. I just wondered if you had stopped beating your wife."

A smile flitted across Jones' face, chased by a more intense frown. "I guess that's one of those questions you are in trouble with whether you answer 'yes' or 'no.'" Jones took a deep breath. "It's not anything I can't handle."

"At the Academy," Clark said, "you were my roommate and best friend. If you can handle it that's fine. If you want to talk to someone, call me anytime, day or night. You got me through some rough times at Annapolis.

"When I made the decision to drop out of the Academy at the end of the second year to marry Sarah it was one of the hardest decisions of my life. You said something I still remember. You said, 'The Navy is a career, but a good wife will last you a lifetime.' I don't need to know what is going on, unless you want to tell me, but you need to get your act together."

Clark squeezed Jones' shoulder and said, "That's all I have to say about that."

Jones nodded his head and swallowed. As they stepped back into the enclosed bridge, the quartermaster sang out, "Captain on the bridge." Captain Bennett walked over to the two junior officers.

"Good morning, gentlemen." His voice had a deep bass tone to it.

"Good morning, Sir," they said in unison.

"Captain," Jones said. "Range to target is 1,000 yards."

"Thank you, Mr. Jones, I can see that. Bring us along side and match course and speed."

"Aye, aye, Sir," Jones said.

Clark's eyes narrowed as he watched the exchange. The captain was not a likeable person. He saw that last night in the wardroom. The steward spilled gravy on the table and the captain chewed him up one side and down the other. The man was a petty dictator who abused power rather than using it. He got the job done, but his men feared rather than respected him. He was an excellent example of bad leadership.

If Clark needed another reason to dislike Captain Bennett, it was his beer belly. It did not hang over his belt, but the web belt cinched the bulge at his waist so tightly it protruded several inches over the buckle. It stretched the limits of what Clark considered acceptable by Navy regulations. Captain Bennett's best feature was his deep, booming voice, which unfortunately, he used to berate everyone around him.

The frigate eased alongside the freighter and slowed to match its speed. "Order the ship to stop and prepare to be boarded," the captain said to Jones.

"Captain," Jones said. "We have tried raising the freighter on all standard radio circuits and got no response."

"Oh, bullshit. Try the bridge-to bridge circuit."

"Captain, we have tried that too."

"Here, give that to me," the captain said, picking up the hand held bridge-to-bridge radio. He turned it to Channel B. "Freighter, this is the USS *Stephen W. Groves*. Stop your engines and prepare to be boarded."

Jones looked at Clark and winked when the captain was not watching. Clark was barely able to keep from smiling. You could always tell a senior officer, you just could not tell him much. Clark decided General Armstrong and Captain Bennett had a lot in common.

"Officer of the Deck," the Captain boomed out. He sounded pissed. "Get on the loud speaker system and order that ship to stop."

The ships were now some fifty feet apart, steaming at less than ten knots. Jones picked up the microphone. "Stop your engines and prepare to be boarded. I repeat, Stop your engines and prepare to be boarded."

The announcement on the *Groves'* exterior speakers echoed clearly across the gap of water between the ships and could be heard inside the enclosed bridge of the *Groves*. It was a little like being pulled over by the Highway Patrol, Clark thought. Of course, a Highway Patrol vehicle would have a blue flashing light and the announcement would be "Pull Over" rather than "Stop Your Engines."

The freighter cruised on and showed no sign of slowing or stopping. Clark looked at the freighter's bridge with his binoculars. The men there were clearly visible and obviously saw the *Groves*. One was gesticulating and pointing at the frigate.

"Mr. Clark, do you suggest we fire a shot across their bow?" the captain said.

"Sounds okay to me, Captain."

"Sounds okay to me," the captain sneered. Captain Bennett's unamplified voice was almost as loud as the P.A. system. "What in the hell kind of answer is that? Is that a yes, a no, or a maybe? My orders were quite clear. They specifically state that you are in charge of this part of the operation."

Now Clark was pissed. You do not talk to officers that way, especially in front of enlisted men. Clark could see Craig Jones looking away, probably wishing he were somewhere else, anywhere else. The other bridge watchstanders were studiously paying attention to their jobs.

"Captain, my orders are to stop and search container ships headed for the Port of Houston. I want that ship stopped. How you do it is within the scope of your responsibility as commanding officer!" Clark's voice was almost as loud as Captain Bennett's. "Is that clear, Captain?"

Clark stood toe-to-toe with Captain Bennett, looking up to the taller man. He would be damned if he would let a pot-bellied Navy commander back him down, even if he was captain of the ship. He had taken worse from General Armstrong and gave it back. Still, Clark felt an undercurrent of embarrassment that the enlisted men had to witness this kind of exchange between officers.

Captain Bennett hesitated for a moment. "My prerogative. Okay. Officer of the deck, put a shot across the freighter's bow."

"Put a shot across the freighter's bow, aye," Jones said.

Jones had barely repeated the order to the phone talker before the 76-mm gun on the bow of the ship fired. The ship rocked to port with the recoil and a fountain of water erupted in front of the freighter.

CHAPTER TWENTY-EIGHT

DEAD IN THE WATER

His dreams of distant thunder faded, merging with the booming reverberations of the metal door of his stateroom as someone hammered it with a fist. Ahmed jumped up from the sweat-soaked sheets. The little room was like an oven, heavy with heat and humidity. It was different from the desert. There the moisture was pulled from your body giving a cooling effect. Here the heat hung in the air like a blanket.

He pulled the door open, angry as the dreams of Safia and his family rapidly faded. "Speak."

The merchant seaman shouted in broken English, "Bridge. Bridge now." He pointed forward.

"What?" Ahmed asked, still groggy with sleep and the heat, but waking fast. The seaman was off and running in the direction he had pointed. Ahmed slipped on his shoes and ran forward. It would do no good to catch him. Most of the crew knew very little English and no Arabic, but it was obvious the action, whatever it was, was forward.

Ahmed ran up the last steps to the bridge and stopped just inside the door. The freighter captain was yelling at Hassan in a language that Ahmed could not understand. The captain reached for the control panel and Hassan slapped his hand away. Hassan then hit the captain across the face hard enough to make his head snap back. The captain took a step backward. His mouth hung open and disbelief pulled his jowls down with his jaw.

"You will hold your course and speed," Hassan yelled back in English. Two merchant crewmen stood as far back from the controversy as they could without actually leaving the bridge.

"What is happening, Mr. Jones." Ahmed said, taking a step closer. He kept his voice calm, hoping to settle Hassan. The old ship rolled slowly as it plowed its way through the furrowed seas. The soft, early morning light put the players on the bridge in sharp contrast. A gull cried out as it circled near the ship.

"This fool wants to stop this ship," Hassan said in an almost normal tone of voice. Ahmed knew that Hassan was at his most dangerous when he was calm.

"Please make him understand," the captain said to Ahmed. "We have been ordered to stop by a U.S. Naval warship. I am not even allowed to reply." He gestured at Hassan. "We must stop."

Ahmed looked at the ship on the port side of the freighter. It was haze gray, functional and efficient looking. A large gun was mounted on the stern, a missile launcher at the front. He turned to Hassan. "Perhaps this is a routine search. All we have is well-hidden. There should not be a problem."

Hassan turned and glared at Ahmed. "You also have become an idiot," he said. "The U.S. Navy does not routinely search cargo vessels. We have been betrayed." Ahmed could tell by the icy tone of his voice that Hassan was on the edge of violence. By the look on the other man's face, Ahmed saw that even he was considered a candidate for the role of the betrayer, as was everyone else on the bridge.

They were interrupted by the boom of the large gun on the bow of the Navy vessel. Ahmed barely saw the flash from the gun before he heard the sound. There was a short whistle, descending in pitch, and a geyser erupted in front of the freighter. The vibrations from the impact shook the ship. Everyone froze, watched the green water fall back into the sea, and looked again at the Navy ship.

The freighter's captain was the first to move. He darted past Hassan and slapped his hand across the bridge control panel. The steady vibration that had become a fact of life on the long voyage died as the engines stopped.

The captain had a smug look on his face as he stepped back. "I am in charge. No bonus is worth this sheet," he said, mispronouncing the word.

Hassan was now completely calm. He took out a pistol. Ahmed watched as the expression on the captain's face changed from one of smug self-satisfaction to creeping disbelief. His face continued its change, sliding further down the scale to horror.

"No," he yelled, putting his hands in front of his face and stepping back.

The bullet from the Beretta passed through both of the captain's hands, tearing out chunks of flesh. It struck his forehead, leaving a hole as big as a quarter, then exploded out of the back of his head, taking half of the skull with it. Blood and brains, gray and red and yellow, spattered the seamen standing against the wall behind the captain. Both ran from the bridge screaming words that conveyed their terror if not their meaning.

Ahmed twitched as a blotch of blood and gore splashed his face. He was feeling numb. "Mr. Jones," he said, his voice an accusation. Hassan turned to face him letting the gun hang by his side.

"You have something to say to me. You disapprove perhaps?"

Ahmed felt a chill run through him, ice water coursing through his veins. "No, Mr. Jones."

"That's good," Hassan said. "Go and prepare the missiles for launch."

"But we are still miles from the coast of Texas."

"I know our position." The gun still hung in Hassan's hand by his side. "We are within range. You yourself have explained the capabilities of these missiles to me."

"Yes, Mr. Jones."

Together Ahmed and Hassan ran to the stern of the ship, down the ladder and along the cargo deck. Their footfalls echoed hollowly on the metal hull. The revenge Ahmed had sought so long was at hand. In the fast pace of the action, would there be time to savor it?

Ahmed opened the rear of the container. He tripped the lever that tipped the wall of boxes at the back of the container into the ocean. Each box contained a large, $2,000 television. The corrugated boxes floated away, slowly filling with water as they settled in the wake of the ship.

"Mr. Jones, will not the American warship stop us from firing the missile?"

"I have a surprise for the American warship." Hassan pulled cartons from the storage compartments in the bottom of the Exocet missile launcher. He removed a squat container. The word "Stinger" was stenciled on its side.

"These are clever little hand held missiles designed by the Americans. They were given by the United States to the Afghan rebels to use against the Russians. When the Russians pulled out of Afghanistan, the C.I.A. tried to buy them back. We offered a higher price." Hassan laughed.

Ahmed thought the laugh was almost hysterical, but it infected him nonetheless. He felt a responsive giggle bubble up to his lips, but held it down.

Ahmed powered up the missile control panel and started the pre-launch sequence. He had to admit it had a certain poetic justice to it. The American Stinger missiles would now be used against an American ship.

"What do you think, Ahmed? These missiles were designed to shoot down Russian planes. Do you think they can sink a ship?"

"A small warship, perhaps."

Hassan laughed. Ahmed laughed, too. It was a great joke. The Americans would not be laughing. Hassan took the Stinger missile and ran forward. He climbed on the top of a cargo container dragging the canisters after him. Laying prone, he spread his feet to steady himself. He aligned the sights of the self-contained unit at the *Groves*. A tone sang in his ear like the buzzing of a bee, telling him the target was acquired. He pressed the firing stud. The Stinger roared out of the tube and traveled the short distance between the freighter and the *Groves* in a matter of seconds.

The high explosive warhead on the Stinger detonated as the missile struck the bridge, bending back metal and crumpling the box-like structure like a can.

"First, take out the command post," Hassan said to himself. "Then the ants will run around in circles."

Hassan lined up the second Stinger on the gun mount at the front of the ship. Again the missile landed on target.

The gun jumped upward and tilted on its mounting with the force of the explosion.

"Now let them interfere with out business," Hassan said.

Hassan didn't know the capabilities of an FFG like the *Groves*. Located amidship was a modern day gattling gun, a Phalanx. Fully automatic, radar guided, it could fire 3,000 rounds per minute. It could shred any missile attacking the ship. If it was turned on, but it was not.

CHAPTER TWENTY-NINE

BOARDING PARTY

Joshua Clark watched as the boarding party hoisted the motorized launch from its cradle and swung it smoothly away from the ship. Under the direction of Craig Jones, the six enlisted men operated as a precision team. Joshua Clark remembered Craig Jones as a plebe at the Naval Academy, always on the verge of competence, but never quite making the grade. Now he was a leader of men and did his job well. Jones saw Clark looking at him and winked.

Joshua Clark tried to forced his hand under the side of his flack jacket to reach a spot near the center of his chest. The flack jacket and life vest were tied confiningly tight and he could not reach the place he wanted. He was starting to chafe from the rough canvas collar of the life vest and the hot sun and the sweat trickling down his back between his shoulder blades did not help. The worst itch was always the one you couldn't scratch.

Clark gave up on the itch, pulled his hand back and let his hand rest on the butt of the .45 automatic pistol strapped to his waist. The pebble-grained grip of the government issue Colt .45 felt good in his hand. He hadn't handled one since summer training at the Naval Academy, but it felt familiar, like holding hands with an old friend. He was sure he could still shoot it. Like riding a bicycle, once you learn, you never forget.

A Coast Guard ensign joined the group as the boat reached the surface of the water. The ensign saluted Joshua Clark. "Good morning, sir. I'm Ensign Bruce."

"Good morning," Clark said. "Joshua Clark." He returned the ensign's salute and then shook hands with him.

"Get the men aboard," Craig Jones said to a chief petty officer. Craig Jones waited with Clark and Ensign Bruce as the men clamored down a ladder to the launch. The boat was bobbing beside the ship, still fastened at the bow and stern, by the cables from the hoist.

"Ensign Bruce will be going aboard the container ship with us." Craig Jones explained. "U.S. law prohibits the Navy from boarding ships in U.S. waters in time of peace. Search and seizure is the responsibility of the Coast Guard, so Ensign Bruce here is 'in charge'. He is going to be our statutory authority for the search. When we pull the launch over, the *Groves* will hoist the Coast Guard flag."

"OK," Joshua Clark said. He vaguely remembered something about the *posse comitatus* laws from military law class back at the Naval Academy. Josh Clark had met Ensign Bruce in the wardroom last night, but hadn't really understood why he was aboard and did not have the opportunity to ask.

The last of the enlisted men boarded the boat. "Our turn," Craig said. "Ensign, you are next."

Clark waited while the ensign and Lt. Jones climbed down the ladder. It was a part of Navy tradition that he liked; the senior officer was last on and first off so he did not have to stand around waiting for everyone else. It did not always work in practice, especially if everyone was standing around waiting to board, but the best seats were still reserved for the officers.

The boat was bobbing around significantly more than the frigate as Clark climbed down the rope ladder. He became aware of the greasy breakfast that he consumed that morning still congealing in his belly. Watching the bobbing boat below brought a bitter taste of fried eggs, which had not tasted so good the first time, to the back of his mouth. Clark refused to accept the fact that nervousness could be a cause of his indigestion.

As Josh Clark stepped on board the boat, he saw a flash out of the edge of his eye and instinctively crouched. The roar of an explosion was followed almost instantly by a shock wave. The frigate rocked to the port side jerking the cleat off the front of the launch as it pulled the bow clear of the water. Joshua Clark caught the gunwale of the launch with his arms, saving himself from falling. One of the enlisted men was not as lucky and fell between the ship and the boat. There was a sound of bones crunching as the boat bounced off the hull of the ship, sandwiching the sailor between the two vessels.

No one moved for a moment as the boat bobbed unsteadily, swinging out on its stern line. The tableau lasted only a few seconds, but seemed longer. Clark grabbed the unconscious enlisted man by his life vest and pulled him from the water.

Joshua Clark looked around. No one on the boat seemed to know what to do. Jones looked dazed and had a bloody bruise on his head. Clark wasn't part of ship's company, but he was senior officer on the boat and a decision was needed, even if it was the wrong one.

"Cast off," Clark ordered the coxswain.

"Aye, sir." The coxswain released the stern line and steered the boat away from the ship.

"Josh, wait," Craig Jones said, grabbing Clark's arm. "That explosion was on the bridge of the ship. There may not be any other officers left to fight the ship. Put me back on board. You handle the boarding party. I may not know enough to do the right thing in my personal life, but I know what I have to do now."

Joshua Clark nodded his head. Command of the boarding party had suddenly shifted completely to him. "Coxswain," Joshua Clark said, "Put us alongside the *Groves*. We will be putting Lt. Jones back aboard."

"Good luck," Craig Jones said to Joshua Clark as he clamored up the ladder.

"Coxswain," Clark said. "Bring us along side the freighter. Move it!"

"Aye, aye sir." The coxswain, a grizzled first class who looked like he had been in the Navy since Jesus was a fisherman, put the throttles on full and banked the boat sharply to the right. Joshua held onto the rail to keep his balance.

Salt spray stung Clark's face as the small boat bounced over the waves and closed the gap of water between the two ships. The freighter appeared to be coasting to a stop. A plume of flame erupted from above the top of a cargo container on deck near the aft end of the ship. Something, a missile, crossed the bow of the launch faster that the eye could focus. It struck the *Groves* near the gun mount on the aft deck. Joshua rapidly shifted his attention back to the freighter. A head was just visible above the cargo container.

"Chief," Joshua Clark said. "That rocket was fired from on the top of the cargo container near the aft end of the ship. Direct small arms fire back there. I want that guy taken out, or at least at a minimum, make him keep his head down."

The chief's smile stretched from ear to ear. He looked like he had waited a long time for permission to use his weapons. "Commence fire!" he bellowed. Clark would have known the chief was boatswain's mate by the magnitude of his voice, even without looking at the rating insignia on his arm. A fusillade of shotgun blasts mixed with the deafening clap from Clark's .45 and popping noises from M-16s used by two of the enlisted men. As the launch pulled alongside the freighter, Joshua Clark could no longer see the individual who had launched the missile. "Hold your fire," he said, "but keep your weapons ready."

One of the members of the boarding party tossed a hook line on to the deck of the ship. He pulled on the line to test that it had snagged something solid, and clambered up the knotted rope. When he reached the top, he turned and hauled up a ladder attached to the rope. Clark and the other men on board the boat climbed quickly up to the deck of the freighter. They crouched by a cargo container, weapons covering all approaches to their position. Several of them glanced over their shoulder at Clark.

Damn, Joshua Clark thought. Now that he had the full load of responsibility, he wasn't sure he wanted it. The lives of these men, and the one woman in the boarding party, were entrusted to him. But, none of them, most of all Clark himself, were really trained for this. Boarding a ship at sea was one thing, but taking it by force was something out of the days of wooden ships and iron men. Where was a cutlass when you needed one? Well, somebody had to make a decision. It was certainly a lot different from the Delta Force where he was along for the ride.

"Chief, you take three men and go forward. Make sure the bridge is secured. I'll go aft and make sure no additional missiles are launched. You two," Clark said, pointing at two of the enlisted men, "Come with me." Clark always prided himself on knowing the names of his men, but these were not his men, and "hey you," would have to do.

Joshua Clark led his group to a narrow corridor between the cargo containers. He looked down the length of the artificial alley. It was like looking into a shooting gallery. What would Sgt. O'Roark do? He certainly would not line up his men and march them between the containers and have them picked off one at a time.

"You two cover me," Clark said. "I will move up to the end of the first container and you two will provide cover. When I'm in position, one of you will move up to the container just past me and we will cover him while he is exposed. Then the last one in line moves up to the container past that. We'll always have two men covering any man moving. Got it?"

"Yes, sir," they both said. One of the young sailor's voice warbled with nervousness when he answered.

Joshua Clark could tell they were both frightened, but they showed no hesitation. They were relying on his judgement. Clean-cut sailors in their early twenties, they were men to be proud of and he was going to do his damnedest not to get them killed.

Clark looked down the corridor between the containers. Waiting wouldn't make it easier. He sprinted forward. Ducked and dodged would be more correct. Though he tried his hardest to run fast, he would no sooner jump over one short cable that attached a container to the deck, than he had to duck under another.

Reaching the end of the first container in the row, he squeezed into the small space between it and the next forward container. The heat from the hot metal seeped into his body. He stuck his arm behind him and waved the next man forward, keeping his eyes on the aft end of the ship. He held his pistol in both hands, pointed aft and upward. He was glad he had the 45, no real room for an M-16 here. Hopefully, Joshua thought, he and his team wouldn't shoot each other.

One of the sailors moved past him and took his position at the next intersection. Then the other sprinted past. Maybe they would make it after all, Joshua Clark thought. As the second sailor neared the end of the next to the last container, he tripped on a steel cable while hopping over it. As he fell forward on the steel deck, his shotgun discharged. Clark watched as a head peered over the top of the container. Clark felt a flash of recognition, but could not place the face. There was something familiar about him. He looked like the same person that fired the missile at the ship earlier, that must be it, but he could not be sure. He had only seen the man from a distance.

The man smiled as he stood at the edge of the container and fired a stream of bullets from an Uzi into the sailor on the deck below him.

Joshua felt a deep throated "No" erupt from his throat as he brought his pistol down to firing position. The sailor one container in front of Joshua stepped into the corridor and Joshua Clark quickly pointed his pistol in the air. He could not get a clear shot! The sailor in front of Clark emptied his M-16's magazine at the gunman.

Unfortunately, the sailor's enthusiasm was better than his aim. The stream of bullets pinged off the metal cargo container. The gunman turned his attention to the sailor and stitched a line of bullets up his torso. Joshua Clark stepped back between the containers as the gunman started firing.

With his head at the edge of the metal container, Clark saw the bullets impacting the sailor, knocking him backward with jerky steps as they struck his flack jacket. It wasn't until they struck his unshielded head that they finally knocked him down. Clark pulled his head completely back into the shielded area between the containers as the gunman jumped down from the top of the container. Clark was only partially exposed during the shooting and he hoped the shooter hadn't seen him.

Clark heard the gunner snap a replacement clip in the Uzi as he walked forward toward his hiding place. The footfall stopped as he reached the sailor closest to Clark. Joshua Clark jumped as the gunner fired another shot. He slowly looked around the edge of the container. Now Clark recognized him. It was the man on the video tape at Gatwick airport. The one who had put the bomb onboard the NorthStar flight with the woman passenger.

Joshua Clark eased himself back out of sight. Footsteps receded aft echoing off the closely-stacked containers. Joshua Clark looked out and saw Hassan's back as the man walked away from him. Clark silently stepped into the container alley and lined up the pistol sights on the man's back. Keep the front sight in focus, he thought. Level the back sight. Let the target stay fuzzy. Lessons from his pistol instructor that had never left him.

He flicked the safety off with his thumb. The gunner stopped. Clark felt a prickly sensation around his forehead. Surely, the gunner couldn't have heard that tiny sound. The gunner slowly turned, lifting the Uzi off his shoulder. Joshua felt uneasy about shooting the man in the back. Probably too many cowboy and Indian movies when he was growing up. Was he supposed to say 'Stop or I'll shoot' in order to make it legal? Should he give the guy a chance to give up?

Screw it, Clark thought as the gunman turned to face him. Clark squeezed the trigger. The bullet struck the gunner in the front of the right shoulder, knocking the Uzi from his hand and lifting him off the deck. Joshua Clark covered the man with his pistol as he walked aft, holding the gun straight out in both hands. He stopped and stood over the prostrate form, the Colt 45 pointed at Hassan's head.

The man was bleeding profusely. No flack jacket here, Joshua thought. He should finish the bastard. No one would know. It would save a trial. His hand shook. Damn it, *he* would know it. He would know he killed an unarmed man. How could he look Sarah in the eye if he did something like that?

Joshua looked aft as another man jumped out of the last container in the line. Joshua Clark covered him with the pistol as the man crouched down and put his hands over his ears. A loud roar shook the container as a large missile flew out of the metal cargo box.

Clark froze for a moment, but only for a moment, as flames from the rocket spilled around the edge of the cargo container. A hot sulphurous blast blew in his face. He turned his pistol toward the missile and emptied his clip at it, aiming high to allow for drop of the bullet and leading the missile.

Now the missile was more than fifty yards away and accelerating rapidly. The booster rockets dropped off as the air breathing engines kicked in. It was at the same time beautiful and horrifying and deadly. The missile started a climb to the right as it disappeared around the starboard side of the ship.

Ahmed, the man who had leapt from the back of the container turned to face Joshua Clark. Clark leveled the pistol at him. Maybe the man wouldn't know it was empty. "Put up your hands and get on your knees," Joshua Clark said. "What have you done?"

A smug look crossed the man's face.

Clark stepped closer and hit Ahmed across his face with the back of his hand. "What have you done?"

"Do what you will with me," Ahmed said. "Your American president will die and many of your leaders with him. You cannot stop the missile now. It will no longer accept further inputs. Now it cannot be stopped."

Ahmed looked to his left. Joshua followed the look, moving the pistol around Hassan as he caught sight of Hassan struggled to a sitting position, holding the Uzi in his left hand.

"Drop the weapon," Clark said, keeping the pistol pointed at Hassan. "Or I'll shoot."

"Really," Hassan said. "My friend may not be able to tell when a pistol is empty, but I can. The Colt 45 locks in the open position when all the bullets are expended. So how will you shoot me?"

Hassan emptied the Uzi into Joshua Clark knocking him backward into the container. Clark fell to a sitting position, legs splayed, arms dangling, unable to move. Almost unable to breathe.

Clark hovered on the border of consciousness, the wind knocked out of him. But the flack jacket had held. He watched in detachment as Hassan attempted to put another clip into the pistol using only his left hand.

Hassan gave it up and pushed the weapon to Ahmed. "You finish him," he said. "And launch the other missile. Target any downtown building in Houston."

"Why do that?" Ahmed asked. Ahmed pulled a Beretta pistol from his waistband. "The first missile was launched successfully. It will take out the Convention Center and the American president."

"Because," Hassan said, anger in his voice, "We want to kill as many Americans as we can."

"But in the downtown area there will be women and children. We are here to kill the American leaders. You said we were going to decapitate them."

"You are weak," Hassan said, disgust in his voice. "To win the war, it is often necessary to kill civilians. Sometimes it will even be imperative to kill women and children to change public opinion. To make the public think what we want them to think."

Clark felt his breath coming back. He was going to make it. "Like in the Tomahawk raid in Libya," he said.

"You Americans are so weak," Hassan sneered. "Yes, of course, like in the Tomahawk raid." He mimicked Clark's voice. "We will do whatever is necessary."

"What do you mean," Ahmed said, turning to face Clark covering him with his pistol.

"Shoot the American," Hassan said. "Shoot him now."

"He means," Clark said, "If it is necessary to blow up a mosque and kill his own people, to turn public opinion against the American people, he will do it."

"You blew up the mosque in Al Jawf?" Ahmed asked, amazement in his voice.

"Yes, yes, of course." Hassan said. "What of it? Shoot the American."

The pistol in Ahmed's hand moved around to point at Hassan. "My family was at Al Jawf," he said. The handgun bucked as Ahmed fired a shot into Hassan's face. The last look on Hassan's face was half sneer and half surprise as the bullet tore out the back half of his head.

Clark jerked back as blood sprayed his face. Seemingly spent, Ahmed let the pistol hang limp at his side. His head hung limp loosely on his neck.

"Is it true what you said?" Clark asked. There was no time for sympathy now. "Can the missile be stopped? If we act quickly we can save civilian casualties."

Ahmed shrugged his shoulders. "The missile flies a course we have programmed. It no longer needs its input signals from us. It calculates its position from your own geosynchronous positioning satellites and from terrain features. It steers itself to the Convention Center and explodes. I know of no way to stop it. It is very fast," he added.

"Help me to the bridge," Joshua Clark said. Ahmed put the pistol in his pocket. Looking lethargic, Ahmed put his hand under the other man's shoulder and pulled him to his feet. Clark felt like his legs were rubber as they walked forward to the bridge. His ribs shot pain through his body with every breath.

When they arrived on the bridge, the U.S. sailors had the crewmembers of the freighter covered. "Chief, get me a line to the *Groves*," Clark said as he got to the bridge. By now, he was moving on his own again. He pushed the pain from his ribs to the back of his mind. No time for that now.

"We get no answer from the *Groves*, sir. The bridge communication circuits may have been knocked out when the rocket hit."

Joshua Clark looked at the pillar of smoke from the *Groves*. She was standing dead in the water. It looked bad, but the ship would survive. "What radio circuits can you give me?" Clark said.

"Any circuits you want, sir," said a man in heavily accented English.

"Try the aircraft emergency circuits," Clark said, picking up the microphone. The man flipped switches and gave a thumbs up signal.

"Mayday, Mayday, Mayday. Exocet missile inbound to Houston's George R. Brown Convention Center." Clark grabbed a chart from the navigation table. "Course of the missile approximate course 320 degrees. Speed 500 knots.

"I repeat Mayday, Mayday, Mayday. Exocet missile inbound to Houston's George R. Brown Convention Center. This is Lieutenant Commander Joshua Clark, United States Navy. Any aircraft acknowledge."

CHAPTER THIRTY

COWBOY

The big passenger jet bucked as it descended from clear blue skies into the cloud layer. What looked like wadded cotton from above, changed to dense fog and rough air as the NorthStar jet eased into it. They flew out of the bottom of the clouds into a hazy gray Gulf Coast day.

"Eight miles to ILS for George Bush Intercontinental," the second officer said.

"Eight, aye," Captain Otis Edwards acknowledged as he twisted on his seat. His butt was sore from hours of sitting, but it was almost over. Another boring flight. He was a bus driver of the air. After the brief flurry of publicity over the emergency landing in Scotland, he lapsed rather quickly back into the groove ... rut was more like it.

Edwards scanned the cockpit instruments while he fidgeted. Bored, yes, but not stupid. Inattention was what killed

267

pilots. The first officer would be landing this one, but that always made his hands itch. It was always harder for him to let someone else land the 747 than to do it himself.

"Captain," the second officer said from his station at the Flight Engineer's Panel. "You had better listen to this. There is something coming over the emergency frequency. I am picking up a transmission from a guy on board a ship who claims he is a Naval officer. He says there is a missile attack on the George R. Brown Convention Center. I'll switch it to your headphones."

Captain Edwards stuck a stick of gum in his mouth. Now that was more like it, a little excitement at last. It was probably some kook on the radio, still, if it was really a U.S. Naval officer, there might be something to it.

He listened to the voice over his headphones. "Mayday, Mayday, Mayday. This is the USS *Groves*. Exocet missile inbound to the George R. Brown Convention Center. Course 330. Speed 500 knots."

"Second Officer," Edwards said, "patch me through to this guy on the emergency frequency."

The second officer flipped switches on his panel and gave Edwards a thumbs up signal. "You've got him, Captain."

"USS *Groves*, this is NorthStar 2 inbound to Houston Intercontinental Airport. What's this about a missile attack?"

"NorthStar 2, this is Lieutenant Commander Joshua Clark. A Liberian freighter has launched an Exocet cruise missile at the Convention Center in Houston. We have no way to stop it from this end. I'm looking for any airborne capability between here and the Convention Center. The president is speaking at the Convention Center. I repeat the president of the United States is speaking at the George R. Brown Convention Center."

"Lt. Cdr. Clark, that is a pretty far-fetched tale. Do you have any way to verify this 'sea story' real quick? If I go yanking this big 747 around the sky and blow a lot of gas searching for a fictitious bogey based on a crank call on the Mayday channel, I reckon it's gonna come out of my pocket."

"NorthStar 2, Clark here. From your terminology you sound like you might be Navy."

"Ex-Navy fighter pilot to be exact," Edwards said.

"Well, Captain Edwards, in the Navy we used to call this kind of 'sea story' a 'no shitter.'"

"I guess that's the password, Hoss. We'll do our best. You'll have to be air control and vector us in. We will do the best we can up here."

"I'm on the bridge of the freighter that launched the missile. We have communications with you and we have just established bridge-to-bridge communications with the USS *Groves*. The *Groves*'s CIC and radar are back on-line, but we have no communications other than the bridge-to-bridge on the hand held unit. Hold on and I'll see if they've got you on the scope."

Edwards turned to the second officer and covered the mike. "See if you can pick up anything on that new collision avoidance radar." Edwards listened to the earphones again as Joshua Clark came back on the line.

"Captain Edwards, Clark here. You're ahead of and to the east of the Exocet. The missile is currently 500 feet above the deck, speed about 500 knots. Come to course 280 degrees, and descend to 500 feet to intercept."

"Come to course 280 degrees and descend to 500 feet, NorthStar 2, aye.

"Lt. Cdr. Clark, since I'm putting on my fighterjock hat, you can call me 'Cowboy.' That's my call sign. If we're going to get burned by the F.A.A., we might as well do this big time." Edwards felt good again. This was what it was all about.

"Call you 'Cowboy,' aye." Clark's answer came over the earphones. "We did not have any handles in the submarine service, so you can call me what you want."

"I've got the stick," Edwards said to the first officer. "You keep your eyes outside the cockpit and see if you can pick up this bogey on visual."

"I think this is a big mistake, Captain," the second officer said, leaning forward to peer out the windows of the plane. "You're going to wind up with your ass in a sling and your license suspended."

"What can they do? At the worst, early retirement. If we do good, we get to paint a bogey on the side of the plane. Let us be bold for a change." Edwards smiled at the thought. Another interview with Oprah Winfrey would not hurt his image either. That had landed him more new dates than he had days off between flights.

The first officer shook his head. "There are bold pilots, and old pilots, but there are no old bold pilots," he said under his breath.

"Well Hoss, I'm still young enough to be bold. The alternative to old and bold might just be death by boredom."

"Captain," the second officer said, "I hold a contact on radar at ten o'clock, 5,000 yards and closing — fast."

"There it is," the first officer yelled. "Bandit at 10:00. One mile below us."

"What's this bandit stuff?" Edwards said. "This is a Navy operation, not Air Force. The correct terminology is bogey. Didn't you see Top Gun? You want to talk about 'bandits' you get the Air Force to make you a movie starring Tom Cruise."

Edwards banked sharply to the right and pushed the throttles forward, putting the big airplane into a steep dive. Edwards could hear screams of the passengers and the muted rattle of food trays and silverware from the passenger cabin. "Get on the intercom, Engineer," Edwards said, "and tell everyone to take their seats and buckle up."

"Maybe we should also tell them to kiss their ass goodbye," the first officer said.

"Do not spoil the fun, First," Edwards said. "This is something they will tell their children about."

"Okay, okay," the first officer said. "Let's talk about how we are going to do it."

"I'll go into a steep descent," Edwards said, "and come in over the missile."

"Then what, Captain," the first officer asked. He didn't bother hiding the sarcasm in his voice. "I didn't load any Sidewinder missiles for this trip. We might have a flare gun in the rubber lifeboat. Maybe I can roll down my front window and give it a shot."

"We're just going to give this bad boy a little nudge," Edwards said. His smile was as wide as his face. "We'll just ease down on top of him and bounce him off the deck."

"As simple as that?"

"It sounds simple to me," Edwards said.

"I just hope you don't kill us all."

"I have no intention of killing any of us. There are still some two billion women on God's green earth who have not yet had the pleasure of my company. I'm too young to die. I'll tell you what we will do though. We'll get him in our jet wash and de-stabilize the guy. That make you happy?"

"Much better," the first officer said, blowing air out of his puckered lips.

Edwards had never realized what a tight ass the guy was. He eased the 747 down in front of and just to the left of the Exocet missile. With the jet throttles to the wall, he was able to match the missile's course and speed, but just barely.

The small missile bucked violently as the exhaust vortex from the big jetliner washed over it. Corkscrewing as the miniature tornado from the 747's wing tips caught it, it whipped violently back and forth. The missile's control surfaces flapped wildly, its onboard computer frantically seeking to counter conditions it was never meant to handle. Its nose pitched down and suddenly it tumbled end to end and broke in half. The pieces shredded themselves in the wind and plummeted the short distance to the ground.

"Lt. Cdr. Clark, this is Cowboy. Splash one bogey."

"Cowboy, Lt. Cdr. Clark. Splash one bogey, aye. Well done, sir."

"Ah shucks, it wasn't nothing," Edwards said.

Edwards switched the microphone to the passenger cabin. "Splash one bogey, you all, and welcome to Texas." He could hear cheering in the background. He was beginning to like that sound.

EPILOGUE

Cherry blossoms were in bloom and the dowdy District of Columbia had a hint of youth and freshness. The clear blue sky, uncorrupted for once by auto photo-haze, made plausible the notion that there were those who choose to live here, and were not merely held here captive to their jobs. Even the most mundane matters had a pleasant aura in the hot spring sunshine.

Clark looked at the men and women assembled in front of him. Those in the military were in formation in the rear. In front of them, seated, were the civilians. Front row center were Sarah and Nicole. He felt his heart grow bigger with pride as he watched them. Nicole said, "Hi Daddy," when she saw him looking at her. Her little girl voice carried clearly. She at least, was not intimidated by the proceedings.

273

Next to Sarah sat Elizabeth Jones, and beside her Craig, his arm in a sling and a bandage on his head. Craig and Elizabeth were holding hands. It looked like Jones might get his act together after all, Clark thought. There was also a strong possibility Jones might also get a medal out of this. Clark had recommended him for one, but the paperwork was still in the pipeline. Jones winked as he saw Clark watching him.

"Lieutenant Commander Joshua A. Clark, front and center."

Clark stepped out of the ranks and performed a right face that would have made his old Naval Academy company officer proud. He marched to the center of the assembled group of men, executed a left face, and marched to the podium.

General George C. Armstrong stepped to the front as Clark approached. Clark saluted the General, fingers straight, forearm rigid. General Armstrong returned the salute with a studied casualness, hand half cupped. A slack salute, but Armstrong probably never had a Marine Corps Major as his company officer when he was a plebe.

Clark tried to keep a grimace of pain from his face as his tightly taped ribs shifted with the movement of his arm. He had little doubt that General Armstrong would rather not be giving him a medal, but Armstrong was first and foremost, a politician in uniform and this was another opportunity to seize the eye of the media. Would that be *Carpe publus*?

General Armstrong's Chief of Staff read the citation into the microphone. "For meritorious valor in the face of the enemy ..." Clark knew the words. Most of them boiler plate right out of the *Awards Manual*.

Still, they had an inspiring ring to them. In the hierarchy of awards, it wasn't at the very top, but it was the highest peacetime award his country could give.

General Armstrong held a steady gaze on Clark as the chief of staff read the award. Clark locked eyes with the General, refusing to blink. Clark knew that even here the General wanted to dominate.

Clark was close enough to see the beads of perspiration on the General's face. A small drop formed on the General's forehead, started moving slowly downward, consolidating with other drops as it gained speed and grew in size. It slowed as it ran along the ridge of the General's nose. It hung on the tip forever. It finally fell. Clark knew the General's nose had to itch, but the General refused to scratch. Valor in the face of the elements. Or pride in the view of the public.

Finally it was over. The chief of staff finished reading the award citation. So profuse were the superlatives heaped on him, Clark was tempted to pinch himself to see if he was still alive. It sounded very much like a eulogy.

Now it was the general's turn to complete his part of the program. He stepped forward, the medal in his hands. As the general lifted his hands to Clark's chest, he smiled. Clark could tell it was for the cameras. There was no reflection of the smile in the man's eyes.

General George C. Armstrong said barely above a whisper, so only the two of them could hear, "Congratulations, you did well." He paused for a second, not long enough for Clark to change his opinion of him, before he added "Boy."

Anger rose in Clark like corrosive acid. His throat closed up and his stomach muscles tightened. Rage gripped his loins and made his arms loose with the rush of adrenaline.

Then the general's eyes twinkled. He continued putting on the ribbon. Clark was surprised he didn't stick the pin through the dress white uniform into his chest. But that wasn't the general's style. He preferred to hit you in the mind. His specialty was psychological warfare, mental abuse not physical abuse.

Clark watched him and calculated. The general was only inches away struggling with the heavy, stiff material of the dress white uniform. In a moment he would step back expecting a salute from Clark, which the general would return.

The general finished. Clark pretended to look down at the medal. He turned slightly to the left, bringing his right shoulder forward. The general shifted his weight, starting to step back. Clark brought his hand sharply forward, fist clenched, catching the General directly in the crotch. Clark smoothly continued his salute, moving his hand upward in an arc, touching the edge of his hat, fingers extended and forming a straight line from the tips to the elbow.

Then it was Clark's turn to smile. His face beamed with joy that knew no bounds. Only someone with exactly the right angle would have seen Clark's hand bounce off the general's genitals. If anyone did see the contact, there was no way to tell that it was not an accident by an overly eager junior officer after receiving an award from a general.

Armstrong returned the salute, his face slack, his mouth open in an "ooooh." It would take a few seconds for the sensory receptors in that part of his body to carry the pain to his brain. But the general was well aware that in a matter of moments the sensation would be excruciating, Clark could see it in his eyes. He watched as the man's jaw tightened, taking up the slack in his face. His face was flush. His eyes grew large. Clark knew there would be no official retribution. How could there be? But there would be hell to pay nonetheless. It was time for a transfer.

There's valor and then there is valor, Clark thought. It's all a matter of knowing who the enemy is, and what is right.

ABOUT THE AUTHOR

Nelson Blish graduated from the U.S. Naval Academy, Annapolis, Maryland. After commissioning as an Ensign, he received an M.S. degree from Michigan State University and attended Nuclear Power School and Submarine School. His first assignment was the USS *Alexander Hamilton* (SSBN-617) where he was Main Propulsion

Photo courtesy of Lou Angora.

Assistant (MPA) and qualified as Engineering Officer of the Watch and Officer of the Deck.

Capt. Blish USNR (Ret.) remained in the Naval Reserves after leaving active duty and attended law school at the College of William & Mary, where he received his Juris Doctorate. While at law school Blish worked at NASA's Research Center, and was licensed as a Patent Agent. He specializes in corporate intellectual property law and has worked for a number of corporations including Philip Morris and Cooper Industries. He is presently Patent Counsel for Eastman Kodak Company in Rochester, New York.

Nelson Blish is admitted to practice before the New York State Supreme Court and the Supreme Court of the United States. He is President of the Western New York Chapter of the U.S. Naval Academy Alumni Association and past President of the Rochester Chapter of the American Corporate Counsel Association (ACCA).

His many professional articles have appeared in Naval Institute *Proceedings, The Marine Corps Gazette, ACCA Docket* and the *Armed Forces Journal*. His literary works have appeared in *New Millennium, Desperate Act, HazMat, Art Times,* and *Voices International*.

His son, Jacob, is a Navy ROTC student at Carnegie Mellon University. His daughter, Madeleine, is a professional ice skater touring with Disney on Ice, Toy Story 2.